Zel

Amanda Meuwissen

Zel – The GriMM Tales
Copyright © 2025 - Amanda Meuwissen

All rights reserved.

No part of this publication may be reproduced, distributed, or transmitted in any form or by any means, including photocopying, recording, or other electronic or mechanical methods, without the prior written permission of the publisher, except in the case of brief quotations embodied in critical reviews and certain other noncommercial uses permitted by copyright law.

Cover artist - Lina Ganef
Map designer – Amanda Meuwissen
Book layout - Amanda Meuwissen
Editor - Greenwing Editing

Printed in the United States of America

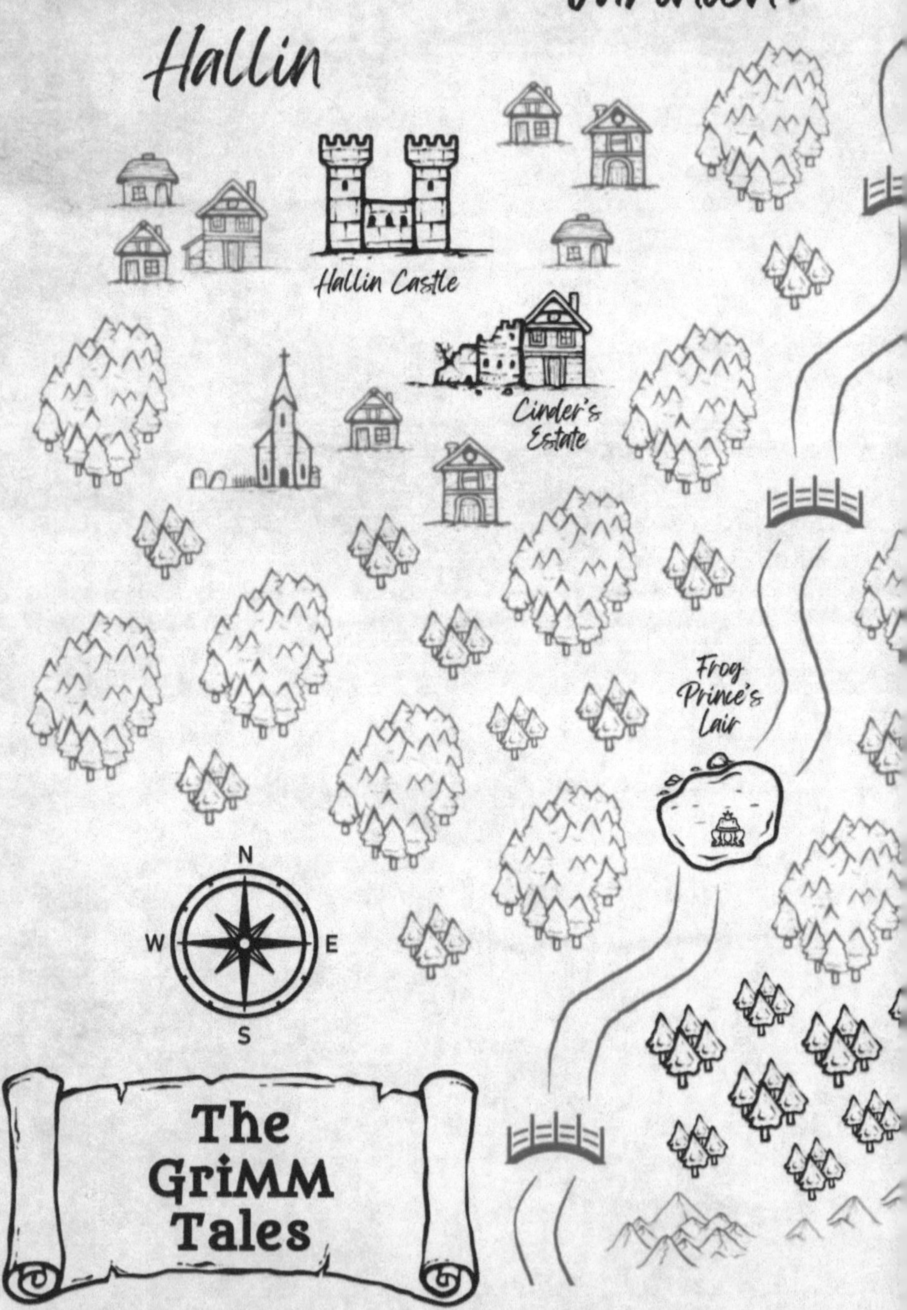

Varinien
Hallin
Hallin Castle
Cinder's Estate
Frog Prince's Lair
N
W
E
S
The GriMM Tales

Falchovari
Evil Queen's Castle
(Rumpelstilzchen's Haunting Grounds)
Shoemaker's Shop
Pied Pipers Music Shop
Sorcerer's Tower
Dark Forest
Miners' House
The Candy House
Old Oma's House
Mines

Prologue

*Once upon a time there was a man and a woman who
had long, but to no avail, wished for a child.*

SOPHIE

"Do you have it?" Gregor whispered.

"Easily, my love," Sophie said, and with a leg up from her beloved, she took hold of the top of the wall surrounding the tower and hoisted herself onto its ledge. Once balanced, she reached down to pull Gregor up beside her.

They needed to be silent now and dropped down into the tower's garden with the faintest of thuds as their boots hit the grass. What grass it was too, lush and green. The garden grew some of the most beautiful flowers, herbs, and vegetables Sophie had ever seen. The rumors were proving true, which meant they must be swift, or risk being discovered by the immortal monster who lived here, a powerful sorcerer who no one had encountered and lived to tell the tale.

An exaggeration, Sophie imagined. How could anything be known if no one lived to tell it? Trespassers were supposedly found outside the wall around the tower as shriveled husks, but others had survived to find those husks. Maybe it was even an outright lie, perpetuated by the tower's inhabitant to keep people away. But whoever lived here must command some magic to grow the most delicious-looking vegetables in all the kingdom.

The monetary reward was worth the risk, and access to such a garden could change the fate of whoever claimed it. Crops had not yielded the usual harvest for several seasons in Falchovari, long enough that villagers and even people in the city surrounding the castle were beginning to whisper of a coming famine.

Lothar, master of the Thieves Guild, had offered a hefty sum to whoever returned with some of the *rapunzel* in particular, lettuce said to be the wellspring of the sorcerer's immortality and the reason the tower and all its secrets had stood for centuries.

The tower's longevity was true at least, for Sophie had seen it in the distance all her life from the safety of the city. Up close, it even shimmered as if infused with magic, or like it was made of many colors warring enough against each other that, in the end, it looked opalescent. If any of the rest was true mattered not, only their success. Nor did it matter whether real immortality was possible for peasants or only for the likes of the evil Queen, who had cruelly ruled Falchovari for almost 200 years.

The garden courtyard was narrow but large enough for a path between the plants that grew all along the interior of the perimeter wall and the exterior wall of the tower itself. Sophie gestured for Gregor to head left while she went right. They were to gather whatever they could in the sacks slung over their shoulders, but their primary goal was the lettuce.

Hood pulled low, in all black clothing identical to Gregor's, Sophie usually would have blended with the shadows, but the moon was high and clear, brightening the courtyard, which was brighter still from the vivid colors of the plants. She made haste, shoveling whatever she could grab into her sack, even flowers they might sell tomorrow. If these plants were as magical as they appeared, surely they would not be easily bruised or wilted.

The tower was at least five stories tall, and only the side facing the heart of the kingdom showed a window at the very top. As Sophie hurried around the tower's base, she saw no sign of any lower windows, nor of a door. The perimeter wall had no door or gate either. Scaling it had been the only option.

She had nearly made it halfway around the tower where she would meet back up with Gregor when she spotted the lettuce growing near a set of especially clean stones when much of the tower's base had moss and vines creeping up it.

Sophie never would have thought that lettuce could look beautiful, but it was. As lusciously green as everything else, and yet the stems of the fabled *rapunzel* were such a vibrant yellow, they almost looked gold. She began to harvest it with gusto, but so entranced was she by its colors and smell—had any lettuce ever smelled so enticing?—that she was lowering her mask and bringing a leaf to her lips before she could stop herself.

The flavor of the lettuce proved its look and smell were no exaggeration of its splendor. Sophie immediately wanted more, and a powerful craving filled her. She braced herself on one of the stones of the tower to reach for another leaf.

The stone sank inward, and the clean stones beside it moved of their own accord as if by magic to reveal an opening into the tower and a staircase leading up.

What treasures awaited inside?

"*Sophie*," Gregor hissed, barely audible but preceded by his hand on her wrist, halting her from the step she had been about to take. "We are contracted for the flora alone. We must go."

Sophie looked into Gregor's eyes, brilliant blue in contrast to her brown, the only part of his face visible with his mask still up, and thought of all the hardships they had overcome since they met and fell in love as teenagers. She thought of how badly they longed to wed, but since they'd had nothing as orphans, they'd turned to the Thieves Guild to have something of a future and now lived as much at the mercy of Lothar as they did the Queen. But having enough to survive didn't mean having enough for a wedding or a future outside the guild.

If they could find something to steal that Lothar wouldn't discover, something priceless they could escape with, maybe even to the neighboring kingdom of Hallin, they could start over and finally bear the child they had been desiring for so long.

All previous attempts at growing a life inside Sophie's womb had failed, and after five long winters of being barren, a new start might be the only thing capable of healing whatever ailed her.

"Sophie," Gregor hissed again, softer, his eyes beseeching her, eyes she had so longed to see in the face of their babe.

"One look, my love, just one, and it could change our lives forever," she said. Perhaps eating the lettuce had bolstered her with something powerful, perhaps it *had* made her immortal, and braver for it. She offered a leaf to Gregor, but he shook his head.

"We can't. We have lingered too long."

"We can. How much grander our wedding, how much grander our *lives* might be if we find treasure Lothar never needs to know about."

Gregor turned his head to look up the stairs, then back at Sophie. "Your face looks aglow, my love. You ate the lettuce?"

"I did. And once we have our true treasure and are safely away, so can you."

Gregor remained skeptical but nodded. He had never been able to refuse Sophie anything. "Lead on then, but let us be quick."

The stairs seemed to go on forever, winding up all five stories to the top of the tower with its lone window. The room the stairs spilled into was a single circular space. Besides the window, there was another door across from where they entered that they assumed led into a closet, for the tower could fit no more within it.

The room was dark, only the window allowing in light, which illuminated a chaise in one area for lounging, a desk in another for study, shelves upon shelves of books all along the walls, and several more filled with bottles and jars, some containing something or another, some empty. There was one shelf covered in trinkets that each looked like the grandest prize the Queen herself might covet and were likely magical.

There was no sign of a sorcerer.

"Hurry. He must be out. Let us not press our luck." Gregor went for the gleaming metallic and bejeweled items on the trinket shelf.

Instead of following, Sophie was drawn to the desk near the closet door. There was an open book upon it, an empty goblet that might have contained wine recently, and a beautiful silver hand mirror beside a matching silver hair brush. The wine goblet was encrusted with every gemstone imaginable, and yet Sophie reached for the brush.

"You *dare*," a voice boomed, and a hand clamped down on Sophie's wrist, more vise-like than when Gregor had done the same below and black as the night sky with pointed nails more akin to claws. There was a glow to the veins in that hand as if violet fire flowed beneath the sunken skin.

Sophie whipped her head around just as another hand gripped

her by the throat and lifted her off the floor. Where had he come from? He loomed in front of the closet door. Did it lead instead to another set of stairs?

He had her now regardless, and he was awful in his majesty. To look on him was like looking into the abyss, when all that could be seen was night sky with ripples of magnificent color. He was the tallest man Sophie had ever laid eyes on. The skin of his face and the hand around her throat did not match the blackness of the hand that had stopped her from taking the brush. The rest of his skin was ashen, almost with a hue of that violet fire. His long wavy black hair sparkled as if dotted with stars that seemed constantly in motion.

He *was* the abyss, with tapered ears like an elf. All that was missing were horns, and he could have been a demon from the depths.

"Sophie!"

No, Sophie thought, as Gregor raced over to them. It was her greed, her vanity, her foolishness that had led to this, and if she could have spoken, she would have screamed at her beloved to run.

The sorcerer yanked her closer, and as he opened his mouth, Sophie's own mouth opened unbidden in response. She felt the same abyss she could see, as her essence was drained from her *into* the sorcerer.

"Stop!" Gregor cried. "I beg of you! Take me! Take me instead! Just *stop*!"

And stop he did.

Sophie fell, dropped from the sorcerer's grasp, and though she would have collapsed, Gregor was there to catch her. She lived, but if the price was her beloved, she would not pay it.

"I had intended to take you both," the sorcerer snarled. "Sophie, is it? You taste especially sweet having eaten of my garden, my *rapunzel*, but your soul is not alone in your body, which may yet save you."

"What are you saying?" Gregor asked with a tremor in his voice, keeping Sophie upright. She soon regained her balance, much as she panted from almost having become the next husk to be found outside the tower.

"What does it usually mean when one body contains two souls?" the sorcerer queried.

As one, Sophie and Gregor looked at Sophie's stomach. She was with child? Finally, at last, she was pregnant.

"I do not tolerate thieves," the sorcerer continued, "especially those daring enough to trespass inside my tower. A boon will be needed in exchange for your lives."

"You would spare us because we are with child?" Gregor asked.

"I will spare you *in exchange* for your child."

"No," Sophie said immediately, with rising horror and a hand placed over her belly as if to protect the babe within.

"I do not mean to raise it," the sorcerer said. "The child, as a child, will remain yours. But all parents part with their children once they reach adulthood, and so too shall you."

"You want our child when it comes of age?" Gregor questioned. "Why? For what?"

"They will come to me here in the tower and live with me for one month to determine if they are a worthy exchange for your transgression. If it comes to pass that they are, we will unite in marriage, and your debt will be paid."

Sophie was already shaking her head, but Gregor placed his hand atop hers on her stomach.

"If we refuse?" he asked.

"Then you will die where you stand, and I will have a meal of all three souls."

Sophie was still shaking her head. The horror of such a fate, to be this monster's bride, she could not imagine cursing upon her child.

But refusal meant it would have no fate at all.

"Take the brush. A gift to seal our promises. Take all you gathered from my garden as well, but heed this." The sorcerer somehow stood taller, his galaxy hair lifting and flowing as if caught by wind around his dark, fierce face. Eyes near enough to galaxies too, housing the doom of worlds, glowed with some of the violet light running through the veins of his blackened hand. He pointed at Sophie with one of those fingers. "Only you are to eat the lettuce. More will arrive for you to consume each day until the babe is born. Then only the child shall eat it, every day, until the day they are of age and ready to come to me.

"If anyone goes against this and eats the lettuce in yours or your child's stead, they will perish instantly. Make no mistake about that. Follow all my instructions and you may yet live to meet your grandchildren."

"Please," Sophie said, hanging her head that she had finally stopped shaking, for looking into the sorcerer's eyes made it too real. "We have waited so long for this child."

"Then enjoy them for all the time you have them. When they are no longer a child, they will be mine. Do we have an accord?"

Sophie could not speak, for either option felt equally damning.

"We do," Gregor said.

"Gregor!"

"It is this or death, my love, to us and the babe before it has even known breath. We have no other option."

"No, you do not," the sorcerer said. "*Do we* have an accord?" he asked again, looking solely at Sophie, as if needing both to confirm so aloud. Maybe he did for whatever magic this pact required to work.

If only she had not been filled with lustful greed for more, they might have had all they had ever wanted without needing to give anything up. But she knew they had no choice.

Lothar would be furious. They could only hope he would be understanding once they returned to the guild and explained that only Sophie could eat the lettuce he had sent them to retrieve.

Though it was not the vow Sophie had been hoping to exchange, she answered the sorcerer, "We do."

ULRICH

"Two more items to heed," Ulrich said, staring down at the thieves. Surely, the woman, Sophie, had not consumed more than a single leaf of his lettuce, but it had been enough that the taste of her soul had been ripe and invigorating.

The taste of the second soul, however, had proven a hundred times as tantalizing. The idea never would have occurred to him had a pregnant thief never darkened his door. At last, might he meet someone who could prove his equal and end the torture of his solitary existence.

"First, be under no illusions that to eat of my lettuce makes you immortal." Ulrich reached for Sophie's cheek and sliced a thin cut with his nail just deep enough to draw a trickle of blood. "My garden serves its purpose, but it is not why I live eternal.

"Second, you will name the child for what you have stolen from me so that you are reminded daily of our pact. Your babe shall be called..."

One

TWENTY WINTERS & NINE MONTHS LATER

ZEL

"Rapunzel!" Gregor yelled, while fending off one of the unsanctioned thieves they had been contracted to stop. His sword glinted in the moonlight and meager candlelight from the windows of nearby homes. "One of the targets is getting away!"

Rapunzel. How silly to have been named after lettuce, but Zel had been born with eyes the same verdant green as its leaves, unlike either parent, and with hair as splendid as finely spun gold in the same golden hue as the plant's stems.

"Rapunzel! Did you hear me? The target!"

He had also been born a boy.

Jolting to attention, dagger still buried in his current target's side—avoiding vital areas, but enough to hurt and incapacitate—Zel looked to his father and finally realized that the last of their quarries had dashed past him and was running down the alley. That man was their true target, the leader. The rest could stand as reminders to others if they survived their wounds, but the leader had to die.

So said the Queen, who did not tolerate thieves she did not own. These men had also killed guards when escaping capture after their thefts, like common bandits beyond the city. They deserved to be put down. They deserved to die. There would be chaos in the streets if the Queen's orders weren't heeded. There would be curses upon anyone who stood against her, and a crossbow bolt between the eyes for anyone who defied Lothar, master of the guild that carried out her work.

"Rapunzel!" Gregor shouted again, just as he skewered his target's shoulder, practically pinning the bandit to the wall. While many citizens, especially in these streets, knew who served the Thieves Guild, it was still best to keep the names of any assassins from being spoken aloud. Tonight, Gregor was clearly as anxious as Zel to have spouted his name so brazenly multiple times.

A mask covered Gregor's face of all but his blue eyes, and he wore a hood like all members of the Thieves Guild. If it hadn't been up, it would have revealed flaxen hair, though more wheat colored than a match to Zel's gold. He was a handsome man, slight of build and naturally smooth-faced, which was lucky, for the same had been passed down to Zel. Maybe that was its own luck, even magically so, because it meant Zel never needed to shave to keep up the lie.

No one outside of their family knew he had been born a boy. No one could ever know, not until the pact was complete, unless Zel wanted to die when he was given to the sorcerer if their ruse was discovered too soon.

The sorcerer expected a bride, and a bride he would receive.

Zel had heard the stories since he was young. Lothar had been as furious as expected when Zel's parents returned from the sorcerer's tower and explained what had transpired. Sophie, Zel's mother, had a cut on her cheek to prove the lettuce had not been what they thought, but Lothar had still sliced her other cheek to confirm for himself that eating the lettuce had not made her immortal.

Immortality not having been stolen from him was what quelled Lothar's rage. He had bidden Zel's parents to prepare for a different outcome to the sorcerer's pact, one that would benefit them all. They would raise their daughter to be the sorcerer's assassin and take all the tower's secrets and treasures for the guild.

Zel being born a boy had not changed that goal. He needed to seduce the sorcerer enough to be kept for the entire month until he discovered a vulnerability in the sorcerer's immortality and where it originated from, but he could not seduce the sorcerer so much that he attempted to bed Zel before their wedding night.

For many winters, Zel had been taught the ways of both seduction and the blade.

He was talented at both.

"The thief is mine!" Zel affirmed, flying past his father with a leap and crouching into a faster sprint, using speed only someone as delicately built and nimble as he could achieve.

Quickly hitting a cross-section at the end of the alleyway, Zel looked left, right, then forward again toward the main streets. The shadows were too dark for him to discern which direction the bandit had gone, but after another scan with his sharp eyes, Zel spotted a figure escaping into a building to his left and gave chase.

Tonight's mission was Zel's most important. With this kill, he would ascend to a full member of the Thieves Guild. The guild had always been an assassins guild when the Queen demanded it—or when Lothar did. They remained the Thieves Guild in name, but every member was trained to fight and kill, even if not everyone ended up having to. Zel had dealt the finishing blows for seven assassinations. Tonight would be his eighth, leaving the sorcerer as his ninth, a number of good fortune to ensure his success.

And he would succeed. He had to, or the lie he had been forced to live for twenty winters would amount to nothing but more misfortune.

The building the bandit had run into was a home, and he had locked it tight behind him. No matter. There was a second story, and the awning over the front door gave Zel the perfect platform to climb and reach the ledge of an open window. He ascended with ease and barely a sound on the awning when he landed or when he leapt from it for the window a moment later. Inside there was a candle flickering, offering enough light that Zel saw when the bandit ran past the room.

Zel recognized him by the bright blue hood he wore, foolishly visible, when Zel's outfit for such midnight prowling was all dark colors, mostly black, as was standard in the Thieves Guild, but with some deep greens, browns, and a violet cloak, adding dimension to what would otherwise be too flat a black against true shadows. His idea, which Lothar had commended when it proved to work.

He kept his hood low to hide the golden brilliance of his hair, the winding length of it tucked beneath his cloak. It had grown so long that it needed to be braided and further twisted around itself to avoid it dragging on the ground. The weight alone should have caused a permanent ache in Zel's neck, but perhaps because of his magical diet of self-named salads, he never ached at all, not there nor anywhere.

Zel never got sick. He never got injured. No one was certain if the immortality his mother hadn't received had somehow been bestowed upon him, but he had never suffered so much as a scratch or scuffed knee. Whenever Sophie had attempted to cut his hair as a child, the shears had suffered for it and became blunt as they failed to give him even a trim.

But while another could not cut Zel's hair, by the time he was six, he had learned that if the shears were in his hands, *he* could. At the time, Zel had threatened to slice it all off, for it was a constant reminder, one of many, of his lot in life, but his parents had pleaded with him not to. Not only did it aid in their subterfuge that Zel was a girl, but if anyone had learned that his hair could be cut by him, they might assume the same was true of any method of harming him. It could have been used against them, when they had needed every advantage on their side to ensure Zel reached adulthood unscathed.

If others wondered how Zel's face-framing fringe remained short while the rest of his hair grew exponentially, they never asked, probably assuming it was some strange part of his magic—and not that Zel occasionally gave his fringe a snip.

Silent as a slinking cat, Zel once again gave chase. He had to stop the bandit before he harmed the owner of this home or slipped away to another. How brazen of anyone to have left their door unlatched in this kingdom for a thief to slip in, when the fight for resources had become one of life and death.

The troubling harvests since before Zel was born had grown worse over the decades until recent seasons when it had been declared a true famine—the Great Famine. Most people barely had one meal with fresh greens, and Zel was gifted magical lettuce daily. It arrived like clockwork on their back stoop every afternoon, and Zel ate it as a salad with dinner. He could hardly complain when the leaves were delicious. What he hated was the envious looks he received from neighbors whenever they saw the lettuce arrive.

Zel remembered vividly the day a childhood bully had attempted to steal some, saying that all the warnings about instant death being the reward for anyone who ate the lettuce other than Zel were lies. But as soon as one of the leaves touched the bully's tongue, he'd melted into a pile of rotting flesh. Zel would never forget that smell, but it had well prepared him to not be fazed by the sight nor scent of death.

The same had happened to one of Lothar's guards, Zel was told, for Lothar had not believed the warnings either. He had been sensible enough to bid another to test it, and Zel's parents had been there to witness the melting of the first flesh pile.

Slicing a throat or piecing a heart or temple with his dagger hardly affected Zel at all anymore. And he could defend as well as sneak. His dagger-wielding hand was covered in a leather gauntlet that extended up his forearm, with several metal plates layered along the backside. With it, he could fend off a blade aimed at him as easily as if he wielded a shield.

Creeping along the wall of the hallway, Zel heard rustling as if the bandit was rummaging through something in the next room. Stealing from some random innocents when he had already been caught in the midst of theft?

Any pity Zel felt for this man fled him, and he readied himself for his duty. He waited. His parents and the other thieves who were called upon as assassins had trained him to have endless patience, for that patience would be tested when he faced the sorcerer.

The bandit exited the room, and just Zel's luck—he was usually lucky, which others guessed was another benefit from the lettuce—he turned in the opposite direction from Zel, leaving himself exposed.

Zel leapt and tackled the bandit to the floor, stabbing his dagger between the man's ribs right into his heart. He ripped the dagger free with a twist on extraction to ensure a swift bleeding out and death within less than a minute. Then he rolled the man over to watch the light leave his eyes. Kills only counted if the final moment of death was witnessed, an old Thieves Guild superstition.

A month from tomorrow, sooner if possible but no later, Zel

would be watching the light leave the sorcerer's eyes, or the sorcerer would be watching the light leave his.

"R-run…" the bandit said with his last breath, but he did not keep his fading eyes on Zel. He tilted his head back to look toward a room at the end of the hall.

Zel noticed the sack the bandit had been carrying, spilled now onto the floor beside the body. It was just clothes. Personal items. Nothing of value. This was the bandit's home, made clearer when Zel looked up and saw a child cowering in the far room's doorway.

"P-Papa?"

There could be no loose ends, no witnesses. It was Thieves Guild *law*. The Queen did not tolerate revenge quests from friends or family of the deceased left alive.

The little girl in a plain nightdress too small for her clutched a patchwork doll to her chest. She stood immobilized and shivering as Zel stepped over her father's body to move toward her. She could not have been older than five or six.

"Are there others in this house?" Zel demanded, using his higher, feminine pitch that was second nature to him now. "A mother? Siblings? Anyone at all?"

The girl shook her head.

Zel lowered his mask and swooped down to her level, grabbing her shoulder with the hand not holding his dagger. "Then do as your father bid you and run. Take everything with you that could prove a child lived here and go. The guild will ransack this house, and if they have reason to believe in your existence, they will find you, and they will not show you the same kindness that I am."

That the girl's eyes did not show blame nor hatred toward Zel for what he had done to her father was a testament to how expected such acts were in this kingdom. "Where do I go?" she asked.

"Wherever you can. But you cannot stay here."

Zel turned back to the dead bandit. Had he been a bad man, or just a poor man turned thief to clothe and feed his daughter? Zel had no way of knowing. He had no way of knowing whether any of his targets had been worse than he was as a killer for hire. But the Queen's words were law, Lothar her arbiter, and guild members Lothar's tools to wield.

Zel was a fool to be taking such a chance on his final night, but if he killed outside necessity or someone deserving, he would be no better than the monsters that held his reins, no better than the sorcerer he would soon be sent to.

Someday, somehow, he longed to be more.

There wasn't time to move the body, but cleanup was the job of other guild members. It would be seen as strange if Zel did it. He needed to circle back to his father, give the girl as much time as possible to escape, then send the cleaners to the bandit's home to confirm the kill. He could only hope the girl would be gone by then.

To her credit, as Zel used the stairs to exit out the front door this time and leave it unlatched for the cleaners, the little girl went straight for the bag her father had dropped and emptied it of the rest of its contents to begin gathering clothes and items of her own.

In this life, this kingdom, childhood was a luxury most did not get.

Zel waited around the bend of another alleyway to catch his breath, which came out in visible puffs since it was late and the autumn season had begun much colder than usual. His father was likely looking for him, after warning the wounded bandits that if they lived, it would be by the grace and mercy of the Queen, and they would do well to never cross her again. Fear was a powerful tool for motivation.

But then, so was hunger.

The girl would be all right, Zel told himself. She had to be. If she crumbled now, she would never survive the winters ahead of her.

Whatever quiver tried to work its way into Zel's hands, he willed it away with a gritting of his teeth. He'd had no choice. He'd had to kill that man, and there was still more killing to be done before he could rest.

Breath calmed and quiet, Zel wiped his blade on his breeches before sheathing it. Missions were the only time he wore breeches instead of skirts. They were more practical for the job, but in truth, he had never minded wearing skirts or other pretty things, rouging his cheeks, or displaying his luxurious locks. He was beautiful enough that pretending to be a girl had always come easily to him, so easy that it rarely felt like pretend at all.

It still wasn't him, not all of him out in the open, and he longed for whatever that might prove to be once he had the freedom to wonder.

If he ever did.

Distantly, Zel heard feet running on cobblestones. *Father*, he hoped, or someone else from the Thieves Guild. Regardless, he had given the girl enough time.

As Zel stepped out of the alley into the next street, he was caught up short by nearly colliding with a passing old woman. How had he not heard her coming?

"Goodness, child! Did you give this old woman a fright! In such a hurry?"

Zel was tongue-tied at first, not only by the surprise of the woman's arrival, but by how frail and shriveled she looked. He had never seen anyone so wrinkled. She wore a black robe and used a walking stick for her hunched posture, likely to keep her from toppling forward.

"My apologies, Madam," Zel said. "I realized the time and felt the need to hurry home."

"As you should," the woman said with an equally aged voice to match her appearance. "'Tis far too late and dangerous to be going anywhere alone. Will you be all right?"

Zel smiled, wanting to point out that the old woman was alone too, but then, when one reached such a ripe old age, they likely didn't worry much about Thieves Guild pickpockets or even bandits. "I will, thank you. These streets are dangerous indeed. You hurry home too."

"Thank you, child," she said. "Although, given what day it is, I can no longer call you *child*, can I, Rapunzel?"

Zel startled yet again, trying to study her face, her voice, but there was something impossible to place about her. "Um... yes. *No*, I mean. I am no child. I became a woman today. Finally twenty. Have we met before, Madam?"

"I do not believe so, dear, but everyone knows you, don't they?"

Most did in these streets. A story like Zel's wasn't possible to keep hidden from neighbors. His true identity was difficult enough to hide. But she must have had a keen eye given most of his hair was still hidden by his hood. "I suppose they do."

"Are you excited for what is to come?" she asked.

"I don't know," Zel answered honestly, "but I am excited to put childhood behind me."

"Good," she said, and then seemed to study Zel's clothing, his breeches especially. If she knew him, then she was local and would also recognize the clothing of the Thieves Guild. If she drew attention to it, he was honor bound to kill her, and he could not risk two acts of mercy in one night. "You've got a spot of red on you, dear. Be well," she said and continued on.

It was no wonder she had lived for so long if she was that wise.

Zel turned to head in the other direction.

"Such a fair and lovely lad," he heard from her.

Zel spun around, because no one should know, *no one*, but when he looked in every direction the old woman might have gone, he saw no sign of her.

Already frazzled by the eventful night, Zel hurried to find his father and to better prepare for what came with the morn.

"You did it!" Rudy nearly bowled Zel over with the force of his tackling.

Zel and his father had returned to the Thieves Guild to applause and merrymaking in celebration of his induction as a full member. Rudy, Zel's closest friend, had ascended to full membership the previous month. He was part of the pickpocketing unit that kept the guild in funds. The Queen could be quite stingy with her coin.

The Thieves Guild in full was made up of the pickpocketing unit, elite thieves for larger jobs, assassins like Zel, guards who were well trained but not as cutthroat or stealthy as the assassins, information brokers known as whisperers who kept their eyes open and ears craned for anything important happening in the streets, and finally, the cleaners. Their job was to ensure that even if citizens knew the Thieves Guild was responsible for something, there was never enough evidence to prove it, and thus Thieves Guild activities remained rumors and guesswork.

Zel's welcome reception meant the cleaners had already confirmed the kill and someone had reported back ahead of them. The little girl must have gotten away, or daggers and swords drawn would have greeted Zel and his father instead. He hoped she would be okay beyond a single night of escape. If an assassin had taken Zel's parents when he was her age, he might not have made it this far without losing even more of his soul to survive in these streets.

"Yes, I did." Zel hugged Rudy back, though he wondered if Rudy would be as jubilant if he'd witnessed the slaughter. Rudy was a handsome lad of Zel's same age, with brown hair, sun-kissed skin, and blue eyes that required a pair of spectacles to see clearly.

The base of the Thieves Guild was beneath the city. There were many secret entrances through the city's undercrofts. One such cellar entrance was in the storeroom of the shop Zel's parents ran as cover—and used for additional funds, most of which still went to the guild's coffers. The entrance led to a series of passages, which eventually led to the guild's primary common room for dining and celebrations.

For being a bit dark and dank, the base was always clean, always warm in the colder months, and cool when it was hot. If missions were successful, food and drink were as plentiful as possible for during a famine.

"Rapunzel did well," Gregor said, hugging Zel in the wake of Rudy's embrace while more cheers rang out from other members. Zel preferred the shortened version of his name, but he could never quite get up the nerve to correct his parents. He had only begun correcting others the previous winter. "Though I think you were a bit more distracted than usual tonight," Gregor added in a whisper.

"Sorry, Father."

"It's understandable, but you came through in the end, just like you will in the month to come." Gregor kissed Zel's temple before releasing him.

The cheers were the most other members of the guild—besides Zel's parents, his teachers, or Rudy—had ever praised him. Even here among peers, Zel was often looked at as something to be wary of, envious of, or worse, like he was some savior set to acquire the fortune they all hoped to share when the sorcerer was defeated. The pressure was great and would get no easier until the deed was done.

Rudy was Zel's closest and honestly only friend because he was one of the few who looked at Zel as simply *Zel*.

Well, when Rudy remembered that Zel preferred his shortened name over Rapunzel. It hadn't been long since he'd begun to request it, but constantly correcting others grew tiresome, especially when so few listened.

Before Zel could find his mother in the crowd, Lothar's voice rose above the rest. The many members in the room hushed and parted to reveal the guild master standing in front of the head table, where he would eventually sit. It and the other tables were covered in various foods and goblets overflowing with wine or ale.

"Three cheers for Rapunzel! Newest assassin for Queen, kingdom, and guild glory!" Lothar shouted.

"Oy, oy, oy!" everyone answered.

It was surreal. The time was finally upon Zel to fulfill his destiny. Amid such revelry, he could almost forget what came with the morn and that he had made an orphan of a little girl tonight.

Gregor pushed Zel forward, and once Zel reached Lothar, he dropped to one knee in a reverent bow. Zel's mask was already lowered from earlier, but Lothar pushed the hood from Zel's head, cupped his cheek, and lifted his chin to make Zel look at him.

Lothar was not unattractive. If Zel were to guess, he would have thought Lothar looked about forty, but Zel's parents had said he'd barely looked five winters younger twenty winters ago. He was long-lived, a supposed blessing from the Queen, but not immortal like he craved. The abundance of magical trinkets he wore was proof of that, from a ring that allowed for brief invisibility, to an earring capable of communication with whomever wore its twin regardless of distance, to any number of other baubles no one person knew all the secrets of, other than Lothar himself. Only someone gifted with magic could craft magical items. The greater the potential of the person, the greater the items they could create. Lothar had no innate magic, but with the guild at his disposal, he had the ability to acquire whatever he might wish for.

One item Zel had always been curious about was another ring, black, possibly even obsidian, with a circle engraved into it bisected by a horizontal line.

Everything about Lothar was a bit paler and brighter than others in the guild. Pale skin, pale hair that was almost silver, slicked back into a long ponytail, and icy blue eyes. For guild members, Lothar's word was more law than the Queen's, but his touch always made Zel's stomach churn.

"Well done, dear girl." Lothar leaned close to Zel's face. "You are ready. The fairest of flowers have the sharpest of thorns, do they not? But they are no less beautiful for it, nor less worthy of being *plucked* in due time."

Just as Zel could not show fear toward the sorcerer come tomorrow, he could not show Lothar his revulsion. "Yes, Master Lothar."

Lothar lifted Zel to his feet. "I have a gift for you. Anna, come!" He snapped his fingers, and a woman stepped forward.

The shabby way she was dressed was the first indication something was wrong.

The collar around her neck was the other.

That was a control collar, one of very few in Lothar's possession. Similarly functioning wristbands were used on enslaved elves to prevent the use of their magic, but those rarely also enslaved their minds since that would have robbed them of their creative abilities, which was what elves were most used for. This type of collar turned its wearer into a seemingly blank slate, silent and obedient. It was said that their true selves were conscious but trapped, so they could only watch as their body obeyed any command given to it by whomever put the collar on them.

Lothar used the collars on traitors.

"Anna was caught stealing from our coffers!" Lothar announced to the room. "She had no excuses, merely her greed to have more than her brethren!"

Grumbles and jeers filtered through the crowd.

"You know what fate awaits such traitors." Lothar returned his attention to Zel. "As a final gift for your induction, it is you, Rapunzel, who will carry out Anna's sentence."

"But... won't that make her my ninth kill instead of the sorcerer as preordained?"

"Do not worry. You are going to have her kill herself." Lothar handed the woman a dagger. "Anna, you will now obey whatever Rapunzel asks of you."

Anna's seemingly blank eyes met Zel's, and to his horror, he believed it must have been true that her mind was her own somewhere within, because he could see the terror shining through.

She deserved this end, didn't she, for daring what she had?

"We do not abide traitors," Lothar went on. "Rapunzel, take your place among our ranks and tell Anna to split open her belly."

Zel couldn't help that he hesitated.

She deserved this... didn't she?

"Remember, Rapunzel. We do not mourn our marks."

"They are already dead," Zel finished. "You heard him," he said to Anna, "split yourself open for your wrongs against the guild."

Despite the fear visible in her eyes, she wasted no time before turning the dagger, stabbing it into her side, and slicing across her middle, deep enough to spill her innards on the floor in front of her.

She dropped, and Lothar kicked her onto her back. Zel knew why, for while this would not count as his ninth kill, he was still expected to watch the light leave her eyes, while her blood pooled toward his boots.

At least the light dimmed quickly.

"To Rapunzel!" Lothar shouted. "Tomorrow, her true task begins!"

"To Rapunzel!" the crowd echoed.

"Enjoy yourself tonight, pretty petal." Lothar stepped over the body as uncaring as ever, while some of his guards came forward to clean up the mess. "And get out of those clothes and into something more befitting of a woman. Unless you desire anything else tonight, as reward for a job well done? Do you, Rapunzel?"

"Only one thing, Master Lothar. Please, call me—"

"Zel!" Rudy panted Zel's name beside his ear, while hoisting him onto the table in the storeroom. Not even he knew the truth, despite being the only person Zel had fooled around with since the first stirs of fleshly yearning set upon them. "God, I love your breasts." He kissed and licked Zel's neck.

"What breasts?" Zel laughed, for he had never tried faking a larger bosom but made a point to remark on his flatness as if it was his unfair lot in life.

Using the cellar entrance into the shop's storeroom, Zel had slipped away first, after whispering to Rudy the common code for their rendezvous, a Thieves Guild saying they had taken as their own:

"Only empty pockets need filling."

It was particularly used among pickpockets, since the pockets of their marks were always full, and their pockets needed filling. Rudy had yet to *fill Zel's pocket*, but the promise that he might always lured him.

Zel and his parents lived on the second floor, so he had gone up to change, then met Rudy back here. The layers expected of a woman could be a pain. Bodice and apron over shirt and outer petticoat, over corset and inner petticoat, all over chemise and stockings. Rudy was adept, however, at getting everything up top undone to slip his hands into Zel's chemise and brush his fingers across Zel's nipples.

He arched into Rudy's touch, always enjoying when his friend did that.

"I prefer small breasts," Rudy said, grinding his clothed cock against Zel's thigh. "Large ones get in the way."

"Oh? And how many large ones have you fondled?" Zel turned his head to tongue Rudy's ear. He did so love being touched like this. He loved touching someone else. He loved the heat it roused in his belly. The difficult part was preventing Rudy from discovering the hardness between his legs.

"I have fondled plenty!" Rudy argued. "But my other girls let me touch them in more places."

Liar, Zel thought. He doubted Rudy had fooled around with anyone else, and if he had, they definitely hadn't allowed him between their legs.

"I prefer your breasts though. I prefer everything about you, Zel. I love you."

It was a shame that was true, because Zel loved Rudy as a friend, but not enough to choose him if he ever got to know choice after the coming month. He also couldn't be sure what Rudy would think once he learned Zel had lied to him all this time. Zel couldn't be sure what anyone would think, but first, he had to survive his predestined month of betrothal. However that turned out, this would be the last time he and Rudy would ever be together like this.

Zel had wanted so many times to confess to him, his one true friend, but his parents had cautioned him against it. It was too great a risk, they'd say. Perhaps Zel's vain hopes at rebellion were what first pushed him to pursue Rudy when they were younger. He'd noticed how Rudy's affectionate glances had become more heated and used his seductive training to encourage it, but always with the caveat, "Just between friends." Perhaps part of him even wanted to slip up and allow Rudy to discover the truth on his own. But at the last moment, he would always default to behaving, to doing as he had been told.

"Ah, ah." Zel grabbed Rudy's hand that was trying to slip up beneath his petticoats and chemise skirt. He often tried to, but a single tut from Zel was always enough to stop him.

Doing this in the storeroom was risky, maybe more so with a celebration in Zel's honor happening below, but it would have been riskier if they'd met in his bedroom. Zel hadn't let Rudy up there since they were fourteen. It would have been too easy to give in.

Rudy groaned at being denied, still rutting against Zel's leg. "You drive me mad. How can you stand not letting me inside you? I know you want it."

Zel did, but even offering his ass would have been too dangerous when Rudy might reach for a cunt that wasn't there. "I am a virtuous lady," Zel said, pushing Rudy away so he could hop down from the table and drop to his knees. "And I intend to stay virtuous until I am wed." He opened Rudy's breeches and tore them down to his ankles.

Rudy could hardly complain about lacking access when their

nearly daily ritual always ended with him finishing, either by Zel's mouth or with his hands. It was Zel who had to wait and finish himself off later with a swift wank. He longed to know the feel of another's hand where he most ached for one, or better yet a mouth. As he sucked Rudy down his throat, he imagined someone else sucking him.

The fantasy had Zel leaking into his chemise and dripping onto the floor. As he lost himself to the hollowing of his cheeks, thoroughly enjoying swallowing Rudy, he hummed to himself, almost unaware he did so.

Rudy held a hand to the back of Zel's head, massaging the top twists of his braids. It didn't take long, and once Rudy had spilled down Zel's throat, he asked, "What was it you were humming, Rapunzel? I didn't recognize the tune."

Zel turned from him, reaching up under his layers to tighten the laces of his corset, and then tightened his outer bodice once he was put back together. "Just something I made up to go along with my favorite poem. You know the one." He sang the start of the same tune, only now he added words.

> "*In the stillest night,*
> *at dawn's break,*
> *a voice began to lament;*
> *sweetly and gently,*
> *the night wind*
> *carried to me its sound.*"

"You composed that?" Rudy asked, finishing adjusting his spectacles and securing his own clothes—breeches, shirt, and vest. The only other layer for a man was linen trunks. Entirely unfair.

"Surely, someone more talented than I will compose a better tune for it someday, but I am fond of my version." Zel returned to Rudy to kiss him on the mouth. He would be a good husband to someone someday, but not to Zel. "You called me Rapunzel again."

"Sorry!" Rudy sputtered. "I forget."

"Funny how no one has trouble remembering to call you Rudy and not *Rudolf*."

Rudy sneered at the use of his given name, and Zel pointed at the expression in earnest.

"See! That is how it feels when someone calls me Rapunzel."

"I know!" Rudy raised his hands in submission. "I am sorry. I called you Rapunzel for nineteen years. Well, I wasn't really calling you anything until we were three or four, but you get my meaning. I am trying. Although, why don't you correct your parents when they call you it?"

"I... don't know," Zel admitted. "I just never manage to. It's silly to hesitate. They weren't even the ones who named me. Are those new spectacles?" Zel hadn't realized until now, but Rudy's frames looked more pristine than he remembered, almost golden.

"The old ones broke." Rudy shrugged, adjusting them again with a quick glance aside.

"Oh? How did—"

Rudy tugged Zel closer before he could finish. "Please, let me feel how wet I made you."

Zel *was* wet, still dripping, but as much as he wanted that, he couldn't allow Rudy to feel anywhere near it. He was tempted. It *was* their last night, and Rudy deserved to know the truth, but Zel couldn't risk it. "Not tonight. Now go before someone catches us. I'll follow shortly. If anyone asks, I'm still getting pretty."

"You are always pretty. But fine. I thought perhaps today of all days I could change your mind." Rudy lifted Zel's hand and kissed his fingers. "Happy birthday, Zel."

Zel was twenty today, finally a man—or woman to everyone else—but at least he had until tomorrow to be sent to the sorcerer's tower.

When Rudy released Zel's hand, he flipped it over and dropped something into it that felt cold and weighty. It was a necklace, gold by the looks of it, with an emerald pendant.

"*Rudy*." Zel held the necklace up to inspect it. "Who did you pickpocket this from? Such a treasure should have been turned over—"

"Do not worry about that. Just enjoy the gift."

Tears welled up in Zel's eyes because it wasn't only that it was a beautiful and clearly valuable piece of jewelry, but that it harkened back to the very first gift Rudy had ever given him.

They were six at the time. They'd played together a little but were not yet close. Several other children were teasing Zel, including the bully who eventually melted, chanting about how the sorcerer was going to chop him up into his own salad someday. If any of them knew it was Zel's birthday, none of them had wished him well but continued to taunt him.

Rudy intervened, chasing them away. The others had been so merciless, they'd pushed Zel to tears, which had only made their taunts worse, saying he'd for certain fail as a member of the guild someday if he was such a "soft and silly girl." But Rudy cheered him up. The Great Famine hadn't fully ravaged the kingdom yet, and they were in a small field of flowers at the edge of the central city, as far as most children were allowed to venture. Rudy sat with Zel, babbling on about one thing or another while linking a chain of snapdragons. Their yellow flowers made it almost look like a gold necklace. Then he affixed the blossom of a green zinnia to act as its pendant and presented it to Zel like a courter.

Happy birthday, Rapunzel.

"I can make you one out of flowers again if you prefer," the grownup Rudy said, clearly having intended the comparison. "I would do anything for you, Zel."

"Rudy, I cannot wear this—"

"Not to the celebration, no, but tomorrow, when you go to the tower, wear it in remembrance of me."

The necklace was truly beautiful, and connected to that precious memory made it even more valuable in Zel's eyes, but as he slipped it into the pocket of his apron, he had to say, "I have told you many times—"

"To not get my hopes up. I know. You are a free spirit, but my heart does not know any better. I will always love you."

The sentiment was almost enough to dwindle Zel's erection.

Almost.

He kissed Rudy's cheek but still bid him farewell for now.

As soon as Rudy left, Zel hoisted his lower layers to take his cock in hand. He didn't think about Rudy while he pumped his prick, smoothing the collection of fluids across his skin. He didn't think about anyone. He simply wanted the bliss of oblivion for a while when nothing else was certain, other than that Rudy was setting himself up for disappointment.

Inevitably, as Zel stroked himself to a harried end, a faceless figure entered his mind. He had begged his parents to describe the sorcerer to him, but all they had ever said was that he was tall, dark, and terrifying, and that Zel could not let his fear show when they met.

Hips stuttering, Zel came into his palm, as he imagined the faceless figure licking him clean. He certainly wouldn't be getting that treatment from the sorcerer, but the fantasy was better than the reality to come. In truth, Zel used a rag to clean himself that he then tossed into the corner, telling himself he'd sneak it into the laundry later.

He tidied himself and prepared to head back downstairs, only to nearly collide with his mother when he turned for the hatch.

Second time tonight. He was definitely distracted.

Sophie had brown hair and eyes to match. Aside from sharing his father's bowed lips and slight build, Zel had often been told he looked like her. The scar on Sophie's cheek did not sully her beauty. Not the sorcerer's cut. That had eventually healed and faded. Lothar's was the one that had scarred.

"Rapunzel—"

"Just this once more!" Zel said. "Rudy remains none the wiser."

"You tempt fate." She crossed her arms sternly.

"What else can one do other than tempt it when one's fate is already sealed?"

Sophie did not move to grant Zel leave to the hatch nor did she look away. She barely blinked. "Are you a man today or still a brat?"

"Why, Mother!" Zel curtsied. "I am a lady."

Sophie threw her arms around Zel's neck so suddenly that he gasped. They were almost equal in height, although Zel was the tiniest bit taller. He remembered how strange it had been the first time he could look her in the eye.

He brought his arms up around her waist to hug her back.

"That boy loves you too much," Sophie said. "It is cruel to lead him on."

"I don't. I have always been plain with Rudy. He leads himself on. If he hates me when this is over, I can accept that." Zel thought he could accept anything once this was finally finished, but perhaps he wasn't being truthful that he could accept Rudy's hatred. He didn't want to lose his friend. He didn't want any of what lay ahead of him other than his freedom.

Sophie was just as fierce of an assassin as Gregor. They had alternated being Zel's seconds on missions. Tonight had simply been Gregor's turn. Both had taught Zel how to wield a blade, but his mother had taught him how to move so stealthily that not even an eagle's eye could notice him in the shadows.

Whether either of those skills would be enough to best the sorcerer would be tested soon enough.

"Happy birthday, my sweet boy." Sophie released him to hand over an object wrapped in cloth.

"Now who's tempting fate?" Zel asked, since the hatch to the Thieves Guild remained open, though he could see down into it that there was no one skulking below to have overheard.

"Open your present."

"You and Father already gave me my new dagger."

"This is just from me."

Curiously, Zel unwrapped the cloth and found the pristine silver brush his mother had used to untangle his hair since he'd had enough hair to get tangled.

The one the sorcerer let her keep.

"You can be whoever you want to be when this is over, my darling Rapunzel."

Whoever he wanted?

Even being an adult now, Zel wasn't sure who that was.

"I might not do away with all my skirts and dresses," Zel said, for he knew that much was true. "I do like wearing them. Maybe with fewer layers though."

Sophie laughed and pulled him in for another hug.

"Also, um…"

"Yes, Rapunzel?"

Zel cringed. "Nothing. I love both my presents, Mother. Thank you."

With so much else about to change, Zel could ask his parents to call him by his preferred name if and when he returned home to them.

When he returned home, successful and free.

There had been much speculation within the guild about why the sorcerer wanted Zel, and why specifically he wanted Zel to ingest all that lettuce, infusing him with some sort of magic, even if not immortality. The reigning theories were, one: so Zel would be a more delectable meal when the sorcerer devoured his soul on their wedding night; or two: that the sorcerer truly did want a bride who would be healthy and vibrant after eating the heartiest of vegetables for twenty winters when much of the kingdom was malnourished.

Zel hoped for the latter, at least until it all unraveled into attempted murder on his part, because then the sorcerer might be kind to him during the month.

Whatever the truth, whatever the sorcerer honestly wanted, he was not going to get it.

ULRICH

All was going according to plan, and at last, Ulrich's final night alone was upon him.

Tomorrow his betrothed would be brought to the tower, and everything would fall into place over the month ahead. It had been centuries since he had enjoyed company, since he had known any companionship at all.

Ulrich wondered who Rapunzel had grown up to be, but no matter who the child, now an adult, proved to have become, Ulrich would not waver from his plan. However much that plan might need adjusting over the coming days, he would succeed. He was certain of it.

The promise of that, as Ulrich looked out of his tower window toward the villages and city and castle in the distance outside the wood, was enough to make him smile and long for the morn.

Two

ZEL

The mirror in Zel's parents' bedroom was one of the more lavish things they owned, though they had not purchased it. It was one of the few items his parents had stolen that had not been taken by the guild. Certain things could be kept for a job well done, and the nearly full-length mirror with its hand-carved wooden frame was something Sophie had requested when she and Gregor wed.

Not really a reward for a job well done, but a promise for a job well done to come. Sophie had stood right where Zel was now in front of that mirror on the day of their wedding, in her wedding dress, with Zel a growing life inside her not yet large enough to show as even a bump.

Zel wore that same dress today.

"You really do look lovely, darling," Sophie said, coming up behind Zel to kiss his cheek. "Whether you wear this again someday for your real wedding or are in breeches and a waistcoat, you will be equally as radiant."

As fair as Zel had often been told he was, he had never looked as beautiful as he did today. No one could have mistaken him for a man in the deep pink and black dress, with luminous sleeves trimmed in gold almost the same color as his hair. A touch of green lace adorned the bottom of the bodice, which was also embroidered with a mix of the same pink, green, and gold, and an addition of violet that all came together with Zel's violet cloak fastened at his neck.

Rather than a bonnet, Zel and his mother had affixed fresh flowers to a headpiece that was near enough to a crown. The cloak, when pulled around him, would hide that he wore Rudy's emerald pendant, but for now, it gleamed beautifully as a centerpiece on Zel's chest. His hair was more intricately braided than usual, though it still hung past his knees, even with countless layers to his plaits.

"Ah, but trim that bit there, will you?" Sophie indicated an uneven strand of Zel's fringe. She handed him a pair of shears, and he clipped the strand to better frame his face.

Perhaps, a month from now, Zel would finally slice it all off. But likely not. He no longer wanted that. He loved his hair. He loved the way he looked in the mirror this morn, garbed in his mother's wedding dress. He just hated the reason.

Zel handed the shears back to Sophie and pulled his bundle of braids over his shoulder to stroke it. It was his, and even if its splendor was from the eating of magical lettuce, he refused to let any part of him be taken away. This pact would end with him gaining, not losing, even if he didn't yet know everything he wanted.

"Are you ready, Rapunzel?" Sophie asked.

Zel fought the usual cringe at the use of his full name. After this was over, he would finally correct them. "I have to be. But may I see Rudy before we go?" He turned from the mirror to face her. "Besides you and Father, he is the only one I will miss if I never return."

"Do not think like that." Sophie brushed Zel's cheek with her thumb and then ran her fingers down his braids as well. "Repeat your mantra, one last time. You will succeed."

"I will succeed."

"You are ready for this."

"I am ready for this."

"You are fierce and beautiful and capable."

"I am fierce and beautiful and capable."

"Now let's find Rudy. But this time, no letting him into your corset."

Zel laughed. "*Mother*."

"I am afraid there isn't time for last-minute visits," Gregor's voice came from the hall. As he stepped into the room, he gasped and held a hand to his chest. "Oh, Rapunzel. You are a vision. As beautiful as your mother was those twenty winters ago."

"Don't lie, Gregor," Sophie said. "Rapunzel is prettier."

"If so," Gregor countered, coming close enough to take one of each of their hands, "it is only because together it was inevitable we would create a child who is the fairest in all the lands." He kissed first Zel's hand and then Sophie's.

"Flatterer," Sophie said.

"I am sure there is at least one person in the kingdom who is fairer than me," Zel said. "But wait. No time? I can't see Rudy?"

Gregor's smile fell. "Before we depart, Lothar demands an audience."

***

The Thieves Guild halls beneath the shop were in a very different state from last night. All signs of their reveling had been cleared away, and there were very few guild members about, as all had tasks to perform or missions to complete. The few that remained were primarily guards, one of which led Zel and his parents to a sanctum several twisting corridors deeper into the guild where Lothar took audiences in private.

Zel's one solace was that his parents were able to join him.

"Master Lothar," Zel greeted and curtsied before the guild master, who sat in a grand chair like a throne at the back of the room, with two guards on either side of him. Just in case, Zel had made certain Rudy's pendant was hidden.

"Rapunzel," Lothar greeted back, already having forgotten to use the name Zel, but that was typical. "No man could resist your loveliness today, pretty petal, not even an immortal sorcerer."

As it turned out, Zel preferred his full name to *pretty petal*. "I will do my duty, and I will succeed."

"I know you will. But I did not call you here only to wish you well. I mean to offer additional incentive."

"Incentive, Master?"

Lothar rose from his throne and approached Zel. "When you succeed and bring back to us all the tower's secrets, you will become a different immortal's bride."

"What...?"

Zel wasn't kneeling, but even standing, he only came up to Lothar's nose. Lothar tilted Zel's chin up like he had last night. "Did you think you would go unrewarded? Return to me with the sorcerer's head, and it is I, a man poised to be more powerful than even the Queen, who will have you for his bride. Something to look forward to." He leaned so close that Zel feared the guild master might steal a kiss. There would be no hiding his revulsion if Lothar did so, but thankfully, he merely stroked Zel's cheek.

"What if I find no weaknesses?" Zel asked. "What if he cannot be killed?"

"I am reasonable. That is a possibility. If so, find the source of his immortality and steal that much from him to bring to me. Your family's debt will be paid. And make no mistake." He gripped

Zel's chin again, this time harshly. "No matter what you think that monster capable of, it is my debt you do not wish to be in."

"Y-yes, Master Lothar."

Zel remained numb the entire way back to their shop. Only once he and his parents were in the storeroom did his knees fail him and he crumpled to the floor, sobbing.

"Rapunzel!" His parents swept down to either side of him, holding him as he cried.

"I-I thought... if I succeeded... I'd be free. I would finally be free. But if Lothar wants me as his bride, when he finds out—"

"We will not let that come to pass," Gregor said. "You will marry no one but who you wish to, if anyone at all. Finish your mission, and we needn't answer to Lothar ever again."

"Gregor?" Sophie questioned.

"We've discussed it, haven't we?"

"As foolish fancy, but—"

"If we follow Lothar blindly even after our debt is paid, we condemn ourselves. We condemn Rapunzel." Gregor held them both closer, gathering his "girls" into his arms. "We deserve more than that selfish brute. The guild deserves more. We could run it so much better than he does. We could save lives instead of only taking them and defy the Queen for superior reasons over just lining our own pockets."

"What are you suggesting, Father?" Zel asked.

"Only what we always planned for as our contingency if worse came to worst. The Queen doesn't care who runs the guild, so long as it appears to serve her. She didn't bat an eye when Lothar took over decades ago by unseating the previous leader. He believes we will hand all that power over to him. We will not. It is ours for the taking. Yours. If you claim the tower's secrets, we can finally stand up to Lothar. We can be the ones who come out ahead, and you can have whatever life you wish. Nothing else about the mission has to change." Gregor brushed the tears from Zel's eyes and kissed his cheek. "We can do this. *You* can do this, Rapunzel."

Sophie looked just as supportive.

They were right, weren't they? They had all feared and followed Lothar for so long, they knew no other way, but if Zel succeeded in claiming all that power and treasure for himself, there was no reason to give any of it to Lothar. It had only ever been discussed as a last resort, but it seemed they had reached that end. Besides, Zel's parents could bring a new age to the Thieves Guild. Zel could too if he chose it. He might even want that life once it was truly his choice to make.

Zel blinked back the last of his tears and nodded. "I can do this."

And when he did, he could finally, *finally* be Zel.

The trip out of the city, through villages, and along the appointed path into the wood and toward the sorcerer's tower took most of the day, meaning they arrived just as the sun was setting, exactly as the sorcerer had requested.

Any travel into the wood was dangerous, on roads or otherwise, even before reaching what some considered the most perilous area—the Dark Forest—but Zel and his parents encountered no bandits nor nefarious magic. It seemed the sorcerer had cleared the way.

The layer of a hand-me-down surcoat lined and trimmed with fur had been added beneath his cloak to keep him warm. It was well-made, if somewhat worn from wear, another item that had belonged to Zel's mother that he was thankful for against the frigidness of autumn. It made the skin beneath his layers no less prickly with gooseflesh when they arrived at the tower he had seen in the distance all his life like a monument to his fate.

He had said his goodbyes to his parents before they left home, keeping the conversation during the journey light so as to not conjure more tears and add any redness or puffiness to Zel's face. He was to be the perfect bride, even if the day he was to wed the sorcerer was a month away. He wanted so badly to hug his parents one last time, but he knew he would begin sobbing again if he did. Instead, when they turned from him to head back down the path on their shared horse, he raised a hand in farewell, they did the same, and Zel steeled himself to approach the wall.

Woe to any bandits who attempted to accost his parents on their ride home, but Zel still worried the clear path to the tower had only been for him. He had to trust that his horse and the few belongings he'd brought with him would indeed be safe while he left them behind.

There had been a note with yesterday's shipment of *rapunzel* telling him to leave whatever he brought with him and the horse he arrived on outside the wall when he approached the tower. It was a guild horse, as was the one his parents rode back on, but the upkeep of any was difficult during a famine. Zel didn't like leaving his things unguarded, let alone a vulnerable animal when times were tough, but he dared not go against the sorcerer's instructions.

The circumference of the tower was narrow, and the wall not much wider around it. Zel's parents had recounted how the garden within was not large either but so lush, it didn't need to be. Even once Zel was only a few strides from the wall, which had no opening, he could almost see around the perimeter where it curved left and right.

To the left, did he see a foot sticking out of the brush?

"Only emp—" A hand clamped down on Zel's shoulder, and he seized its wrist, flipping the offender end-over-end to land hard on his back in front of Zel.

"Rudy!" Zel released his friend, allowing him to scramble to his feet. Rudy was bundled up as well, but the hood had fallen from his head. "What are you doing here?"

"Being reminded to finish our code in full before surprising you, apparently. How could I not come? When you didn't meet me to say goodbye, I had to follow so I could see you one last time. You wore my pendant." The emerald had jostled loose from Zel's surcoat, which Rudy could see after adjusting his spectacles.

"Of course I did." Zel clutched it. "But Rudy—"

Rudy swept forward, lips already puckering, as he took hold of Zel's cheek.

"Are you *mad*?" Zel lurched away. "He could be watching us right now!"

Rudy glanced over his shoulder at the tower. Silent as it remained, when he looked back at Zel, he straightened his shoulders and nodded. "Forgive me. Then I am merely a friend wishing his friend farewell. Do you remember five years ago, I think, when Carl tried to kiss you like that?"

A smile tugged at Zel's lips. He remembered.

While wariness of Zel had always been rampant among their peers, the more his beauty had grown as he reached maturity, the more the boys tried to press their luck. Zel always rebuffed them beyond honing his skills of seduction, only willing to risk actual intimate activity with Rudy, but Carl had not taken no for an answer.

"You yanked him back from me by the hair and readied to punch him." Zel chuckled.

"And you, with the speed and grace of an alleycat, seized me by the arm to stop me. As soon as Carl breathed relief, you punched him so hard yourself, his eyes watered for an hour." Rudy chuckled too, and the familiar ease of his company almost helped Zel relax. But he couldn't relax. Not for the next month.

"Because I do not need rescuing," Zel said, echoing the words he had said back then. He didn't, not like when Rudy had given him the flower version of this pendant.

"I know. But I will always be here in the unlikely event that someday you're wrong. I will be thinking of you, Rapunzel. *Zel*. I love you," Rudy finished in a whisper but looked Zel square in the eyes as he said the oft spoken words. "We will see each other again."

As Rudy darted back into the trees to follow the path Zel's parents had taken, everything in Zel ached. He could only assume Rudy had his own horse hidden somewhere. It had been foolish of him to come, and Zel couldn't have said he shared Rudy's affections, but it had still been nice to see his friend once more. The romantic fool.

Now for the task at hand. Zel's eyes returned to the foot to the left of the wall. He neared it, but before he could be certain if it attached to a body or was simply a lost boot, the stones in the wall parted, creating an entrance for Zel where none had been before. Wary as he was, he stepped through the opening.

The wall immediately closed up behind him, and the chill in the air dissipated. Fragrant smells assaulted Zel. Grass and herbs and flowers. It was the height of spring here, like another world from the autumn cold he had left. As the sun finished setting into darkness, Zel remained in light with the rising of the moon.

He followed the same path he had been told about by his mother and eventually came upon a patch of familiar lettuce. He touched their leaves, verdant green with gold stems. He was overdue for his daily salad, but if the sorcerer wished for him to eat more today, he would provide, Zel assumed.

First stone over, third stone up, and—when Zel pressed it, a door into the tower opened just like the wall had. The sorcerer probably could have opened it magically, but Zel knew his way up, almost as if he had been here before. He had been technically, but as a still barely formed babe in the womb. He also noted how, up close, the tower's outer surface looked iridescent, like rocks or cave walls when wet.

Ascending the steps, each story up felt more and more like heading to the gallows. He was everything he should be. Everything the sorcerer should want. But he could not predict everything that would be asked of him. He could not predict anything. The only weapon he carried was his dagger, hidden in a sheath on his thigh beneath his skirts. He hoped to not need it until the month was up.

When he reached the top of the tower, the door was already open.

Everything beyond was dark, so before Zel stepped forward, he called out, "Master Sorcerer? May I enter and present myself to you?"

"You may," a voice boomed back, deep and resonant enough that Zel felt it in his bones.

He dared to enter the tower's room, and as soon as both feet crossed the threshold, candles and large sconces on the walls lit up to brighten the space like the dawn. Zel gasped, for the sorcerer stood before him a mere stretch of his arm away, tall, dark, and terrifying, just as his parents had said.

And so... so beautiful.

"Quite beautiful," the sorcerer said.

"M-my lord?" Zel sputtered. Had he said that out loud?

The ethereal man stepped closer to Zel. His skin had a violet tint to it, as did his long, wavy black hair. Eating of his garden was clearly what had grown Zel's hair so long, for the sorcerer's also dusted the ground, only his was so like the void of the night sky that Zel could see stars moving in it.

His tapered elf ears were sharp, but his gaze was sharper, piercing with the swirling heavens in his eyes. Elves, by nature, were not immortal, though one aspect of their magic seemed to age them more gracefully than their human contemporaries. Zel couldn't be sure if the sorcerer even was an elf or something else, but his outward appearance must have stopped aging from whenever he'd achieved immortality. He could have as easily been mistaken for thirty as his supposed centuries. He wore black and violet robes that covered most of his tall, broad body. He was imposing to be sure, and Zel wondered what the rest of him looked like beneath his clothes.

"You are more beautiful than I could have envisioned," the sorcerer said. "Twenty winters ago, nearly twenty-one now, your parents made an attractive pair, but you outshine them for how you are a blend of their fairness."

"And a bit of something else?" Zel asked. He stood frozen as the sorcerer circled him, smelling like moonflowers and sage.

"Yes. A part of my magic is also in you. Much magic in fact." He was behind Zel then and drew back Zel's hood. How different to have the sorcerer do that instead of Lothar. Then he unclasped the cloak at Zel's neck to remove it and bid him, "Remove your surcoat as well. It is warm here."

It was the perfect temperature, just like in the garden.

The sorcerer continued to circle Zel, taking both surcoat and cloak, though he didn't appear to hold either any longer when he came around Zel's other side to stand before him. He looked Zel up and down in the wedding dress and flowered crown.

"Look at you. Ripe with my magic."

"But why?" Zel asked when the sorcerer tried reaching for him. "To ensorcell me? Is that why you wanted me this way, to bewitch me into being the perfect obedient bride for you?" He had always feared that once here, the sorcerer would be able to control him without him having any agency at all.

The sorcerer lowered his hand, his left, while the right remained hidden in his robes. His expression looked almost amused. "Only weak minds can be bewitched without a magical device in play, and even then, never the heart nor soul. Do you feel bewitched by me, Rapunzel?"

"Please, my lord, call me Zel." He felt immediate panic for having asked that. "Unless you prefer—"

"It is your name, and names are powerful. Your preference is what matters... Zel."

Zel shuddered. The way that single syllable rolled off the sorcerer's tongue was sinful. And though he had given Zel his name, he accepted the request so easily. "I wasn't certain. You named me, after all."

"As a reminder for your parents, but you made the name your own. I respect that."

"May I know your name, Master Sorcerer?"

"You may." He held his left hand out to Zel, but this time turned it palm up in offering for Zel to decide whether to touch it. The nails on that ashen colored hand were pristine, lovely even, but almost unnaturally sharp. "I am Ulrich. And yes, you may address me as such."

"As you wish, Master Ulrich." Zel placed his hand in the sorcerer's grasp.

"If you insist on titling me, lord is fine, but I am no one's master. Not anymore." Ulrich lifted Zel's hand to his lips and kissed it, gentle with his hold so that even where his nails pressed against Zel's skin, they did not prick him. The aura about Ulrich was indeed terrifying but also alluring in a way Zel had never felt with Lothar. Nor with anyone.

"Perhaps I find you a bit bewitching," Zel admitted.

"Good. A bride should not fear a future bridegroom. Nor look upon him without desire. But I assure you, there is no spell that could dictate how you feel or act toward me, and no item I would use to force such a thing. I abhor that kind of magic, for I prefer truth." Ulrich lingered, the grip he had on Zel's hand stroking down his fingers.

Zel's loins stirred. This was better than the worst-case scenario, but still not ideal if Zel couldn't temper him. At least in some things, Ulrich was superior to Lothar if he didn't condone magic like what infused Lothar's control collars. "My lord, would you grant your future bride a request?"

"Ask, and we shall see."

"Would you promise to not bring me to your bed until we are wed?"

A smile softened the intensity of Ulrich's gaze. "Do you expect me to be a brute?"

"I do not know what to expect, only what I have been told. You do not seem like a brute."

"May I ask something of you, Zel?"

"You may."

"Are you a virgin?"

A spike of fear pierced Zel's heart. "Y-yes."

Ulrich fixed him with an unwavering stare.

"The, um, virtue expected of a bride remains intact."

Ulrich chuckled. "Now that is an honest answer. Are you generally honest, Zel?"

"Generally."

"As am I. You are not to be mistreated. This month is for me to know you."

"To assess my worth?"

"Yes."

"And if I displease you before the month is over?"

"Are you going to displease me?" Ulrich asked.

"I cannot say, but so far you have not displeased me."

"Another honest answer." Ulrich leaned forward, lowering his towering height to Zel's level. "I respond viciously when wronged, against trespassers, thieves, and liars in my midst, but to one who shows me their true self, I can be kind. Shall I show you around the rest of the tower?" He snapped upright again, leaving Zel to mull over the obvious threat.

"There is more to see?" Zel glanced around.

The room was also as his parents had described. A lone window looked out toward the heart of the kingdom. There were shelves of books along the walls and more filled with bottles and jars. One shelf was covered in magical trinkets. There was a chaise in one area and a desk in another beside a second door, which, given the size of the tower, could only lead to a closet or to another set of stairs.

Or so Zel thought.

With a motion of his arm, Ulrich bid Zel to follow him across the room toward that second door. When they reached it, he pulled a key from a pocket inside his robes and handed it to Zel. The key was brass but polished enough that it almost looked gold. It had an intricately shaped bow. The oval within the bow's empty space almost seemed to shimmer like a rainbow stretched across it. The stem was long, but the three key bits were short, each decreasing in length to an almost tapered end.

"Oh yes," Ulrich said. "There is much more to see."

ULRICH

Zel's parents had indeed been an attractive pair, though Ulrich hadn't honestly cared whether or not their child would inherit their beauty. He had not asked for beautiful. He had asked for his rules to be followed, and they had been. Those foolish enough to have eaten the lettuce when not bidden to had gotten their punishment, but Zel had not gone a single day since birth without eating at least a leaf of Ulrich's lettuce.

The green eyes and radiantly golden hair were proof of that.

Zel glowed with all that magic, a truly magnificent bride-to-be and already dressed in a wedding gown. Ulrich was almost tempted to take the young mortal to his bed that night. It had been so long since he had known another's touch. But he was no such brute, and after all, Zel had asked so sweetly for him to wait.

What a marvelous deceiver. Perfect to be the sacrifice to achieve Ulrich's goal.

"Go on." He motioned for Zel to use the key on the lock. "Insert it and give the key a quarter turn. Then open the door."

Zel seemed cautious, smartly so, but did as requested and turned the key one click to the right.

Three

ZEL

"It's a washroom," Zel said with no small level of disappointment. He hadn't been certain what he expected, but given the intricacies of the key, something more magical than a place to relieve himself and wash up at the end of a long day.

"Every home needs such a space, does it not?" Ulrich said.

Zel's old home had one, but only because he hadn't been able to risk using a public bathhouse. Otherwise, it was rare in smaller homes. "Wait." He looked back into the tower proper, then forward into the washroom again. Both were equally spacious, which shouldn't have been possible. From outside, the tower looked no larger than the main room.

"Close the door, relock it, and give the key a half turn next," Ulrich instructed.

The key was magic, Zel realized, and he hastened to do as told to see what the next room contained. Half a turn of the key, and he reopened the door to one of the largest rooms he had ever seen, filled to the brim with treasure.

"I hardly remember anymore what is in there." Ulrich regarded the contents of the room as if he were looking upon something entirely benign. "Anything important to me is on the shelf in the main area. If we are to wed, all that is mine will also be yours. You are free to remove anything you like from this room and claim it as your own."

"Anything?" Zel almost dared not enter the magical space. Everything he'd ever needed had been provided by his parents or the guild, and his wants were forced to be minimal. The only item he had ever been able to keep from a mission was a silver cloak clasp, which Lothar had given him after his first kill. The only other item of value he owned was the pendant from Rudy.

"I need none of it." Ulrich gestured Zel inside. "Go. Pick out something as a betrothal gift for thus far proving worthy by following all of my instructions."

Where was Zel to begin? There were mounds of gold and gemstones. Overflowing chests, which themselves were jewel encrusted. There were statues. Fine art. Armor. Weapons. On one weapons rack was a dagger so lovely, it put Zel's recently gifted dagger to shame, but he couldn't very well choose a weapon as his first trinket.

Stepping inside the room, Zel turned to his right and saw a large open chest with piles of silks, other rich fabrics, and spun thread waiting to be made into bolts or as embroidery. Beside the chest was a walnut-colored loom.

"Is there something special about that loom, my lord?"

"You have a good eye," Ulrich said. "That loom is one of my most useful treasures. There are different types of magical spinning wheels and tools for weaving cloth. Some can contain dangerous spells. Some can change the nature of what it creates. That loom, at the introduction of thread or even full fabrics can turn the materials into whatever manner of garment the user envisions."

"I could... have that?"

"You needn't even remove it from this room to call it yours. Should you wish to use it to turn any of the fabrics or spools of thread into garments, you can do so at your leisure."

Zel stood in awe. His parents could never afford much for gifts. Rudy giving Zel the pendant had been a gamble. All treasure was guild property, unless Lothar deemed it otherwise, and magic in the hands of common folk was practically unheard of outside of elves, and most of them were enslaved.

"Your ensemble is lovely for our first meeting," Ulrich said, not entering but leaning against the doorframe, seeming all the more magical for how the gemstones and fine metals glittered near him, reflecting off his periwinkle skin and twilight hair.

"It was my mother's," Zel said.

"It suits you. But what would you make, Zel, if you could create anything to wear?"

Zel had never been asked that. What would he have, what would he want if he could have anything? He approached the loom and all the fabrics and materials for weaving beside it. "I would have a simple dress, one lovely and colorful but all one piece, with no complicated bodice, and no need for corset or petticoat beneath. Instead, I would wear linen trunks like a man, or perhaps breeches." Zel yanked his hand back from where he had set it upon the loom. Why had he said all that?

"Do not be startled," Ulrich said. "If you touch the loom, it plucks from your mind what you truly desire, so you need only will its use. Let me show you your room next, and should you wish to return here to create a garment before dinner, you are welcome to."

How dangerous to have admitted that Zel would prefer to wear clothing that was a mix of masculine and feminine, yet Ulrich seemed neither bothered nor suspicious to have heard so. "Thank you," Zel said.

He exited the treasure room, relocked the door, and Ulrich told him to give the key a three-quarter turn this time. When Zel looked into the next room, it was a spacious bedchamber, complete with canopied bed, wardrobe, chest, a desk of its own like the one in the main room, and a mirror on the wall with an intricately carved frame like the one in Zel's parents' bedroom, only this one was made of gold.

Even more miraculous was that Zel's things that had been in his horse's saddlebags were on the bed waiting for him. Zel raced over to check the contents, and all was accounted for.

"And the horse?" He looked back at Ulrich.

"Returned to your family with my gratitude."

"Will they be able to attend our wedding?"

"Should we wed, they will be welcome to join in celebration the following day."

Then Zel was on his own until his mission was complete, be that his wedding day or sooner if he learned Ulrich's secrets.

He had not expected any help, but anything new he learned would aid him in forming his plan.

"I will leave you now to settle in until you are ready to join me." Ulrich bowed his head and turned to go.

"My lord!" Zel called after him. "May I assume that a full turn of the key opens into your bedchamber?"

"It can." Ulrich peered over his shoulder. "A full turn can lead wherever I wish it to. Take your time, change if you desire, explore to your heart's content, and please, catalog whether there is anything you require that I have not provided for you. When you are ready, use the key with a full turn to find me."

He left and closed the door behind him.

The nervousness Zel had been able to hold at bay until now swept over him. He was here. He was doing this. And at least so far it seemed as though Ulrich's intentions were genuine. He wanted a bride as payment for Zel's parents' trespassing, and he had given Zel everything he could want to ensure his comfort.

Zel, who was going to do everything in his power to slay the sorcerer before the month was over.

There would be no slaying tonight, so Zel unsheathed the dagger from beneath his skirts and hid it under his mattress. He unpacked what little else he had into the chest and wardrobe, discovering that his cloak and furred surcoat had already been placed within the wardrobe on metal hooks. He set his silver hairbrush on the nightstand between the bed and window.

There was a window here, just like the one that faced the heart of the kingdom. Zel approached it to look out, and it faced the neighboring kingdom of Hallin. Zel was certain a second window could not be seen from the outside and assumed that this one, in this magical room, was invisible to anyone who looked at it.

How wondrous; but as enchanting as the sorcerer had proven to be, Zel could not falter. His future, his *life* depended on it, as did the lives of his parents if forced to face Lothar's wrath.

He would change, he decided, and removed his flowered crown before venturing back into the main chamber. The sorcerer was not there. The room remained lit by candlelight and sconces, and Zel allowed himself a moment to look it all over, especially the original treasures that had tempted his parents.

Everything was immaculate, all expensive looking or ancient, like fanciful leather tomes tucked between strange trinkets that Zel dared not touch when he did not know their purpose. He was surprised, even pleasantly so, to see some of his favorite collections of poems and bard tales among the sorcerer's books. Some were even quite modern for a being who had supposedly lived here for centuries. Did that mean the sorcerer sometimes left the tower, or did he acquire such things from unwanted guests?

Zel spared a glance outside the window, wondering how far along the path through the wood his parents had gotten, and how surprised they would be when they returned home and found Zel's horse waiting. He hoped Rudy would be well too, following in their wake.

He should dress for dinner and rejoin the sorcerer. *Ulrich*, Zel reminded himself. It had never suited him to know the names of his victims, but in this case, he must use it. He needed to charm Ulrich to better learn his secrets, his weaknesses, his undoing, without charming him so much as to be found out.

Would Ulrich go back on his promise to wait until they wed to bed him? If he grew too eager, the ruse would be over. Zel had to take this one moment at a time and always come out ahead as the true manipulator of what was to come.

He took the key and used it to return to the treasure room.

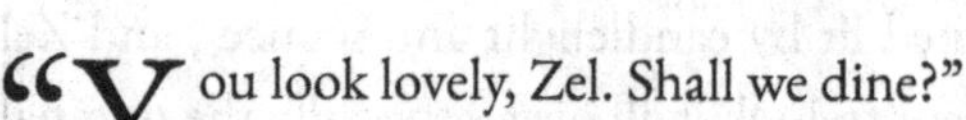

"**Y**ou look lovely, Zel. Shall we dine?"

Zel had assumed—and hoped—that his full turn of the key would not yet bring him into Ulrich's bedchamber. If it had, he worried his seduction might take a dangerous turn too soon, but his guess was right, and instead, the door opened to reveal a stately dining hall fit for the Queen herself.

Ulrich sat at one end of a long table in a high-back chair,

though he rose at Zel's entrance and bowed like a proper gentleman greeting a lady. He was dressed the same in his black and violet robes. Zel had used the loom to create exactly what he had said he wanted—a simple, single piece dress with breeches beneath as his only undergarment, no corset nor bodice, only a silk sash cinched at his waist. It was the most comfortable he had ever felt outside of his assassin gear, and he still looked convincingly feminine. He also still wore Rudy's pendant. He knew it was foolish to wear something a commoner shouldn't have, tempting Ulrich's curiosity when the pendant's origin was complicated at best, but the weight and meaning behind the token helped Zel feel grounded and somehow safer within the monster's den—however unlike a monster Ulrich had acted thus far.

What he had bid of the loom was to take what had been black and violet fabrics and add starlight shimmers to the combination as a mimic of Ulrich's hair. It was as if literal stars dotted Zel's dress as he moved, in brilliant contrast to his golden braids.

He also carried one of the books he had found in the main room. He set it beside him on the table when he took his seat across from Ulrich. Food had already been laid out, waiting for him to fill his plate, including a salad made from the *rapunzel* in the garden.

"You still wish for me to eat your lettuce?" Zel asked.

"I do. Do you not care for it?"

"It is some of the most delicious food I have ever eaten. But it leaves me curious."

"You know what it does. You are healthy and brimming with magic because of it. Your hair could never have grown so long or so silken if you were not infused with magical essence."

Because Zel's hair could only be cut by him—and as far as anyone else knew, not at all—it had often been speculated that it was where his magic was contained. "But I cannot wield magic."

"Would you like to learn how?"

"Anyone can learn?"

"Anyone can learn almost anything with the right tools. Talent is a factor, but lacking talent only stops those unwilling to put in the work. It is even possible for magic to occur spontaneously from someone with seemingly no power at all, although quite rare."

Zel wondered if that was how the sorcerer had learned—hard work over natural talent. "Perhaps not on our first night," he said.

"Please then, eat. If the wine is not to your liking, I can conjure a different vintage, ale, anything you like." Ulrich began to fill his plate, so Zel did the same.

He took a sip from the wine before taking his first bite of food, and it was worlds different from the vinegary swill served to guild members. "This is wonderful, my lord."

Ulrich raised his glass. "To the month ahead and a deserving end when it is over."

"*Prost*," Zel toasted, and after taking a larger gulp, he turned to his food. It was all just as delicious as the lettuce. "Do you have servants who prepared all this?"

"Not living ones."

Zel paused, wondering if undead had touched this food.

"Not any longer, I mean," Ulrich said. "Magic can accomplish much. I know many spells to cook and prepare food, so long as I know the recipes, but I tend to my garden myself, and I still need to catch and kill any game we eat."

"You leave the tower then?"

"Often. If you are wondering why no one has reported seeing me, who is to say whether I look like this when I leave?"

A shapeshifter. Good to know. "You eat, clearly," Zel indicated as Ulrich finished a bite.

"Why wouldn't I? But it is not food nor water nor wine that

sustains me. Do you know what does?"

Zel thought of the foot he had seen outside the tower wall. He thought of the stories he had heard and the many bodies reported to have been found around the tower for decades. Centuries. "Souls you drain from others, as you once attempted to drain my parents."

Ulrich's starlight eyes held Zel captive. "Understand that it would not kill me outright to stop consuming souls. But it keeps me... lively, even if it is not what keeps me alive."

It was still possible that Ulrich's true goal was to consume Zel's soul as some magically enriched meal. It was also possible that the game Zel ate now had once been an unfortunate trespasser. But he could not waste time on wondering unless it furthered his goal.

"Do you resent your parents or me for how things have come to pass?" Ulrich asked.

"I used to," Zel answered plainly. He had long since decided that he would be honest in everything he could, for it would add legitimacy when he had to lie. "As I got older, I understood why they risked what they did."

"Did you?"

"They had nothing. Stealing from you gave them the promise of a possibly better future together. Anyone would have taken risks for that."

"I suppose they would."

"But I also do not resent you. They trespassed. They stole from you. You were in your rights to punish them. Yet you spared them. Now *I* have a chance for a better life. One I hope I can share with them eventually."

Ulrich smiled and took up his wine glass again to sip from it. "Let us get through the month first."

"Of course."

They ate for a while with idle chatter. If this had been a normal arranged marriage without subterfuge and all that was at stake, Zel might have been truly charmed by his betrothed, however intimidating he may have been. Ulrich was certainly attractive. Entrancing. Regal.

But it was Zel who ought to be doing the charming and learn all he could.

When their meal was waning, Ulrich asked, "Are you going to tell me about that book of mine you brought to dinner?"

"I know this book." Zel lifted it. "I know all its stories. It pleased me to see it on my future bridegroom's shelf."

"Do you have a favorite story within?"

"Many."

"Pick one and read it to me. I am interested to know how your thieving parents educated you."

Was that a bait? "They are more than thieves, my lord," Zel said plainly, if a bit stilted.

"Forgive me. Tell me then, what else are they?"

Assassins was not the answer Zel planned to give, but he could still be truthful. "They own a music shop, Pied Pipers. Piper is our surname. They sell instruments there. Sheet music. Supplies for writing music. Even books like this one of beloved stories that have since been made better by being set to music. It is a cover for the Thieves Guild, yes, but they chose for the shop to be about music. Their love for stories and song is no lie, and they instilled the same in me."

"Well then, tell me, Zel, instead of reading one of your favorite stories to me, could you sing one?"

"I can do better." Zel rose from the table. "Might my magical lord provide a violin?"

Ulrich did so with no more flourish than lifting his hand from beneath the table, and there he held one, summoned, Zel assumed, from the treasure room.

Zel went to him and placed the book in front of Ulrich, turned to a specific page to follow along. It was when he took the violin that he saw Ulrich's right hand for the first time, as it had held the bow. Ulrich had been using his left for everything, and it was clear why given the state of the right.

Zel's parents had prepared him for it, but to see it was jarring. Not only was it blackened, with its veins glowing violet, but it was almost husk-like, just skin over bone.

"Thank you, my lord," Zel said, paying the hand no mind for now. He would learn its secrets in time.

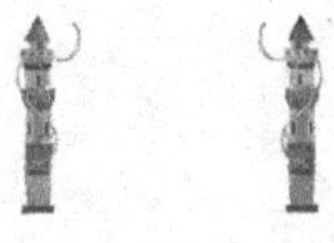

ULRICH

How wonderous Zel was thus far. Ulrich had envisioned much of how this encounter might go. So far all was as he had hoped for, yet even better and more surprising than he could have guessed.

Especially when Zel lifted the violin and began to play while singing.

"A fiddler skilled,
though love eluded her,
she played her woes
beneath the forest's shade,

and from her music,
unfit suitors stirred for her,
a curse, perhaps,
that love could not invade."

"First came the wolf,
with hunger in its eyes,
who sought her touch,
demanding like a beast.
She slipped from its grasp,
escaping with a sigh,
fleeting like the shadows,
her heart uncreased."

"Next came the fox,
dressed in charm like a liar,
riches it promised,
which she knew as fake.
Fooled it in turn,
she took all it had acquired,
and left it in tatters
for her own heart's sake."

"Then came the hare,
timid and fearful,
who hoped gentleness meant
the songstress would yield.
But stronger still,
her will remained cheerful,
for against such weakness,
she never would kneel."

"At last, a man,
steady and kind,
loved her freely
and honored her mind.
For true love is selfless,
a rare gem to find,
not beastly nor cruel
when hearts entwine."

Lovely. The song and the performer.

Ulrich applauded, studying Zel, who curtsied and smiled. How lovely indeed. Someone other than Ulrich might never have guessed that the beautiful golden-haired muse had been sent here to kill him. But Ulrich knew.

What happened to Zel when the time came was yet to be decided.

Four

ZEL

Zel stared at the ceiling of his bedchamber. He hadn't really looked at it when he was exploring his room before and unpacking his things, but it was tall and domed, with a translucence through whatever the magical ceiling was made of, so he gazed upon the bare night sky.

Beautiful as it was, how was he expected to sleep when there was still so much to be done? He had twenty-nine more days and nights to succeed, yet it already felt like too little. Ulrich was powerful. Everything that had ever been speculated about the sorcerer in the tower had so far proven true, given his treasures and the ease with which he wielded magic.

Zel knew little of elves. There were some in the Thieves Guild and throughout the city, most slaves, occasionally free or even more rarely high standing, but certainly none as capable as Ulrich. Maybe he was something other than an elf and merely looked like one—a question among many that Zel needed to answer.

Tomorrow, he would begin prodding for information, but gently, so as to not arouse suspicion. At least the luxuries that accompanied this task were pleasant to experience. Zel loved his new dress. He would have to make more like it, since he had been given leave to do so. He'd loved the food and drink as well. He even loved the tower, with its hidden rooms and anything and everything Zel could have thought to ask for.

It felt too easy, but maybe because the challenge remained ahead of him. Most important was for Ulrich to never discover that Zel planned to kill him.

Or that Zel was a man in disguise, playing pretend.

Although, like usual, Zel didn't feel like he was pretending, but he knew better than to assume anyone else could understand. Least of all a sorcerer who wanted a bride.

Well, maybe least of all Lothar.

Zel was most curious about Ulrich's blackened hand. How far up did the damage go? Was it damage? Was it evil, or the source of Ulrich's magic the way Zel's hair was the source of his?

Though, was Zel's hair the source of his? And could he actually wield magic, or had Ulrich simply said that to appease him? Ulrich was charming, but Zel could not be certain if he was honest. The true nature of someone was rarely discovered in a day.

It was rarely discovered in thirty, but Zel had to try.

He also had to try to sleep, or he would be exhausted come morn—

A scream pierced the night, and Zel swung upright in bed. That hadn't come from inside the tower, but somewhere below.

Tossing aside his sheets and quilt, Zel leapt out of bed to go to the window. He wore a linen chemise that he preferred for sleep. It was soft and well-worn, since he hadn't grown much since he was sixteen and had used the same nightdress from then on.

The window did not have any glass, but was simply an opening in the stone wall. No wind or cold from the autumn night filtered in, and Zel was surprised any sound could penetrate what was clearly a space enchanted to act like glass.

As he neared it, he wondered, should he ever need to escape the tower quickly, could he use his hair to do so, like rappelling down rope? But how, when it would need to be tied to something that he then wouldn't be able to untie it from? And besides, surely he would tear the hair from his scalp to have the full weight of an adult dangling from it, even if only his slight form.

What a foolish notion.

Zel peered outside, down the five stories to the garden, the wall, and the clearing around it below. In the moonlight, he could see a shadowy figure sprawled on the ground outside the wall, partially hidden. The body he had nearly investigated earlier, or someone new?

Another shadowy figure caught Zel's eye, darting toward the tree line. A larger, more menacing shadow chased it, and when it caught the fleeing figure, it formed into the obvious silhouette of the sorcerer. Zel knew it had to be Ulrich, for even in the dark and a good distance away, the height, the robes, and the flowing hair were all him, and he sparkled like the night sky above.

He lifted the other figure off the ground, high into the air, and Zel's vision seemed to zoom in, focusing more clearly. Something invisible was being sucked from the man, from his open mouth into Ulrich's, and as it drained away, the man's body shrunk in on itself until it was nothing but a husk with empty eyes.

Ulrich didn't drop the body but tossed it over his shoulder. When he returned to the wall, he picked up the other body and tossed it over his other shoulder, carrying them both like sacks of fertilizer. That was clearly what they were used for when not left outside as deterrents, because the wall opened to permit Ulrich, then closed behind him, and when he dropped the bodies into his garden, they melted like the flesh pile that Zel's childhood bully had become.

Ulrich looked up, and Zel foolishly ducked out of view. He shouldn't have done that. He had shown fear, when it was obvious to Zel now that Ulrich had made certain he heard and saw all that on purpose.

Zel did eventually sleep, though he couldn't say he slept well. In the morn, he used the washroom without running into Ulrich. He was glad his braids had mainly stayed in place, for it was difficult to style his hair on his own. He did not feel the need to bathe yet, and his hair required washing very seldomly, but once he did wash it, he might have to get creative with how he formed it into plaits.

Zel frequented the treasure room without running into Ulrich either, creating a new garment for the day with the loom. Since it was effectively spring on the grounds, he made a spring dress, a simple one-piece again but shorter, only to his knees, so the bottoms of the breeches he wore beneath showed through. He found he rather liked that look, complete with stockings and the more comfortable shoes he wore on missions, but again, no corset or other undergarments. Like before, he also donned Rudy's pendant. It was a simple indulgence but one that further bolstered him to succeed, so he might see his friend again someday.

He still didn't run into Ulrich when he returned his nightdress to his bedchamber. He had not asked about washing his clothes, but there was a basket in the corner of his room. He tested a theory and placed the nightdress in it. The basket swirled with sudden water, then with suds like soap, then the garment spun faster until all the water was gone and it was suddenly dry and clean. Zel pulled it back out, amazed. The garment now smelled like moonflowers and sage.

Like Ulrich.

Zel did the same with his mother's wedding dress and the dress he had worn to dinner, and then placed all the items in his wardrobe. He imagined he would quickly fill it using that loom and doubted he would wear any of the other clothing he had brought if he could make whatever he liked.

Hungry afterward and ready for breakfast, Zel decided to try a full turn of the key to find Ulrich, wondering if the sorcerer waited for him in the dining hall again. He slipped back out of his room and into the main area of the tower.

"Ready for something to eat?"

Zel gasped, not having expected to find Ulrich after two times of him not being there. And he was *right there*, a reach away from Zel, wearing a different, brighter colored robe than yesterday's—this one like a long, shimmery teal vest over black underlayers. His hair seemed to have its own current of wind around it, like it was constantly floating as the stars danced through its curls.

Ulrich reached for Zel, and he lurched backward, nearly tripping into his bedroom.

Damn. He could not afford to do that.

"You recoil?" Ulrich frowned.

"I-I didn't mean to, my—"

"Because of what you saw last night?" The frown faded almost immediately to a gauging stillness. "It is different knowing something compared to witnessing it, is it not?"

He was testing Zel. That was the point of the whole month. To assess his worth. "I have seen worse, my lord," Zel said. He had. His melted bully, for one. And Anna. The viscera of a close-up kill was worse than seeing a man turned into a bloodless husk, even if that husk had melted afterward. "Do you hunt your prey?" Zel asked.

"Why bother? Plenty cross my path on their own, seeking riches or power or the fame of having slayed a myth. It is very rare that I show such trespassers mercy. Do you think me vile for that?"

Another test? Again, Zel could only be honest. "It is not vile to kill to survive. To kill to defend, or to protect. Even to kill simply for gain if it helps ensure the rest."

"The ends justify the means if it protects you and those you care about?"

"That is what I believe. Do you think me vile for seeing it that way?"

"I think you pragmatic, Zel. There are far worse things than me in this world, even if, once, I was the worst. Breakfast?" Ulrich did not gesture back through the magical door but to the center of the main room, where Zel realized a small round table had been placed and was set for breakfast with bread, meat, cheese, and something steaming that smelled like...

"Coffee?"

"Do you partake?"

Zel stepped free finally of his bedchamber and closed the magical door behind him. He followed Ulrich to sit with him at the table. "I have rarely had the chance. It's considered a luxury. I first tried it at fourteen and hated it. Then again at eighteen and found I had come to enjoy its bitterness."

"You will enjoy this then," Ulrich said, pouring some for each of them from a pitcher into porcelain cups, "for the best coffee is balanced. I thought it would be nice to eat out here this morn. There is a better view of the sunrise." He nodded toward the lone window, for it faced the direction of the rising sun, which looked lovely brightening the kingdom, even if much of the land was suffering from the Great Famine.

Like last night, Zel contemplated that if they were not surrounded by past and future deaths, this would have been a nice way to spend time with a betrothed. Also like last night, everything about the meal was wonderful, especially the coffee.

But Zel had a duty. He must learn all he could.

"My lord, may I ask how and when you were... the worst?"

Ulrich smiled thinly while sipping from his cup. "Have you not heard tales of the Immortal King before your current Queen?"

"You mean, you're..."

"Have you had enough to eat?"

"I... I would not say no to more of this exquisite coffee."

"Then keep your cup while we take a walk."

"We are going outside? I am not dressed—"

"Not outside the tower. Not today. We will be taking a walk through time and memory." Ulrich stood, and when Zel stood after him, the porcelain cup of coffee he held was suddenly refilled without the tip of the pitcher, and the rest of the food and the table and chairs vanished in a swirl of color.

Once more, Ulrich led Zel to the magical door.

"Give the key a full turn."

ULRICH

The door opened not into a dining hall but onto a balcony. Rather than a view of the neighboring kingdom, like outside Zel's bedchamber, this balcony looked upon the past.

"Where is this?" Zel asked, moving slowly to the balcony's railing with an expression of ravishing awe. Such beauty, even while clutching a cup of coffee. Maybe more so for the domesticity added to Zel's profile.

"My homeland to the north, many, many centuries ago." Ulrich moved to stand beside Zel and waved his left hand, showing the passage of time in his home country rapidly over many changes of the seasons. What started as a distant view of rolling hills and farmland became the building of villages, cities, and finally, a shining castle to make it a kingdom. Ulrich paused the plunge through time around when he was a boy.

"You *were* an elf," Zel said, as the view zoomed in like they were traversing the kingdom in a flying carriage instead of remaining stationary on a balcony, and it became clear that the people who walked the city streets all had pointed ears and an elegance only elves possessed. "*Are*, I mean." Zel cringed with the correction.

"I am, and I am not. Past tense is a fitting choice." Ulrich waved his hand again, and the view moved them through the city down a dark alley, where Ulrich as a boy was but a slim and bedraggled mortal, his dark hair shorter and in tangles, and his skin closer in color to a warm, ruddy brown rather than ashen and indigo.

"I was an orphan," Ulrich continued, "a nothing in the eyes of most people. All elves have some magic, but mine was limited and useless when what I needed was food and water."

As he spoke, the scenes continued to play, at first showing him as a beggar, trying to earn coin for pity by creating illusions to dazzle a mostly uninterested audience.

"Needs and wants are different though. Greed is for the wealthy, who step on others to get more when their needs are already met." Some of those wealthy were shown tossing coins at him while sneering and complaining about his presence in their streets. "Envy is for those with little or nothing, but can be just as destructive given time, feeding into a hunger for revenge when the belly is starving.

"I wanted more than to be like the wealthy and powerful I envied. I wanted to take all they had and put them in my place instead." Ulrich's young face showed it all with the way he sneered back at those who dropped their coins as soon as they were no longer looking. "I would have given anything to achieve that, and so I decided one day that I would give everything."

The scenes rapidly changed as Ulrich filtered through dozens of unimportant memories, pausing to let Zel witness the gathering of his fellow orphans to better share resources, and the mentors he began to acquire.

There were five others around his same age who became closest to him. In Ulrich's displayed memories, and not with any conscious effort on his part, they each had a haze about them of a specific color. It was easier to remember them as shades than people with names, for to think on them more deeply might stir inklings of remorse too belated to explore.

A boy shrouded in red who could blend with the shadows and dazzle with sleight of hand. A girl tinted orange with an affinity for animals, who was often more comfortable in their company than with people. Another girl bathed in yellow, much larger and stronger than the rest and quick to defend or fight. A third girl in shimmering green who could captivate anyone with the stories she told. A boy awash in blue was perhaps the frailest among them, but his desire to help others made him an optimal healer.

Last of all was Ulrich, exuding almost the same violet color as he did now, who even as a boy was a determined natural leader and could better than any of them infuse his magic into items, however minimally at the start—and eventually into sustenance, which was the precursor to his garden.

He often looked back on these memories in his solitude. The spell was like a living journal, but he could not interact with any of it. He could not change anything that had come to pass. He could only bear witness, and there were certain events he had not relived since the days when he still dreamed.

"I suppose I built something quite like your Thieves Guild at first, so those of us with nothing could start to build up something of our own. I also began trading in whatever I could get my hands on to learn more magic and spells, ones from far off kingdoms. Ones forbidden. Ones called evil. By the time I had enough power to pull myself up from the slums, I no longer cared who got crushed by my ambitions, just like the powerful had never cared about me."

Zel gaped when an adult Ulrich, ruler of his legion of the downtrodden, killed one of his followers simply for speaking against him. In the memory, Ulrich warned others that they would suffer the same fate if they dared similar transgressions, and his five closest friends stood by his side, unbothered by their leader's display of cruelty.

Present day Ulrich watched Zel's reactions to the scene, thinking the young thief looked sorrowful and sympathetic but not condemning. Zel saw Ulrich's actions for the unfortunate necessity Ulrich had believed of them too. Once. But although most of Ulrich's other followers remained loyal after that, growth of their underground and magical abilities eventually drew attention from above.

Ulrich showed the battle that erupted soon after, leaving many dead, while he and the others were forced to the borders and barred from returning. He could almost feel the heat from the fires lighting up the streets and smell the sweat and blood from those fighting as his people retreated. As they left their home. He knew Zel must feel it too, for the hairs on Zel's arms would prickle whenever someone used a spell, from ice swaths misting the outer walls of homes to the reconfiguration of inanimate objects, like swords becoming limp lengths of rope, or clothing transforming too large or too small to trip up its wearer—a rainbow of mystical carnage.

Yet still, Zel watched with rapt attention, never judgment or revulsion.

"My remaining followers and I were driven out by others we were not yet powerful enough to best." Ulrich moved the scenes swiftly through their travels until ending at a more familiar kingdom, although not yet as built up as the one Zel knew. "Falchovari was young and innocent then and easily awed by traveling elves with magic tricks to distract them from their purses."

The sequence of a growing kingdom began again, only this time Ulrich was already strong, and he was part of what built rolling hills and farmland into villages, the city, and finally, the shining castle that truly made it a kingdom.

Ulrich was its first and only king.

"In life, if you have ambition, you make friends easily. When you start to gain enemies, your friends aid you. When some of your followers doubt you, you are already too powerful and control them with fear. When you make the choice to pursue power for the sake of subduing others rather than for self-betterment, it becomes your sole purpose, and those who remain with you become more like you, continuing the cycle of cruelty and dominance."

It had with his companions, and he showed Zel as much, for those original five were just as corrupt as Ulrich by then, taking what they wanted and sneering at those beneath them.

Red's mastery of shadows meant citizens eventually feared they might be consumed by his darkness—or that parts of them would be if he was feeling cruel. Orange lived mostly in the shape of animals, listening in on the citizens for dissension, so that meeting a bear in the wood often meant one had said too much. Yellow magically buffed her physique so often that it became an obsession until nothing else mattered, certainly not protecting others even when they begged for it. Green did not suffer insufficient recitations of her bard songs, and if a performer displeased her, she would make them relive what they sang—specifically those tales that ended tragically. Blue was so distorted by disappointment in what often became of the people he aided that he turned instead to killing children before they could grow into bandits or grooming them to become more like him. Which fate was worse was often debated.

As the most powerful among them, Ulrich was also the most corrupt, never satisfied with what he had. He sped through scenes to show him on his throne, closer to how he looked now, but surrounded by beauty fawning over him and presenting to him their skills, like dancers, musicians, and the best courtesans. He sometimes did not wait to take them to bed, but fondled them on his lap, right there in his throne room.

He showed very little of his carnal encounters, but Zel's blush proved that his betrothed's virginity in most ways had not been a lie. Despite having experienced it all firsthand, rewatching those moments stirred next to nothing in Ulrich's own loins. No, they stirred not for the past.

"All power has its limits, Zel, but I sought to transcend that too." Ulrich lifted his right arm, stretching out his bony black hand with its violet veins. "To achieve immortality, a price must be paid."

Again, Ulrich moved the scenes forward, pausing on one with his hand already black, clutching it as he knelt upon the floor of a room he kept vague to Zel's view. He would not show Zel what had led to that moment, how he had achieved it, but together they watched the aftermath.

The pain Ulrich had been in was followed by a surge of power infusing the rest of him, setting him aglow, and causing the stardust-like appearance he had now, for a part of the void, the unknown, the absence of everything that existed beyond the touch of magic lived within him and would forevermore because of what he had done.

When the void grew hungry, his arm ached, and the next scenes showed no signs of his former friends, only him devouring the souls of his citizens to subdue the pain both there and deep within him where he continued to crave more. Eventually, he craved nothing but souls, for soon, the scenes, similar to those before of Ulrich being fawned over by dancers, musicians, and courtesans, showed how disinterested he had become of their company. He still hungered, but his cravings, his desires, his spark of life was gone.

Those scenes seemed to trouble Zel least of all, perhaps because of having seen that none of it happened overnight. Ulrich had been tainted over years of poor decisions and selfish living, until *living* wasn't what he could be called at all anymore.

"What I had not accounted for was that it would all ultimately grow stale. Everything does if it never ends. And so, I left and came here. Tell me, Zel, do stories persist of how the Immortal King made his exit?" The final scenes showed Ulrich in the wood erecting the tower to keep others away, and yet also needing the foolish thieves and wanderers who came calling, so he could continue to control his hunger and the pain he had willingly accepted when he thought the payoff would always be worth it.

"The stories do not say that the Immortal King and the sorcerer in the tower in the wood are one in the same, only that he grew tired of ruling and vanished." Zel, still clutching the now cooling cup of coffee, looked at Ulrich, and then down at the blackened hand that had lowered to clutch the railing. "The longer you go without feeding that way, the more your arm pains you?"

"My arm pains me every second a soul is not passing between my lips, but yes, it worsens the longer I go without."

Zel set the porcelain cup on the railing and reached to place a hand upon Ulrich's.

Ulrich inhaled sharply, not because he was shocked Zel would dare such a thing, but because the pain, for the first time since he'd lost his true hand, receded. He had not anticipated that. "Fascinating."

"My lord?" Zel blinked up at him worriedly.

"Zel, might I touch the fall of your braids?"

Color filled Zel's cheeks, same as when the scenes had shown a few sordid moments. "Y-you may. I appreciate that you asked first."

"I never used to ask for anything, but constant worship grows stale too, for what can anyone believe of a slave who has no choice but to obey their master? Surrounded by fear and lies, all that remained of any truth in my life was the pain." Ulrich lifted his black hand from beneath Zel's. At that moment of disconnect, it ached again, but with the first stroke down Zel's braids, not only did the pain subside, but Ulrich's hand swelled, plumping back to life almost as if it was normal, even a little less black in color.

Zel's head snapped toward the reinvigorated hand to stare. "Is this why you wanted—"

"I did not expect this," Ulrich cut off Zel's question, for he had not. The magic in Zel was to serve a different purpose, but this development was not unwelcome. Just like the touch of Zel's skin, as soon as Ulrich was not touching the strands of hair, the pain returned, and in this case, so did the shriveled blackness. "It seems the effect is only temporary."

Zel clasped Ulrich's hand and brought it back in contact with the braids. "My mother used to help me with my hair, since it is difficult to manipulate such volume alone. Its length is not always a blessing since it cannot be cut."

"It cannot be?" Ulrich had wondered about that.

"Well, *I* can cut it, but only me. We did not want others knowing that and thinking of ways to use it against me. I only used the knowledge to manage the hair around my face." Zel brought Ulrich's hand up to touch the fringe.

The hair was so wonderfully soft, but especially because Ulrich felt no pain while touching it. "Did you ever wish to cut its length?"

"Yes, but I have grown fond of it. I would gladly keep it this way forever now if I could style it on my own more easily."

"Perhaps that could be the first magic I teach you."

Zel's eyes brightened. "I would like that. But even if you do, would you perhaps like to help me with my hair each day? When you have the time or desire to, of course. It is your brush my mother always used to comb it, and now that brush is mine. The silver one?"

"I remember it. And yes." Ulrich allowed Zel to move his hand from hair to delicate cheek, while enough strands still brushed it to keep it plump. "I would like to assist you. Tomorrow then. For now, would you like to help me in the garden, Zel?"

"That sounds lovely, my lord."

Lovely. So lovely.

Perhaps Ulrich had not accounted for everything with his would-be assassin after all.

Five

ZEL

Zel had learned so much, and all he had asked to know was how and when Ulrich had been the worst.

He truly had been. He was the Immortal King! The current Queen had ruled Falchovari for two centuries, but countless centuries before her name had even been uttered, the Immortal King had been written and sung about as a beast from the underworld who'd surfaced to spread malice and cruelty like a plague. There could be no viler being in all the histories, and Ulrich had not shied from showing Zel how true most of it was.

Not all the old stories were true though. If they had been, there would be no way to kill him, but Ulrich was no beast. He had simply been an elf once, who self-taught his way to power and sacrificed much for the immortality that he now seemed sick of. Yet the pain his arm caused him pushed him to devour more and more souls if only to keep the ache at bay.

If all *that* was true and not merely a convenient lie, would it be a kindness to slay him? Could he be slayed, mortal once but unstoppable now? It all had to do with that cursed arm. That was Zel's best clue.

Ulrich had been genuinely comforted to have Zel touch it, or to run his shriveled, claw-like fingers down Zel's braids. The arm had returned to life in those moments as if blessed by Zel's magic. Ulrich had certainly seemed genuine at least, especially in his surprise that any of it was possible. He hadn't expected it, and if Zel could continue to surprise him, he had the upper hand, so to speak.

Even if killing Ulrich wasn't a mercy, surely slaying such a monster was justified. Ulrich had not sought retribution for his centuries of evil, only seclusion. And he still killed, horribly so. Only trespassers, thieves and possibly murderers who dared to enter his lands, but hadn't Zel's parents nearly been counted among those slain, and by extension, Zel himself? Was he, as a thief and murderer, any different?

Zel could not think on it all too much, or he would falter, when it hadn't even been a full day on this mission. He instead had to focus on one of the most important tenets of the Thieves Guild.

Do not mourn your marks. They are already dead.

They had gone outside into the garden after their visit to the past, enjoying the spring weather that beyond the wall would have been bitter autumn. Ulrich had shown Zel how he tended to the plants, even how he used the rich red fertilizer that had become of the people he drained. If Zel had not grown up among assassins, he might have thought it sickening to use the remains of people to garden, while sharing stories and songs with their killer.

As things stood, the morn was quite pleasant in Ulrich's company. The sharp scrutiny that had been tainting his words and presence had softened.

After the midday meal, Zel asked if he might pen his parents a letter, and Ulrich gave him leave to do so, promising he would ensure the letter reached its destination once ready.

Zel kept the letter simple. He was well, he was optimistic about the future, and they needn't worry but wait to see him again when the month was over. He and his parents had worked out a code for him to use to give them hints of his progress without anything seeming suspicious should Ulrich read the letter, which Zel expected he would.

> *I have continued to eat my daily lettuce, as expected of my betrothed, but being here, I swear that only one leaf would be enough to sustain me.*

One leaf, *one lead* to grow on to ensure the month ended successfully.

Zel had been alone at the desk in the main room, but the moment he finished and blew upon the ink for it to dry, Ulrich appeared to help him send the letter off. With a wave of his hand, the rest of the ink dried. With another wave, the parchment lifted from the table, folded upon itself into the shape of a bird, and flew out the window toward the heart of the kingdom.

Some of Ulrich's magic was terrifying. But some, like what was always said of elves, was beautiful. He was beautiful, and strangely, the darkness in him did not obscure that beauty as much as Zel had expected.

"It must have taken your mother hours to tend to these locks."

"Oh, it did. Thankfully, my hair does not require much washing. It mostly keeps clean on its own. We would only brush it out and re-braid it weekly, unless it got especially tangled or dirty." Zel suppressed a moan in response to Ulrich's nails running over his scalp after the last of his previous braids had been unbound, both the normal, though still pointed nails of Ulrich's ashen hand, and the claws of the one that was usually black.

The skin did not remain black while in contact with Zel's hair, proven again this morn, as Ulrich prepared to brush out Zel's locks like they'd discussed. It had always felt nice when Zel's mother did so, but with Ulrich, the act of fingers combing through his hair almost seemed worshipful. The reverence and peace on Ulrich's face could be seen plainly in the mirror in front of Zel.

They were in his bedchamber, with Zel seated in front of the mirror and Ulrich behind him. After he roused, Zel had freshened up and changed into another new dress made from the loom, but had waited to do anything with his even more tousled braids until Ulrich came to him.

As long as there were fabrics to manipulate, Zel liked having something new to wear each day. Today's dress did have a bodice. He did not miss wearing a corset, but a less constricting bodice over a dress was nice and helped give an extra cinch to his waist that almost made his flat chest present more feminine. He liked, however, that Ulrich's attention did not stray directly there but moved freely over all of him, equally captivated by every part of Zel.

Zel was used to being stared at, lusted after, especially by Rudy—and oftentimes Lothar—but this felt different. The longing from Ulrich was different. But then, Ulrich had been alone for ages, without another's touch for all that time too. If Zel had gone centuries without touching or being touched, he would have grown mad with desire.

Pausing finally in what had become a very pleasant massage of Zel's scalp, Ulrich took up the brush that had once been his. Zel's unbraided hair was so long, Ulrich had stretched it out along the floor nearly to the doorway. Given how long Ulrich's hair was as well, he clearly knew how to handle such length. He moved first away from Zel to begin brushing out the golden locks from the ends, and slowly, section by section, worked his way up.

At first, Zel could watch with a turn of his head. Ulrich had forgone robes today and wore pantaloons that went to his ankles, not the higher breeches and stockings Zel was used to on Falchovarien men, and a tunic-like shirt that was tightly fitted over his chest and open enough to show his collarbone. It was all very dressed down and becoming on him, and made sense, given he was on his knees to brush out Zel's hair. The former Immortal King and fabled sorcerer of the wood was on his *knees*. And out of his usual robes, his figure was quite trim despite the broadness of his shoulders.

Zel wanted to run his fingers through Ulrich's starlight locks with the same reverence that Ulrich was offering Zel's.

Perhaps so long having daily dallied with Rudy and now going without *was* making Zel mad. Once Ulrich came nearer, Zel had to turn forward, and the closer Ulrich returned to Zel's scalp, the more Zel felt it. The more he enjoyed it. The brush from Zel's crown down toward the nape of his neck was the best, but especially when Ulrich's clawed nails followed in the brush's wake.

Only when Zel's hair was glossy from the attention, and all combed through, did Ulrich begin to braid it. He formed the foundation, setting up the right sections, knots, and tucks near Zel's scalp. With him there, so close to Zel, pausing often to merely touch Zel's hair or alight his long fingers on Zel's shoulders, a familiar tingle began to travel through Zel, pleasant and hot.

If this had been Rudy, the young pickpocket would have slid his hands into the top of Zel's dress by now.

Zel tilted his head, exposing the length of his pale neck, chest heaving to show his interest, however subtly. He should not yet be coaxing Ulrich into intimate acts, but he wondered purely for his own sake what it might be like to feel those pointed nails and claws reach down to circle his nipples.

"Zel, do you feel the way the magic rises with heat in your belly?"

"*Yes.*" Zel met Ulrich's violet eyes in the mirror. "But is that... magic, my lord?"

Ulrich grinned. "It can be. Let me shoulder the brunt of the work, but some of this next magic will come from you." He ran his hands down Zel's shoulders, down the whole length of his arms to his wrists and took hold of them, spreading them outward. He manipulated Zel's hands like someone leading a choir or band of players. "Now, envision the sections of your hair lifting on their own."

"That is all?"

"You were born with magic inside you, Zel. The talent is already there."

Zel tried, focusing first on Ulrich, on his touch, on his motions with Zel's hands, and how being in contact with him made the heat, the tingle that had already been building within Zel, grow stronger. Then he imagined his hair lifting and starting to twine into more and more braided sections.

"That's it, Zel. Don't stop."

Zel gasped, for he could see the hair behind him in the mirror, and it was indeed starting to lift and move. It followed the motion of Ulrich's hands on Zel's wrists, but eventually, it was Zel leading, Zel choosing how to conduct them, somehow able to envision it all, even the parts of his hair he couldn't see.

Ulrich never released Zel's hands, even when it was all by Zel's direction that the movements continued.

"There we are." Ulrich lowered Zel's arms, but his touch lingered on Zel's wrists. Their eyes met in the mirror before Zel took in the way his bound hair looked from the front. It was perfect. He reached back to pull his braid over his shoulder, stroking it more to marvel at the intricacies of the design rather than for comfort like he usually might.

"Does it look all right at the back of my head?"

"See for yourself." Ulrich produced a silver hand mirror that matched the brush.

Zel took it, stood, and turned away from the wall to use the hand mirror to reflect the larger mirror behind him and the full length of his braids twisted into one glorious whole. It looked even better than how his mother had woven it for their trip to the tower. "And I did this? With *my* magic?"

"I barely had to help at all by the end." Ulrich smiled more softly than his teasing grin. He looked so handsome in his minimalist clothing. "Eventually, you won't even need my touch."

Zel clutched the mirror to his chest. "I very much doubt that, my lord."

It was flawless double-speak, enough flirtation that Ulrich glanced down Zel's body and back up to the flush in Zel's cheeks—a flush Zel didn't need to fabricate.

Zel worried his bottom lip, holding Ulrich's gaze, and then tried to hand the mirror back to him.

"Keep it. You already own its partner, and a perfect match should not be separated."

Perhaps *that* was flawless double-speak. Zel needed to hold back, draw things out until he knew more, knew enough, but a part of him wished that his two large lies to Ulrich did not have to be so.

"Breakfast?" Ulrich turned to the door. "And then, afterward, shall we take a walk?"

"Through time and memory again, my lord?"

"No. This time, we will be leaving the tower."

ULRICH

It seemed Zel had been prepared to be kept like a prisoner, for being led to the tower wall, which parted for them like curtains drawn aside, filled that lovely face with wonder.

Ulrich had reminded Zel to dress for autumn, and while temperature hardly affected Ulrich, he dressed in kind. He also donned one of his many guises to dull the sparkle of his hair, his skin tone a more even brown rather than tinged with indigo, and his eyes less aglow. He could have been any free elf out for a stroll with a charming companion on his arm, and it was very much how he had once looked before amassing his power and immortality forever changed him.

Of course, few people went out for casual strolls in this wood, for it was a place traversed only with necessity or ill intent. It meant the forest was quite empty of distraction and rather peaceful most of the time, since Ulrich feared nothing.

"You are staring, Zel," he said, noting the constant flicks of Zel's eyes up toward his changed appearance.

"My apologies. You are still handsome, but it is strange to see you muted. This is how you looked in the memories you showed me. Why not look this way all the time if you can?"

"It would be a waste of magic when I am in my own home, and in truth, I rather like that other appearance. It's distinct, boldly declares my power, and is a reminder of all I have become."

"As well as adds a mystique of ethereal beauty." Zel smiled, seeming quite genuine with the compliment. "I suppose glamours to trick the eye come easily to you?"

"Do you assume I trick you too?"

"I was raised to take nothing for granted, my lord, and to always assume a smile hides something sinister. For in this world, it usually does. But I believe the version I see of you in the tower is the real you."

"It is. Although, the truth of someone goes much deeper than what one sees on the surface, does it not?"

Barely a waver of lost confidence betrayed itself on Zel's face. "I couldn't agree more."

Such a talented liar, but lies alone were not enough to condemn Zel. Ulrich had more to learn over the month ahead before he decided Zel's fate for certain. "Had you been in the wood before your trip to my tower?"

"A few times," Zel said. "Never unaccompanied, and I never felt quite so at ease in them as I do with you, but an all-powerful immortal does soothe the nerves. Did you have a destination in mind, or shall we—"

"Not that way." Ulrich blocked the step Zel had been about to take down a path to their left. "Oh, you *can* be at ease with me, Zel, but certain territories within this wood are respected between its denizens. No need to stir the wrath of anyone who otherwise leaves me in peace, and I leave them in peace as well."

Zel peered around Ulrich cautiously, where distantly down that path could be seen a thicker density of trees with a shroud of darkness about them as if no light could penetrate. Even in autumn, with many of the leaves turning colors and falling at their feet, bare branches themselves were thick enough to hide most of what might be stumbled upon in there, with additional thick and dark fir trees.

For most mortals, to go that direction would not end well.

"The Dark Forest?" Zel whispered.

"I am sure you have heard many tales of it." Ulrich leaned down to whisper as well. "And yes, nearly all of them are true." His breath must have been warm on Zel's skin amidst the cold around them, for gooseflesh prickled the pale skin near where Ulrich exhaled.

"Well then," Zel said with a shiver, "I certainly do not envy anyone foolish enough to head that way on purpose, unaware of the dangers."

"Agreed." Ulrich led them forward instead.

Zel was on his right. Ulrich had not specified it that way, but Zel had naturally gravitated there and held onto Ulrich's right arm. Now, leaning a little closer, Zel slid the hand nearest to Ulrich down his arm until their fingers entwined—Ulrich's blackened and pained ones, and Zel's soft but strong.

The comfort throughout Ulrich's usually aching veins was instant.

"Are all denizens of the wood, the Dark Forest in particular, immortal like you?" Zel asked.

"Some, I believe. Others with stipulations. I am not friendly enough with any of them to know all the details."

"Do any of them know your details?"

"No one knows everything about me, Zel, not even my old apprentice." That caught Zel's attention just as Ulrich had intended, but he did not elaborate.

"Am I your new apprentice, my lord?" Zel asked.

"You are more than that as my betrothed."

"And despite not sharing all your secrets with your apprentice, would you with a bride?"

So very clever, Ulrich thought, as he looked at Zel. "I would."

"Then might I ask..." Zel brought them to a halt along the path they trod down. "Will you always be this way? Pained by your arm, I mean?" Zel gently squeezed Ulrich's hand. "There is no way to reverse this curse you bear?"

If Ulrich did not already know Zel planned to betray him, he might have believed the question was borne of genuine concern and curiosity. "There might be," he admitted, but he had no intention of elaborating on that yet either.

They had reached their destination.

Ulrich darted his eyes into the trees around them.

"My lord?" Zel followed Ulrich's gaze.

"Sit tight and have no fear," Ulrich said, lifting Zel's hand to kiss the chilled and seemingly delicate fingers in his grasp. "I will let no harm come to you. But we are not alone." Ulrich tore his grasp from Zel's and darted into the darkness of thicker trees, leaving Zel, so very lovely and alluring, even bundled against the cold, that any bandit would gladly take the bait.

Ulrich watched from the shadows, having gone the opposite direction from the hiding place of the bandit who was watching them. He had not known exactly where he might find a highwayman in wait, but he knew the most likely places along the paths in the wood where it was dangerous to tread alone.

For mortals, anyway.

Zel spun the correct direction moments before the bandit revealed himself. Ulrich made note of how Zel's hand jerked, as if reaching for a dagger that wasn't there. Good instincts. Honed.

"What a fool your escort is to leave such a fragile flower alone," the bandit said, circling Zel with his own dagger drawn.

Zel's entire countenance shifted. No longer politely composed and demure, Zel went taut like a wolf ready to spring forth and rip the man to pieces with bare hands and teeth. "You would do yourself a service to walk away," Zel warned.

"Why would I do that, pretty petal, when your company would be so sweet." The bandit lunged, but a fire filled Zel's eyes, and a snarl formed, as if that nickname was especially unwelcome.

The bandit meant to frighten, overpower, and claim—not injure. Not initially. So Zel easily deflected the first blow, showing off the true skills of a Thieves Guild assassin. No skirts or long flowing braids could hinder Zel's fluid and elegant movements. Being smaller and weaker than the bandit meant little, for Zel was fast and knew exactly how to redirect the bandit's strength against him.

A second swipe of the bandit's dagger was deflected, a third, then a fourth came at such a perfect angle that Zel was able to twist the bandit's arm, spinning him to have his back to Zel and his arm pinned behind him.

The bandit slammed his head back, too tall to strike any part of Zel, but enough disruption for him to break free. Still having hold of his dagger, the bandit turned and launched himself to tackle Zel to the ground.

Zel caught the trajectory of the bandit's arm bringing the dagger down. It stopped, a mere prick away from nicking the skin of Zel's neck. Zel did not look afraid at all, and Ulrich knew why. Zel had fallen on purpose, ended in that exact position on purpose, for that hold would make it only too easy to tilt the dagger upward and pierce through the hollow of the bandit's throat.

Impressive, but as much as Ulrich wanted to watch Zel complete the act, he also wanted that soul.

Ulrich pounced from out of the trees much like the bandit had. He was half shadow, like the haze of clouds over the face of the moon, as he hurled the bandit off of Zel, sending the dagger skittering across the dead grass and brittle leaves. Ulrich rose like shadow too, towering to an even greater height, and the guise of a mortal elf fell away to reveal his abyssal majesty.

He lifted the bandit from the ground by the edges of his dirty, tattered surcoat. The man barely got out a scream before Ulrich was siphoning his soul from that open mouth and swallowing it like wine. It tasted just as heady, lessening the sharp sting of Ulrich's senses like wine could too. But as he had told Zel, this was the only time when Ulrich felt no pain at all.

Aside from touching Zel.

The eventual husk of the bandit stared blankly, still alive for the briefest of moments before Ulrich dropped him to the cold ground with a crunch.

Ulrich turned toward the still horizontal figure of Zel on the path. There was the fear Ulrich had caught a glimpse of when he looked up at Zel's window that first night. Clearly, Zel worried about becoming one of Ulrich's future meals. Good. It was good for Zel to feel some fear. Fear could lead to so many useful truths.

Ulrich straightened his robes, immediately veiling himself again in his disguise. "This one we can leave." He looked at the body and then back down the path toward the fork that led to the Dark Forest. "Herr Candy will find use for it."

Without elaborating further on that either, Ulrich returned to Zel to offer a helping hand.

"Thank you, my lord." Zel took it, also straightening disheveled clothing once back on solid ground. There was a stiffness to Zel's posture that Ulrich did not think was solely because of him. "I could not have survived such an encounter without you."

Liar, but Zel did not know Ulrich had been watching the entire time. "Are you all right?" he asked.

"Of course." Zel's eyes did not say the same, and Ulrich kept their gazes locked in wait for the truth. Zel sighed. "He... called me a name I do not care for. Pretty petal? Lothar, who runs the Thieves Guild, also calls me that. He has never wronged me directly, but his attention has never sat right with me. He controls the guild and all who are in it. He scarred my mother, when the mark you left on her healed. And he covets my company. He has made that much clear."

A swell of possession overtook Ulrich. He did not like the thought of anyone coveting Zel's company, and definitely not anyone acquiring it. He was glad to know that this Lothar had not gotten what he wanted thus far, but now Ulrich wondered who had.

Zel had been honest about being a virgin, but also about that not meaning *untouched*.

"How disappointed he must have been when you left," Ulrich said, picking a few stray leaves from Zel's hair. "Pretty as you are, I will be certain to never call you that myself... *little cabbage*," he ended on a whisper.

Zel laughed, and the clouds cleared from those vivid green eyes. "Cabbage? Shouldn't it be 'little lettuce'?"

"Lettuce can be frail. But cabbage, while similar, is stronger than it looks." Ulrich continued to smooth Zel's hair and pick out debris from the tousle on the ground. He took his time, because only with his fingers in contact with those locks did he feel as if he might never need another soul again, especially with Zel's eyes on him.

Eventually, the chill in the air, or perhaps Ulrich's lingering closeness, caused Zel to shiver. Ulrich saw the added gooseflesh forming across Zel's skin. Saw the invitation wrought with hesitation in Zel's eyes. All of it seemed so real, despite knowing there were lies hidden within the truths.

"Shall we return to the tower?" Ulrich suggested.

"To do what, my lord?" Zel smiled, banishing at least a little of that hesitancy.

"By the time we return, we will have worked up an appetite again."

"Oh?"

"Aren't you starting to crave something, Zel?"

"Are you, my lord?"

"For *lunch*. Then afterward..." Ulrich bent closer, so his lips were right beside Zel's ear. "I will give you time alone before dinner."

Zel's inhale was audible when Ulrich almost bent low enough for his lips to brush Zel's skin, but then he didn't. He lifted his head, reached with his blackened hand, and led Zel by the small of the back, turning them to return in the direction of the tower.

If Zel was disappointed by the tease, nothing was spoken to express it.

The question remained: did Zel deserve the fate Ulrich originally had planned?

And now, another question had surfaced: regardless of what Ulrich decided, would he indulge in Zel first?

Because gods above, he was starting to want to.

Six

ZEL

It was a nice lunch. A nice, quiet afternoon. A nice dinner. Even the earlier stroll in the autumn chill had been pleasant—until they were interrupted.

Zel would have killed the bandit without remorse if another moment had passed before Ulrich came to his rescue. Someone like that, more intent on the kill and defiling his victim, was worth little consideration from one's conscience. And then, seeing Ulrich swoop in like moving shadows, reforming into his glorious self, and sucking the man dry of his awful soul, more than only fear had stirred within Zel.

Little cabbage. It wasn't so different an endearment from pretty petal, yet somehow it was worlds different all the same. Zel was tempted, so tempted, to succumb and simply be Ulrich's bride.

But he couldn't. Wanting a bride meant Ulrich expected a woman, and he had made it clear he did not suffer liars. Ulrich's wrath would be great if he discovered Zel's secret. If Zel failed to kill him before the month was up, that wrath might be turned on Zel's parents. Even if they escaped Ulrich, Lothar's wrath could very well be worse.

If a bandit deserved death, did not also the vilest villain the kingdom had ever known? Ulrich had changed during his solitude, clearly, but he was still something preternaturally fearsome. He was still *evil*. Wasn't he?

And now Zel knew from Ulrich's own admission that there might be a way to reverse the curse embedded in his arm, to undo the exchange that gave him immortality for the price of his pain. Zel merely needed to discover what that was. He could not get distracted by how much he enjoyed Ulrich's company or his touch on Zel's skin and in his hair. The mutual bliss their contact caused could only lead down a doomed path.

Zel had gone many winters wanting more from Rudy and not being able to submit. Of course, he had only wanted the *physical* from Rudy. If something physical was all he could have now, he could weather a lack of Ulrich's touch with an abundance of his own.

Given his scuffle on the ground, Zel had decided to bathe before bed. His hair dried quickly, magically so, but it was easiest to let it dry during the night. While it was wet was the only time it felt heavy to Zel.

The Thieves Guild had its own bathhouses beneath the city, but as Zel could not risk using them, his parents had given the excuse when he was young that they feared for his safety there, and once older, he had given the excuse that his hair would get in everyone's way. Their home above the Pied Pipers music shop had always had its own washroom, but not so lavish or filled with minerals and oils as the one provided by the sorcerer with a quarter turn of the key.

There were two basins large enough to submerge in. One had a table beside it with all the accompaniments for cleansing. The other emitted more steam, clearly intended for soaking once cleansing was done. Zel took his time, and once he was clean, he lay back in the soaking basin with his hair hanging over its edge and spilling upon the damp floor.

The ceiling here was like the one in Zel's bedchamber, translucent to show the night sky, without any real threat of the elements. If Zel had doubted so in his room, he knew for certain here, for tonight was overcast, and when it started to rain, the droplets fell upon the invisible ceiling as if Zel was in a bubble.

For as long as he soaked, the water in the basin did not cool, despite Zel seeing no method for heating it, and his skin never wrinkled. He could stay for as long as he wanted, and while he did, he watched the rain and drifted a hand down between his legs.

Zel trusted that Ulrich was not watching—he had to trust that or never bathe or change his clothes at all while here—but he also allowed himself the indulgence of imagining Ulrich might be watching.

Or that Ulrich was the one doing the touching.

"Ah!" A gasp left Zel as he dragged his thumb across his slit. Ulrich's hands, even the shriveled one, were large and powerful in contrast to Zel's, making him feel strangely secure whenever they touched him. Like on his shoulders. Or the small of his back.

Or how they might feel touching Zel's shaft and circling his head.

The soaking basin was large enough that Zel could imagine leaning against a taller, broader body, encased by Ulrich while sitting in his lap. Those strong arms would encircle Zel's waist, powerful hands taking hold of him to fondle and stroke him, where none other than Zel's own hands had ever touched before.

Zel didn't mind that, without the contact of his hair, Ulrich's blackened hand would remain shrunken. It wasn't unpleasant to feel those fingertips. That hand was warmer too, maybe because of the pulse of magic in its cursed veins. Zel envisioned it doing the stroking, the blackened skin still soft, while Ulrich's other hand held Zel's sac, squeezing and gently pulling.

Zel's breath began to quicken. The rain didn't drown out the sound, for he couldn't hear the storm at all. He could only see it and kept his eyes skyward to enjoy the dance of the raindrops while Ulrich stroked him faster and nuzzled into his hair, whispering:

"Come for me, little cabbage."

Zel did, with a bitten off whine and a sag lower into the water—alone, with no firm body beneath or behind him.

While the rest of the night was Zel's to do with as he wished, he couldn't stay in the basin forever, and besides, the water was no longer clean.

As soon as Zel stepped out over the basin's edge, the water swirled like it had in his laundry basket, and it was clean again as if wholly renewed. The same had been true of the other basin that had become milky with soap and other elements but was crystal clear now for its next use.

Magic was a wonder, but because it was tangible.

Fantasy could not replace truth.

Zel dried himself, dressed in his sleep chemise, and gathered up his damp hair into a bundle to carry it. There was a mirror in the washroom like in his bedchamber, and catching sight of himself, minimally covered though he was and devoid of any powders or paints on his face, even he could have believed he was a woman.

Would he have preferred dressing as a woman if he had not been forced by necessity? He had often wondered that but could never be certain. He liked to think he would have. It felt right to be a man, but it felt right to be a woman too. He simply wished he did not need to lie and could be both by his own choosing.

Could someone be both? Be neither? Be themselves and be

accepted whatever the answer? Zel hoped so. Somewhere. If he succeeded in his mission—not only in killing Ulrich but in keeping all the secrets and treasures of the tower for himself and his parents—he would no longer need to wonder, for he would be free to live as whatever and whoever he wished to be.

Even if he didn't yet know who that was.

Zel retired to his room. When he got into bed, he continued to watch the rain pinprick the ceiling and let his mind wander to other dangerous thoughts. But so what if they were dangerous? If he had already been fantasizing, why not allow the indulgence of imagining that Ulrich's reaction to discovering the truth beneath Zel's skirts might be a happy one?

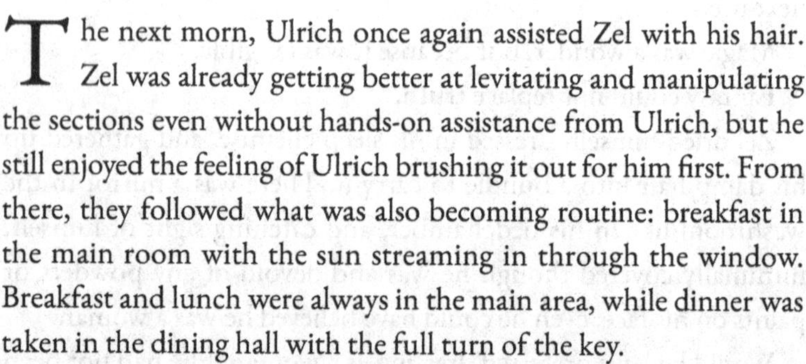

The next morn, Ulrich once again assisted Zel with his hair. Zel was already getting better at levitating and manipulating the sections even without hands-on assistance from Ulrich, but he still enjoyed the feeling of Ulrich brushing it out for him first. From there, they followed what was also becoming routine: breakfast in the main room with the sun streaming in through the window. Breakfast and lunch were always in the main area, while dinner was taken in the dining hall with the full turn of the key.

After breakfast, before Zel could ask what they might do that day, Ulrich bid Zel to use the key just so. Having already eaten, Zel knew it would not lead to the dining hall. He had a few guesses about where it might go instead, but when he turned the key and opened the door, he was still surprised.

Ulrich moved into the room past him.

"Do you wish to teach me how to defend myself, my lord?" Zel asked, stepping forward to join Ulrich and letting the door close behind them.

The space was as large as the dining hall but with weapons racks lining a central square like a fighting ring. Zel was familiar with such arenas in the Thieves Guild, mostly for training, but also, occasionally, for entertainment. He had learned hand-to-hand in such a space long ago, as well as how to wield a blade.

The very type of blade, a dagger, that Ulrich took from one of the racks.

"I do not believe teaching you is necessary," Ulrich replied, and hurled the dagger at Zel's head.

Zel caught it by instinct, expertly grasping the hilt and readjusting his grip to suit his style, while squaring his stance for a fight.

Ulrich smirked.

Damn. Zel had not intended to play his hand so openly. Then, as he straightened his posture and looked at the dagger, he realized it was his. This trap had layers, for this was the very dagger Zel had hidden beneath his mattress that first night.

"You went into my room?" he questioned.

"I did not. A simple spell. It periodically sweeps the tower for anything dangerous that does not belong to me and brings it here. My apologies." Ulrich bowed. "You could have simply told me. Having something to protect oneself with is smart, as are having the skills with which to use it." Ulrich claimed another weapon from the nearby rack, this one a sword. The sword was simple but beautifully crafted, steel with an intricately designed guard and pommel and a black grip. Ulrich took to the ring, brandishing it and settling into his own fighting stance.

"My lord?"

"Show me, Zel, what you are truly capable of." Ulrich sprang at Zel with the speed and ferocity of a trained duelist.

Zel deflected Ulrich's thrust with another rush of instinct. First rule of dagger versus sword was he could not let his opponent keep him at a distance. Zel ducked beneath a slash and leapt closer. He feinted toward Ulrich's most vulnerable opening before striking at another that wasn't, hoping to get Ulrich to overcompensate, but the sorcerer spun out of range like he'd seen the move coming and immediately thrust at Zel again.

Zel parried but only barely, focusing on the second rule of dagger versus sword—*speed*. He went for a riposte, a quick counterattack that brought him back into close range for a stab. Ulrich parried that just as quickly, grabbed Zel by his wrist, and spun him, pulling him back against him and holding Zel's own dagger to his throat. The move was almost identical to how Zel had grappled with the bandit yesterday, but being shorter than Ulrich gave Zel the advantage.

He stomped Ulrich's foot in the same instant that he threw his head back to collide with Ulrich's chin, all as he had been taught, ingrained in him since he was strong enough to hold a dagger's weight. He wrenched his arm free, using the momentum to spin back around, aiming for Ulrich's throat, wondering if his immortality meant the blow would naturally be deflected or still puncture him only to heal.

The dagger did not make contact to see which was true, for Ulrich used his sword like a shield, locking their blades together. Ulrich had been dueling one-handed to match Zel, but with both hands on his hilt now, Zel could not break their binding in his favor. Instead, he kicked, knocking Ulrich's foot out from under him. Ulrich scarcely parried Zel's next stab, so Zel refused to let up. He pushed, slashing and stabbing in quick succession to keep Ulrich on the defensive.

Back and back, they moved until Ulrich was close to being

knocked out of the makeshift ring into one of the weapons racks. Another strike, another; Zel would not yield. His life depended on it, or so his instincts told him.

Then Ulrich *laughed*, and the resonance, the surprise of it, caused just enough of a distraction for Zel to pause.

Ulrich swept his sword in a half circle to force Zel's dagger downward, nearly disarming him, and then swept his blade point up to align with Zel's throat again. This time not even speed would be in Zel's favor to bring his dagger up and deflect a killing blow.

That was when he realized that while Ulrich was smiling in the aftermath of his laughter, Zel was smiling too. He *had* fought like his life depended on it, but he hadn't been truly afraid. He had enjoyed that. He had only ever enjoyed sparring with his parents before. Not that they gave him any quarter, and they still fought dirty, just like they'd taught him to, because fair never saved anyone's life. But there was a comfort in not having to hold back, in trusting that one's opponent would not hold back either, yet that trust also meant believing a killing blow would never follow through.

Not yet.

"It seems I lost," Zel said, although he couldn't resist tapping the point of his dagger against Ulrich's thigh.

Ulrich glanced at it, seeing that Zel was equally poised for a deadly skewer, and a far more emasculating one, given how low the blade had been deflected. "Hm. If I were mortal, it seems we both would have lost." Ulrich disengaged, sweeping his blade down to point at the floor, as if it bowed just before he did.

Zel lowered his dagger and bowed in kind. He had trained both in his daily clothes and in assassin gear. Wearing breeches and a simple dress without a corset certainly made sparring easier than in his old outfits. Usually when in a dress, Zel was more hindered. Even more comfortable like he was now, he couldn't say for certain if he could defeat Ulrich if they fought for real. Would they come to another standstill? Had luck been on Zel's side today, like it usually was, or had Ulrich gone easier on him than things appeared?

If Zel found a weakness to exploit, the only way to be certain of a killing blow would be to catch Ulrich unaware.

Like Ulrich had caught Zel. If that magical sweep for dangerous items happened daily, then Ulrich had possessed Zel's dagger for a lot longer than only this morn.

"It was a test, wasn't it?" Zel asked, while Ulrich went to place his sword back on its rack. "Not just this, now. Yesterday too. You wanted us to encounter that bandit. You let him attack me on purpose to see what I would do."

Ulrich looked over his shoulder with a knowing smile. "You were never in any real danger."

"But what did you hope to learn?"

"Oh, little cabbage, I hope to learn everything." Slowly, Ulrich returned to where Zel stood in the ring. He seemed taller in his pride. Pride toward Zel? Pleased with him? Pleased by something. Who was the real swindler here? Zel honestly couldn't say. "Tell me, do you hide a sheath beneath your skirts?"

Zel reflexively tightened his grip on the dagger. "Not today." That was true. Zel had seen no reason to risk carrying his dagger before now. Did Ulrich think Zel simply skilled at fighting, or did he guess, did he *know*, how many people Zel had killed?

"Pity," Ulrich said, reaching to brush some of Zel's fringe from his forehead, which had grown damp with sweat. "I might have put it back for you."

Heat swelled in Zel's gut. He *was* being bewitched. He had to be. He wanted nothing more than to lift onto his toes and kiss Ulrich then, not as some tactic, but too real, too honest, too much something Zel wanted only for himself.

Before he could, Ulrich stepped away.

Zel loathed how disappointed he was. He could not risk becoming compromised like this. He didn't even know what games Ulrich was playing or what he truly wanted from Zel. Were these tests merely to weigh the worthiness of a bride? Zel didn't know, and yet, only days in, and despite having made progress with his mission, compromised he was.

"About the dagger—"

"I remember your parents, Zel, and you have never denied being part of their same Thieves Guild. Did you think I expected you would come to my door without their same skillsets or ability to defend yourself?"

"I suppose not."

"You hadn't noticed the dagger was missing. Which tells me you had no intention of using it unprovoked. It is immune now from the magical sweep. You can keep it wherever you wish."

But Zel *had* planned to use it unprovoked. He *did*, just not yet.

Not yet.

Not until he knew how to divest the sorcerer of his immortality and kill him.

Kill Ulrich.

"Thank you, my lord," Zel said. "I hope we can spar again someday."

He had no choice.

He had no choice.

Even as Ulrich's smile made Zel's knees feel weak. "As do I, little cabbage."

ULRICH

Zel was a talented member of the Thieves Guild, there was no doubt about that. A talented *assassin* sent to ensure Ulrich's demise.

Ulrich had pushed things by saying he might have re-sheathed Zel's dagger. But Ulrich's beautiful *little cabbage* was difficult to resist, deceptive though the assassin may be. Zel's comforting touch and magical hair aside, there was something entrancing in those green eyes. Only time would tell just how much of a liar Zel proved to be.

ZEL

Our dearest Rapunzel,

Your mother and I are overjoyed that your time with the sorcerer is proving fruitful, and we believe that in getting to know one another, there will be no doubt in him that he could have no finer bride.

We arrived safely home after our parting with you at the tower to discover your horse had arrived ahead of us, a sign we took to mean you were well, but to hear from you directly adds much needed comfort.

We hope to see you again soon, but rest assured that the music shop thrives, and business continues at a sharp pace compared to the previous season.

We love you dearly.

-Your Devoted Father

Most notably coded in the letter was that *sharp pace* meant Lothar was still giving them assassinations to carry out while Zel was away. Just because the time had come for their grand ruse did not mean his parents could rest during the month. Lothar always had contingencies and would not risk anything other than business as usual to alert the Queen of a plot in the works to undermine her power.

Tucked in with Zel's parents' letter was one from Rudy. Whether they knew he had slipped it in was uncertain, but he too kept to a code.

Zel,

> *The city is not the same without you, my friend. I think of you often. Should you ever need anything that your betrothed cannot provide, trust that your friends in the city will always be there for you.*

> *Don't forget: Only empty pockets need filling.*

> *Please continue to let us know you are well. While the sorcerer might be judging your worth during this month, we know it is he who could never be worthy of you.*

-Yours, Rudy

Coded to some extent or not—offering Thieves Guild assistance should Zel indicate distress—it was still daring and dangerous for Rudy to say such things if Ulrich were to read the letters, which Zel assumed he did.

Or perhaps he did not, if it was true that he had not rummaged for, found, nor removed Zel's dagger, but had merely acquired it from a spell. A week had passed since that sparring match, which meant they were nearing the halfway mark of their time together. Zel couldn't be sure when another "test" might present itself, or if every word, every action, every breath he took was under scrutiny.

His pleasant days with Ulrich had mostly been the same since then, yet never dull. They would go for walks, tend to the garden, share stories and music, dine together, spend time apart too in such tasks as reading, writing, and simple relaxation, and every morn, Ulrich would brush out Zel's hair and help him to braid it with magic.

Their magic.

Zel continued to eat his daily lettuce with every evening meal, and maybe because he was in the tower, maybe because of the presence of Ulrich, and actually utilizing Zel's inner magic more than simply having good health, he felt his magic more too. He felt invincible.

Invulnerable.

Immortal?

The thought struck Zel just as he was finishing his own letters to send back to Rudy and his parents. He had taken to keeping his dagger with him for whenever they might leave the tower. It rested next to him now since he had used it as a letter opener. He took up the dagger again and contemplated just what immortality meant.

Zel had not been able to prove whether a cut against Ulrich could mark his skin, draw blood, and then simply vanish, or would his skin be like stone, like steel, and deflect any blow against it the way others could not cut Zel's hair?

With the dagger tip pressed to his index finger, Zel pushed it forward.

"Zel!" Ulrich was there, as if he'd manifested from the walls. He took the dagger from Zel to set it back on the desk and held his injured hand, where a small pool of blood oozed from his fingertip. "Why would you harm yourself purposely like that?"

Zel imagined Ulrich taking the finger into his mouth to suck the blood from its tip, but Ulrich did no such thing. He grasped Zel's finger with his blackened hand and curled his own fingers around it.

Ulrich's hand flared to life the way it did when in contact with Zel's hair, and the pain Zel had been feeling vanished instantly.

Did Zel's blood have the same effect on the curse?

Ulrich's eyes said he was equally surprised. When he uncoiled his fingers, the blood and cut were gone. And for the first time, Zel noticed something carved into Ulrich's palm, for just before the last of the blood disappeared, absorbed into Ulrich, it looked vibrantly red—a circle bisected by a horizontal line.

Zel knew that symbol from somewhere.

"I'm sorry, my lord," Zel said. "I had always wanted to do that, but my parents wouldn't allow it."

"Injure yourself? Why? Surely, you have bled before?"

"Not that I can remember. Since only I could ever cut my hair, I always wondered if only I could pierce my skin. The thought occurred to me that I might be even more invulnerable now. Maybe... immortal?" He blinked up at Ulrich, who hovered over him at the desk.

"You are not," Ulrich said.

"Yet? My lord would not take a bride without ensuring she would be by his side forever, would he?"

Ulrich's concern faded to his more knowing look. "Our month has many days yet, Zel."

Whatever that meant, for it did not answer the question.

Ulrich kissed Zel's finger before releasing his wrist. It was not as desirable as the heat from Ulrich's mouth encasing it, but enough to stir within Zel a flutter of southbound heat. "Now you know. You can injure yourself. So please do not do that again. And despite what may seem like magical luck up until now and the imperviousness of your hair, you are not invulnerable to outside harm should someone land a blow against you. Do not test that theory either. Unless you would like for me to prick you next?"

Oh, more than Zel could admit concerning another type of *prick*, but he wisely shook his head.

"Good."

"My lord, were you watching me?" Zel asked.

"Not actively spying, if that's what you mean." Ulrich shifted to lean against the desk. He appeared so ethereal to Zel, like it wouldn't be possible to touch him without bursting. Zel couldn't be sure whether it was Ulrich's magic alone that had healed his finger, his own healing intensified even if not to the point of immortality, or both. "But I can always see you, Zel, always find you when you are within the grounds of my tower, except for when you use the key and are in one of those rooms," he added with a nod at the magical door.

"You cannot see me at all when I am in there?"

"When you are in my chambers with the full turn of the key, I am already with you."

"Yes, and I had assumed as much for my bedchamber and the washroom, but you do not see me even when I am in the treasure room?"

"Why would I need to? I already told you that my truest treasures I keep out here." His next nod was to the shelves of trinkets that had tempted Zel's parents all those winters ago.

"May I ask you why that is?" Zel turned in his chair to look at the items. "You get thieves frequently enough. Why risk having what is precious to you so much easier to take?"

Ulrich grinned. "By all means, attempt to take something from that shelf."

Apparently, Zel had walked willingly into his next test. Although part of the test might have been to gauge whether or not he had tried to take something from the shelf before.

He had not.

There was a myriad of items, all made from precious metals, bejeweled, or both. Zel couldn't guess at any of their magical properties, such as a gold and silver necklace with entwined snakes for its pendant.

Or a set of golden scales balanced by a skeletal hand steadying its fulcrum.

A glass orb on a small silver pedestal with swirling green mist within.

A book made of strange leather, ominous compared to the tomes on the other shelves. It was embossed and bejeweled, yes, but its silver clasp to lock it seemed to be a closed eye. Zel did not want to guess whether that eye could open.

There were many things, but also what appeared to be a gold and emerald hairpin.

Zel chose to reach for that. As soon as he had plucked it from the shelf, it vanished from his fingers, and when he looked up, it was back on the shelf where he had found it. "No wonder you needn't worry about thieves." Before being interrupted by Ulrich,

Zel's parents must not have managed to try taking anything from the shelf, or they would have mentioned its trick. "Might I ask you about some of them? *Why* they are precious to you?"

"Most are because they are part of my history or some strong memory." Ulrich joined Zel in front of the shelf. "But yes, you may ask about them."

Zel pointed out each of the items that had most caught his eye.

"Notice how the pendant is an ouroboros?" Ulrich said. "It protects the wearer from harm but at the slow cost of time left on their life. It is gradual enough that one might not notice, but greater injuries can mean decades lost. I used it to assassinate a neighboring king, knowing he would foolishly take the bait and charge into battle wearing it.

"The scales weigh intent. Most thought it weighed whether or not someone was lying to me, but lies can have purpose. If someone wished to use lies or even truth against me, however, it would weigh their treachery and remove that same weight from their body."

"Remove...?" Zel repeated with a shudder.

"It is best to not imagine it. But I used it on anyone who attempted to get close to me, whether to serve me in my rule, in battle, or in my bedchamber."

Zel's fear spiked.

"It has since lost its magic from overuse," Ulrich finished.

"The magic in an item can run out?"

"It depends on how it is made. The scales needed to be charged regularly. Since I lived alone for so long, I stopped bothering."

Thank God.

"The orb can look anywhere one desires," Ulrich continued, "but only places the onlooker has been before. I mostly use it to see how my old homeland fares." He ran a hand over the glass, and the green mist cleared to show a vision of a kingdom similar but still somewhat changed from what Ulrich had shown Zel of elven lands.

Then Ulrich turned his attention to the book.

"One of my first teacher's spellbooks, filled with forbidden magic. I was only to use it when in her company. I did not follow that rule. Eventually, when I was poised to surpass her, she used her own soul to lock the remainder of its contents from me. I used to show her my exploits that she failed to prevent, but I let her sleep now."

Zel instinctively sidestepped away from the book, since it seemed the eye could open when prompted. "You can't release her?"

"No. That type of magic is irreversible, but she knew the danger when she sealed her fate."

"What of the hairpin?" Zel asked.

That item Ulrich took from the shelf, and unlike when Zel had taken it, it remained in his grasp. "There is a simple spell on it, one I put there to ensure it never tarnishes but is always as pristine as the last day it was worn. It was my mother's."

"Your mother's? But I thought you were an orph—"

"A tale for another time." Ulrich made to place the hairpin back on the shelf but then seemed to change his mind and motioned for Zel to turn around. He carefully placed the hairpin within Zel's braids.

When Zel turned back to Ulrich, the silver hand mirror had been summoned, and Ulrich used it to show Zel how the gold and glittering emeralds peeked just above the crown of his head.

"I have never felt right wearing it," Ulrich said, "but better for someone to. Keep it."

Zel was humbled, for unlike the magical loom, this was something personal to Ulrich. "Thank you. Is the mirror magical too?"

"In a way. It is capable of reflecting the greatest beauty in all the lands."

"I do not believe any mirror can do that."

"No? To me, it is doing so right now."

Zel felt some of the heat from his gut spread upward to fill his cheeks.

Then, with a quick sleight of hand, the mirror returned to where Ulrich had summoned it from—which would have been the nightstand in Zel's bedchamber—and began to straighten the items on the shelf to make up for the empty space of the hairpin. He did so with his blackened hand, and after a moment, the violet veins glowed a little brighter, and he cringed.

"May I?" Zel asked. When Ulrich nodded, Zel took the hand in both of his, watching the change in Ulrich's expression as Zel's touch eased him. "You do not reach for me anymore without asking first."

"I should always have done so, and I thought that was your preference, given how you've flinched and even recoiled at times."

"It *is* my preference," Zel confirmed, "but you can ask more often, since it soothes your pain."

"Zel, have you heard the old adage: be careful what you wish for?"

"Of course."

"If you grant me such leave, I might never stop touching you."

Zel felt his cheeks flush hotter. It was in moments like this that he forgot he one day had to betray this man. "When we are wed, I would welcome that." He would if it weren't a lie that they would ever reach such an end.

Ulrich's gaze softened in a way Zel did not think he had seen from the sorcerer thus far. "Then I have something to look forward to. Might I ask about one of your trinkets now?"

"My dagger?"

"Your pendant."

A bit of Zel's fear resurfaced. He could not be certain whether or not Ulrich had seen Rudy that first day. It was too risky to lie, and so he released Ulrich's hand to lift the pendant from his chest, fingering the emerald. Emerald and gold just like the hairpin now in Zel's braids. "From my dearest friend, Rudy. Rudolf, but Rudy as I am Zel. We have always been close."

"The one who wrote to you?" Ulrich glanced back at the desk. "I do not read your letters, I assure you, but I noticed the name. Are those ready to send?"

"They are."

Ulrich waved a hand, and they folded themselves and flew off out the window like last time. New letters came in the same way.

"The truth is... Rudy is in love with me," Zel admitted, "and it pains me that I have never felt the same. I have been plain to him about my feelings, and it would have complicated things for me and you of course, but he never gives up. I think part of him still hopes we might end up together someday. He doesn't care that he is breaking his own heart."

"Forgive me for saying so, but wouldn't a true friend heed your wishes regardless?"

Zel fought a cringe. He knew that, but Rudy would still be his friend even if it finally got through to him that they could never be more. Wouldn't he?

"Although, I have heard it said that what you describe is one of the main problems with love," Ulrich continued. "The heart does not know when to quit, even if it heads toward doom."

"*Heard* it said?" Zel questioned, distracted from his wondering about Rudy. "You have never been in love in all your time alive?"

Ulrich seemed to contemplate that. "Not that I am aware of, and I have also heard it said that if one does not know, one has not loved. I have often wondered about it, especially in my centuries alone, with only stories for company. A good romance can be more thrilling than the most epic of battle scenes. Surely, to experience it would be just as thrilling."

Yes, Zel had often wondered the same. "Do you have a favorite love story?"

"I am not going to sing it for you."

Zel laughed. It amazed him how often Ulrich could cause that reaction. "You don't have to sing it, but I would love to hear it spoken. Come, tell it to me." Zel took Ulrich's blackened hand again and led him to the chaise. They sat with Ulrich's hand in Zel's lap to keep it soothed. He could feel the grooves of the bisected circle carved into Ulrich's palm, which he was still curious about. Zel even deliberately pulled his braid into his lap, so it too touched Ulrich's hand, plumping it to near normal life.

Ulrich sighed deeply. "Do you know the tale of *The Bard and the Fairy Prince*?"

"I do not." Zel honestly didn't and wondered how old that story might be. Perhaps it even came from Ulrich's elven homeland.

"Then you, little cabbage, are in for a treat. How does one begin such things? Oh yes. Once upon a time..."

Zel listened with rapt attention to the deep, resonant tones of Ulrich's voice telling him a love story. He was continuing to earn Ulrich's favor, as was his mission, but in doing so, he was forgetting to not allow Ulrich to earn his.

ULRICH

"Once upon a time... a prince was born to an elven queen and a human king—or so the prince thought. Some called his mother queen of the fairies for all her magic, but she was neither fairy nor honestly an elf. She was from the depths, the unknown, born of wild and dark magic, and when the prince learned of this, it darkened his heart to match his heritage."

Part of that fairy tale was very personal to Ulrich. He didn't know if it was based on anything truthful, but he did know what it was like to be the cause of one's own demise in the pursuit of power to defy one's birth.

The fairy prince, who just as easily could have been called a half-demon, went on a journey very similar to Ulrich's, amassing magic even if it meant stealing it from good, kind people from other kingdoms who had never wronged him. The difference between the prince and Ulrich was that the prince had a warrior bard he hired to protect him who eventually tried to convince him to give up his quest for power and choose love instead.

Such an option had never been presented to Ulrich. Love of family had meant little. He lost them too young. Love of friends had never been enough to sway him. He had swayed most of them. There was never a true love in Ulrich's life, never any connection to another that could have prevented his downfall once he realized too late it had all been for naught, and none of his pursuits had ever led to happiness.

Happiness, it seemed, was the quelling of the ache in him that had persisted for centuries. Happiness was touch he had not realized he had been starved to know again. Happiness was found in these brief, pain-free moments with Zel.

Which he had to strive to not give into.

This was not how the month was meant to go. Zel's willingness to touch and be touched was welcome, but Ulrich had always known willing companions. He had slain many in his long life, but he had never wanted nor needed to take anyone unwilling into his bed. Everyone who had ever ended up there had asked for it, wanted it, offered themselves wholeheartedly, whether for power, favor, or simply the pleasures he could provide. His magical scales to weigh intent had helped ensure that.

Zel was willing too, even to listen to a love story that Ulrich had never dared imagine he might mimic. Zel, who it seemed sometimes forgot, had the goal of assassination while here. But if killing alone was enough to condemn someone to what Ulrich had originally planned for Zel, then the tale of *The Bard and the Fairy Prince* would not move Ulrich as it did. The story gave hope when Ulrich had long since stopped believing he could have any. That anyone could.

He was continuing to gauge Zel's worth for the month's end, but in doing so, he was forgetting who each of them was to the other and that the outcome was never meant to be marriage, even if Zel passed every test.

"And they lived happily ever after?" Zel asked once the story had reached its end.

"Yes," Ulrich said, "I suppose they did."

Eight

ZEL

Sometimes, Zel would look out toward the kingdom of Hallin before bed and spot the shadow of Ulrich walking into the wood for who knew what—likely for a soul or possibly to hunt game, since they never went without meat each day. Sometimes, Zel would see Ulrich catch his prey around the perimeter of the grounds when some foolish bandit came upon the tower—or if a deer did. Sometimes, Ulrich would even look up, and rather than ducking out of view like the first time, Zel would smile, imagining that Ulrich smiled back at him, even if he couldn't see Ulrich's face clear enough in the dark.

Whenever Zel spotted Ulrich outside the tower like that, he would take to his bed imagining the sorcerer ascending and climbing in through the window to join him. He never did. He never snuck into the washroom either, and Zel believed Ulrich did not watch him while there or in his bedchamber, or he would have already known Zel's secret.

One of them anyway.

Zel had learned many things in the subsequent days since the tale of *The Bard and the Fairy Prince*. He continued to keep Ulrich's interest and continued to feel interest of his own, much as it pained him when he remembered his true goal. Most interesting, at least for Zel's mission, had been a couple nights after Ulrich shared that favored love story.

They had dined together for the evening meal, but later into the night, they had still not left the dining hall. The wine flowed, more than any night before, as discussion turned to each of their first teachers.

Ulrich talked of the first person to teach him magic beyond the minimal amount he had been born with—thankfully not the same as the one whose soul sealed the magical book on the main room's shelf—and Zel reminisced not of his parents but of a different teacher, one who had taught him the basics with the blade before his parents honed those skills.

Sadly, she passed away during a mission.

"Mission?" Ulrich had inquired.

"Um... we call any order for a particular theft a mission." Which wasn't a lie, but it was if implying Helga had died from anything other than a failed assassination.

Ulrich eyed Zel with a glassy haze.

A drunken haze.

"My first teacher did not stay long enough for me to know her fate," Ulrich said. "A traveler through our kingdom. She was ravishing. Not the most beautiful person I have known, mind you," he added with a fixed stare on Zel's face, "but if ever in my past I could have given up my ambitions for love, she might have earned it and turned me from my path."

"Just as the bard saved the prince?" Zel referenced Ulrich's favorite tale, though not without a stir of jealousy, even if that teacher had only been a potential love for Ulrich. Surprised as he had been to learn Ulrich had not known love in his life, Zel had come to like that truth. He liked knowing Ulrich's heart had never belonged to another.

"Precisely," Ulrich said. "But I think I mourned more for the fairy tale not lived than the woman. It takes someone special to tempt one with both." His drunken eyes had centered on Zel, more heated than ever.

"Are you well, my lord?" Zel asked.

"Too well." Ulrich chuckled, tearing his gaze away to stare into his wine goblet. "I think it best that we suspend our merrymaking or regret it come the morn."

"Being immortal does not spare you the effects of strong drink?"

"How unfair if it did. But I am spared the ill effects later. You, I imagine, are not. I would not want to put you at such... dire risk should we continue."

Zel rarely suffered too badly after a night of merrymaking with drink, but he had never woken after a rough night completely unhindered. He did not think that was what Ulrich was saving him from, however.

They parted and retired to their separate chambers, but what mattered was what Zel had learned. Now he knew how Ulrich might be put in a vulnerable enough state for a blow to be struck. He just needed to learn how to make that blow matter.

Since Ulrich's tongue seemed loosened while intoxicated, Zel also began laying the groundwork to propose a different sort of outing, one during which he might discover the final pieces of the puzzle needed to slay him. Zel did so perhaps too slowly, but it saddened him knowing he might have a way to complete this mission, and he stalled well into their third week, until he could no longer risk wasting another day.

While Zel had a moment alone, resigned to finally move forward with his plans, he perused Ulrich's shelf of dearest treasures. He eventually realized he had his braids over his shoulder and was stroking the plaits. Typical when anxious, but he had been doing it too often lately. If his hair hadn't been magical, he might have pulled out clumps by now.

The only other things that could usually ease Zel when he felt like this were stolen moments with Rudy in the storeroom—currently not an option—or encouragement from his parents. Usually not an option, since Zel was in the tower and they were hours away back in the city, but in front of Zel was an orb with green mist swirling within it that could show anywhere its activator wished to look upon.

Although Zel couldn't remove anything from the shelf, he could still touch its contents. He ran his fingers over the orb and imagined his parents in their music shop, which at this hour would just be closing.

"Any letters today, Soph?"

Zel snatched his hand back. He hadn't expected to be able to hear what he looked in on. He hadn't heard anything when Ulrich touched the orb, but then, Zel's father's voice had sounded like it echoed within Zel's mind, not from the orb itself. Perhaps only the activator could hear what was shown.

Zel quickly returned his fingers to bring the images and sound back.

"...normal to not receive one every day," his mother spoke the last half of her answer.

"I know. Doesn't mean I don't worry every second our little Rapunzel is away."

The pair were shuttering the shop for the night. They didn't look like assassins while in normal clothing. Or like thieves. But then, who did when not in the midst of such acts?

"She is not so little anymore," Sophie said.

"Soph, when it's just us, I think you can say *he*."

"Can I?"

Gregor looked over from where he had latched the door closed to Sophie counting the day's coin to separate out what would go to the guild. "What do you mean?"

"Just that." Sophie shrugged. "When this is all over, do you think Rapunzel will live as a man or remain a woman?"

Gregor approached her with a scrunched brow. "I suppose I had never thought about it. Rapunzel hasn't had a choice in the matter until now. Has he only ever dallied with boys?"

"You have to ask?" Sophie chuckled.

"Well, how does one discuss such things with their child?"

"I thought most fathers and sons got quite bawdy about such talk."

"It's different with Rapunzel than if we had a real so—oh. I see your point."

Zel had rarely heard himself spoken of in such a way. When he thought, it was with I's. When others spoke to him, it was with his name. It was only in overhearing other people talk about him that he had to hear he's and she's. And usually, just she's.

But perhaps neither sounded right.

"I am fairly certain Rapunzel has only ever dallied with Rudy," Sophie said—which was correct.

"Then I imagine Rapunzel will live as a woman."

"Gregor," Sophie chided. "That is hardly definitive evidence."

"I know. I just rarely think of Rapunzel as a son. He's my daughter!" Gregor laughed. "*She* is. Goodness, this is difficult when we do not have the one person here who can tell us which is right. And it's all our doing, not Rapunzel's choice at all." Any mirth between them dwindled as the last coin for the guild was set aside. "Our dear child has had to sacrifice so much. We have too, but... Oh, I hate this, Soph. I hate that our child must pay for our mistake."

"My mistake," Sophie muttered.

"Don't start that again. There's no guarantee the sorcerer wouldn't have caught us before we scaled back over that wall, even if we hadn't gone up the tower first. Eating that lettuce might have been what saved us and Rapunzel. I wouldn't trade any of our sacrifices if it meant our babe would never be born." He reached across the front counter where Sophie had been doing the counting and took her hands.

"Neither would I," she agreed.

"I just wish Rapunzel was free to live as whoever and whatever he or she wishes to be. I wish that for us too. Can you imagine if it all actually goes to plan, the full plan, and we take over the guild? Nobody is loyal to Lothar. They only fear him. We could run things so much better."

"It still surprises me how much I want that, when once I wanted a life for us outside the guild," Sophie mused. "Though I'm fairly certain other members will still fear us if we take over using the sorcerer's magic."

"Only at first! We'll earn their loyalty until they learn they needn't fear us at all."

Sophie brought Gregor's hands to her lips and kissed both sets of knuckles. "I hope for that future too. Soon. Rapunzel will not fail."

"Rapunzel will not fail," Gregor repeated. He helped Sophie sweep all the coins for the guild into a separate bag that they would bring to the communal coffers, like they did every night. "What's this?" he asked of a piece of parchment resting beside the till.

"A recalculation of yesterday's sales," Sophie explained. "You were short."

"I was?" Gregor studied the parchment. "This isn't your handwriting."

"Rudy did it, when he was helping me restock earlier. He noticed the discrepancy."

"That boy," Gregor said with fondness. "He's been here nearly every day. Still trying to earn Rapunzel's favor?"

"I don't think that's it precisely," Sophie countered. "Well, he *is*, but he made me promise to not say anything about all he's been doing for us. I think he simply sees it as right to aid us, because like him, we are without our Rapunzel."

Oh Rudy. He always had been more selfless than the average pickpocket. Zel missed him. Other than Zel's parents, Rudy had been his only constant, even without counting their physical dalliances. For so long Zel had wished he could love Rudy the way Rudy loved him, but dear as Rudy was to him and always would be, he couldn't wish for that any longer, not after knowing Ulrich. Not after knowing what truly wanting someone felt like.

Gregor sighed, seemingly lost in thought.

"What?" Sophie asked.

"Whether Rapunzel lives as a he or she, if it's a man our child chooses to marry, we'll never be grandparents. Does that ever bother you? I'm not saying it bothers me, but—"

"It doesn't bother me," Sophie said, "because it isn't a parent's place to want grandchildren. It's a parent's place to want their child to live freely and happily, better than they did, whether that includes grandchildren or not, and regardless of whatever it does include. Besides, just because Rapunzel might not father a child and cannot birth one doesn't mean grandchildren are out of the question. We were orphans after all."

Gregor looked over at Sophie with pure adoration.

"What now?" She chuckled.

"How did I get so lucky as to have a woman as wonderful as you in my life?"

"As I recall, I pursued you, and you were wise enough to let me catch you."

"Too true."

They kissed, an act taken as easily as breathing. They loved each other as if no other choice had ever entered their minds.

Zel wanted that too.

"Now," Sophie said, "let's play a little something before dinner, shall we? I have had this song in my head all day!" She claimed a violin from one of their displays, while Gregor pulled out his flute.

What Sophie began to play and sing, which Gregor soon accompanied, was the same song they used to play and sing to Zel as a lullaby.

The moon is risen, beaming,
the golden stars are gleaming
so brightly in the skies;
the hushed, black woods are dreaming,
the mists, like phantoms seeming,
from meadows magically rise.

And lo, there Zel was, so near the Dark Forest, the deep, *black woods*, far from home, longing for the comfort of his parents beyond just their faces and voices.

He sang the next verse in harmony with his mother.

How still the world reposes,
while twilight round it closes,
so peaceful and so fair!

> *A quiet room for sleeping,*
> *into oblivion steeping*
> *the day's distress and sober care.*

Zel had to finish the mission for their sakes.

"I will not fail," he whispered. "I will succeed. I am ready for this. I am fierce and beautiful and capable... because of you."

He joined them again by singing.

> *Look at the moon so lonely!*
> *One half is shining only,*
> *yet she is round and bright;*
> *thus oft we laugh unknowing*
> *at things that are not showing,*
> *that still are hidden from our sight.*

"Zel?"

Zel snapped his hand away from the orb, and the images and sound halted. Ulrich had exited the magical chamber only a few strides away from him.

"You needn't stop on my account." Ulrich approached with a soft smile, as handsome and majestic as ever. "May I ask what you were looking in on? What you were singing sounded lovely. I think I might even know that one. But are you all right?"

It seemed unbidden moisture had flooded Zel's eyes because when he blinked, his vision blurred. It was only a song, and he was certain Ulrich couldn't hear what came from the orb anyway, so he returned his fingers to it. "I was checking on my parents. I miss them more than I realized."

Another easy truth, but omission still felt like lying when Zel wished he didn't have to.

Ulrich stepped closer, watching Sophie and Gregor through the glass.

"Is that your music shop?" he asked.

"Yes. Pied Pipers."

"Would you often sing and play together?"

"Almost every night. Sometimes for members of the guild too."

"I am sorry I cannot hear you all together. If I touched the orb, the vision would vanish. It is only intended for one. But... would you perhaps play that song for me from the beginning?" Ulrich produced what appeared to be the same violin as the one Zel had used on their first night and many since.

He looked back at his parents in the orb, bid them a silent farewell, and removed his hand, returning the contents to green mist and stopping the sounds of music in his mind. But Zel could create his own. "I don't suppose you know how to play any instruments to accompany me?" he asked as he accepted the violin.

"I am afraid I never learned, but I do know the words to that song."

"I thought you wouldn't sing for me."

"Not *alone*," Ulrich scoffed. "But in harmony with you, Zel, I can try."

Once again, Zel was charmed, but for the first time...

It *hurt*.

Zel moved to the middle of the room, and as he began to play, and then added his voice, Ulrich harmonized with him using his deep, haunting resonance. He had a lovely voice to be so timid about it, but it surprised Zel that playing and singing with Ulrich filled him with the same joy he used to feel at home with his parents.

Do not mourn your marks. They are already dead.

Zel had to finish this. He had to.

Tomorrow night, he would move forward.

Tonight, he would enjoy what he could.

ULRICH

"You wish to go to the city? To a tavern?"

"I wish to accompany *you* to a tavern, my lord," Zel explained. It was the next night, nearing the evening meal. "Or are we to never leave the walls of this tower other than for strolls through the wood? You did say you leave often. Do you never go into the villages or city?"

Ulrich was no fool and allowed his smile to reveal that he knew he was being goaded. "I sequestered myself in this tower to stay away from others, remember? But yes, I do visit the city from time to time. In disguise, of course."

Zel had already dressed for the occasion, it seemed, in one of the outfits brought along rather than one made from the loom, complete with bodice, petticoats, and—Ulrich assumed—corset and chemise. The more traditional garb wouldn't prevent stares, however, pretty as Zel was.

Zel also wore the pendant from Rudy that Ulrich begrudged, but it matched the gold and emerald hairpin Ulrich had given Zel, which helped assuage his jealousy.

"Then tell me, my lord, will you grant your bride-to-be this request?" Zel held out a hand to Ulrich, who had been reading while lounging on the chaise.

Ulrich set his book aside, took Zel's hand, and stood. "How could I refuse? But I assume you expect some magical transport to get us there promptly?"

"We wouldn't arrive until nearly tomorrow otherwise. I imagine you have your ways."

"I do. We will need to gather some of the *rapunzel* to bring with us, so you do not go without tonight when we have our evening meal."

"I had a feeling you would suggest that and already have some in my pockets." Zel opened one to show Ulrich the bursting of greenery.

"And where will we be going?"

"Hessen House. A bit rowdy at times, but it has the best options for food and drink."

"I do not know it. I can blink us out of existence to arrive somewhere new in an instant, but I can only do so to places I have been before, much like how the orb works. Once in the city, you will have to be our navigator to this rowdy tavern known for its food and drink." Ulrich took Zel's arm, and as he did so, his simpler elven guise overtook him, also forming more appropriate attire for a young man of the time. Sorcerer robes were not the current fashion. "Do you have everything you require?" he asked.

Zel squeezed Ulrich's arm and looked up at him with a bat of those alluring *lying* eyes. "I do."

Nine

ZEL

The trip was instant and jarring with the change in scenery, going from the walls of the tower to a claustrophobic alleyway that Zel assumed Ulrich had chosen because it was unlikely to have anyone down it. The smells of the city hit Zel just as suddenly, some pleasant like desserts baking for after the evening meal, some rank like rotting garbage and excrement in the deeper slums of the back streets. Either way, he was home.

As he and Ulrich ventured onto a more heavily traveled thoroughfare, Zel got his bearings and turned them in the direction toward the tavern. It wasn't far from where they'd arrived, a familiar area to Zel, though thankfully far enough from any Thieves Guild entrances that he hoped to not see anyone he knew. The goal of the evening, however, was worth the risk.

Most shops were closing and street vendors heading home, but as they passed a flower seller, Ulrich stopped her.

"My good lady, might I purchase the remainder of your stock?"

"You want the lot?" She tilted her basket. "They're not the

freshest, mind you, but I can give you a discount."

"They're suitable enough," Ulrich said. "Whatever you think is fair for them is fine."

He made the exchange with the seller, a mere pittance of coin for Ulrich, and then, in the shadows of another side street, he removed the glove from his right hand so he could trim the stems with his claws.

Zel hadn't noticed the glove until now, and Ulrich only wore the one. It seemed that even in disguise, he couldn't hide his blackened arm with magic, but had to wear a glove to hide it. Zel had noticed as much all those days ago during their stroll through the wood, but since Ulrich hadn't worn a glove then, he hadn't taken note of the importance. Here there was a much greater chance of curious eyes and questions.

Whatever Ulrich did to the flowers next, they came out bound together into a perfect miniature bouquet and seemed rejuvenated where their petals had previously looked brown and brittle. They were cornflowers, now a lovely shade of indigo, as if untouched by the Great Famine.

"It's temporary but should last the night." Ulrich tucked the flowers into Zel's bodice as a nosegay. All the unpleasant smells of the city faded with its presence.

"Thank you, my lord. And here I thought someone who had never known love might not know romance either."

Ulrich fitted his glove back over his cursed hand. "I've been keeping up on my reading."

Zel chuckled.

"One other thing." Ulrich reached inside Zel's cloak so suddenly that he gasped, and tension filled his body, though it was different from the tension that had once made him recoil from the sorcerer. Zel felt overheated, even in the autumn chill, growing colder as the sun set.

But all Ulrich did was pull Zel's hair from out of hiding beneath his cloak and perform a little extra magic.

Cornflowers like the ones in Zel's bodice bloomed from his braids, adorning the length as well as parts he couldn't see but could feel, like at the crown of his head.

"Now, you are even lovelier," Ulrich said.

Zel instinctively stroked the braids, careful around the blossoms. It was his little gesture of comfort, yet with Ulrich, the flutter of nerves he felt was its own contentment.

No one, save perhaps Rudy, had ever done something for Zel so spontaneously sweet. But not the flower pendant when Zel and Rudy first became friends nor the gold and emerald version as a token of Rudy's feelings evoked in Zel what he felt receiving this gift from Ulrich.

He needed to remember who was meant to be doing the seducing here.

"Lead on." Ulrich let Zel's braids fall back behind his shoulders and took his arm.

It was strange having lived here all of his life but having been away for weeks. It felt the same and yet foreign to Zel too. He had known a taste of freedom, even while on a mission.

Passing more and more people heading home or out to various taverns, Zel realized that Ulrich's hold on him tightened the longer they walked.

"If you worry I might wander off or flee from you—" he began, but Ulrich hushed his concerns.

"I believe if you wanted to do either, you would have done so already."

True. Ulrich had never locked Zel away or barred him from going where he pleased. But he still kept tightening his hold the more people they passed.

People they passed who cast appraising glances at Zel.

Ulrich was jealous. Possessive. Which was what Zel needed. He needed Ulrich to want him, but he also needed to stop being pleased about that for any reasons other than for the sake of the mission.

When they reached Hessen House, it proved rowdy indeed, even at this early hour. It was one of only a handful of establishments that always had enough food and drink for its patrons—for the right price—no doubt from some deal with the Queen to help combat the pitfalls of the Great Famine. It still wouldn't be much or anything like the meals Ulrich provided and meant coming early was the only way to ensure a decent seat along the wall rather than standing at the taller tables in the center.

Zel wondered as they searched for a table if Ulrich might change his mind about the locale with so many patrons about, but the sorcerer seemed more at ease now. Perhaps because a crowd meant most onlookers at Zel were accompanied by their own companions, courters, and wives.

An empty table appeared and in an ideal location, secluded yet not outside the throng of merrymaking, with a clear view of the area reserved for bards and players. Whether by Zel's luck or Ulrich's magic, they claimed it quickly.

They dined, with Zel sneaking bites of his *rapunzel* while eating his stew, and the din of the tavern was never without music. They even conversed a bit with a neighboring table, which hosted two younger married couples whose children were being looked after by one of their mothers. The couples were already drunk but in good spirits, so when one of the wives mentioned how much she adored the flowers in Zel's hair, he plucked one out to tuck it behind her ear.

They also drank. And drank. And *drank*. Zel did not need to come up with excuses for them to stay, for Ulrich seemed content, enjoying himself as much as Zel was. Honestly.

There was an eventual lull in the music for the bard who had been playing to be replaced by a full band, and the standing tables in the middle were moved closer to the ones along the walls, leaving room for dancing.

They could indulge as much as they wanted with Ulrich's unlimited coin, and Zel was contemplating their next drinks when Ulrich's hand slid onto his knee.

Zel looked at Ulrich, feeling the heat in his cheeks from all they had drunk so far flood lower and spread through his loins. He was supposed to be working, manipulating, but Ulrich was so handsome. So compelling. Zel wished he looked like he normally would, with starlight hair and a purplish complexion, but the shape of his face was the same, even if he was dimmed from his true radiance.

"Thank you for this," Ulrich said. "I went too long without partaking in such things."

"I worried you might not enjoy this as much as I was hoping."

"I am in good company. And while one can, one should *live*, should one not?"

While one can...

The desires blossoming in Zel's gut turned sour.

"Indeed," he said. "So let us keep living. I will fetch us more drink. It gets difficult to obtain service once the dancing starts." Zel slipped from their table, out from under Ulrich's hand on his knee, like a fleeing coward.

He had Ulrich right where he needed him, drunk and compliant enough that it would be easy now to ask him more about the curse and learn what Zel required...

To kill him.

Zel blinked a rush of heat from his eyes. Let it keep to his cheeks from drink, or his loins from Ulrich's touch. But not tears. He could not afford tears.

He moved for the bar, which was crowded with others trying to secure more drink before the new band of players began. Zel's beauty commanded a bit of chivalry, however, even from stumbling louts, and several parted to make way for him.

"Yes, please, barkeep, two—"

"Ain't you a pretty thing?"

Zel's beauty also commanded *unwanted attention* from stumbling louts. Such a presence pressed up against him from behind, and hot, ale-tinged breath struck Zel's cheek. "Thank you, sir, but I—"

"Have a dance with me, will ya? Though I'd rather see more of what's under that cloak, to be honest. Ain't you warm enough, pretty?"

"I am quite comfortable, and I'm afraid—"

"Dance with me." He tugged Zel's arm, whirling him around to face what was a perfectly unremarkable man, but one well into obnoxiously inebriated. "I ain't taking no for an answer."

Every instinct in Zel wanted to flip this man on his ass, but that would call attention. It would signal that he was from the Thieves Guild, and the evening would be ruined. "Sir—"

The man tugged Zel's arm again, forcing him onto the dancefloor and into his arms. Zel could easily escape, but could he do so without causing a scene? The music was just starting, and other drunken patrons crowded in around them, drowning Zel in the throng. He couldn't see their table anymore, being shorter than most of the other dancers.

Perhaps it was good the crowd rushed in quickly. Surely, Zel could spin out of the man's grasp and escape amid the other bodies.

He had a tight hold around Zel's waist though, too tight, and was starting to drift his hand lower.

Zel prepared himself to grab hold of that hand and twist it, throwing himself out of reach with the momentum, but he didn't get the chance.

"I believe you have acquired an already spoken for dance partner."

The shadow of Ulrich appeared, a brief flicker of his true form showing itself, as he swept Zel into his arms and shoved the man aside in one graceful motion. Whatever else he had done to the man, whether magical or just brute force, the lout was sent scurrying for one of the exits, holding a hand to his mouth like he might expel everything he had drunk.

Zel was in awe. The song was an upbeat waltz, modern within the past few decades, yet Ulrich, holding Zel close, fell into step with those around them effortlessly. The difference was that his hand at the small of Zel's back was welcome and did not wander.

"Thank you, my lord."

"You follow my lead beautifully, Zel. Assuming I have permission to continue dancing with you beyond the rescue?"

"You do," Zel said.

Ulrich danced far better than the drunken oaf had, well enough to draw a different kind of attention to them, but once the band moved on to a second song, Zel realized they had wound up back at the bar. He mourned no longer dancing with Ulrich, but the bar had been his goal, and the barkeep pushed fresh goblets their way as if having expected them. Perhaps he had witnessed what happened and knew to have drinks ready.

Perhaps Ulrich continued to command the night's events.

They claimed their cups, but Ulrich grabbed hold of Zel around the waist again and danced with him one-armed back to their table. They laughed when they collided with its edge upon reaching it, but not a single drop spilled from their goblets.

They drank. They listened to the music. And there was soon no question as to whether or not Ulrich was using his magic, for the air in the tavern began to sparkle like twinkling stars. Swirls of colored lights sprang to life in unexpected corners, twirling along with the dancers. It was like being in the heavens, on a night when more than stars dotting inky blackness could be seen, but swaths of pink and teal and violet.

Like Ulrich himself when no disguise dampened his brilliance.

Zel was delighted to watch it all with Ulrich beside him. A few less inebriated patrons noticed the illusions, most assuming that this elf or that one must be responsible, for their race was known for creating beautiful enchantments. The drunker among the patrons simply enjoyed it.

"It's lovely," Zel said, as the next song began. "The magic even moves to the music."

"You added your magic," Ulrich said, leaning in closer to Zel, "so I added mine."

"*My* magic?" Zel questioned. They were close enough that, when he glanced up, the barest lean from Ulrich could have bumped their noses.

"Your voice. You have been humming along to the songs."

"Have I? I didn't realize."

"You have a lovely voice. Though everything about you is magical to me, Zel."

Zel was feeling warmer by the moment. "Praise be to the lettuce?"

Ulrich chuckled. "Oh no. You surpass anything mere *rapunzel* could give you, little cabbage. That is why you are Zel."

Zel felt warmer still, but in his eyes like earlier. In his chest. In his gut. Between his legs. What magic was this, he wondered, for his whole body felt aflame, and he wanted to launch himself at Ulrich as much as part of him feared he might burst into tears. "Drink can make one... truthful," he said, bold enough to move his hand onto Ulrich's thigh. "But also feverish. Flush. My virtue is crumbling, my lord, for all I can think about is getting on my knees beneath this table and taking you into my mouth."

Ulrich's disguised eyes flashed with their usual violet fire and swirling galaxies. His chest heaved, not with need for breath, but with the same rising desire. He seemed about to say something, or equally like he might pull Zel to him and kiss him. Zel leaned closer too, enough that a kiss, whether chaste or bruising, would be so easy to claim. But then he might never want to stop.

"I'm sorry!" Zel lurched away before any kiss could be taken. What was he doing letting himself want and wonder? At least something he *could* blame on the drink was a sudden need to relieve himself. "I... I fear I am going to ruin this moment far worse than postponing it if I don't make my way to the latrines just now."

Ulrich huffed a laugh. He was clearly disappointed but nodded.

Zel did need to piss, but he was also being a coward again. He had to clear his mind and think through a plan to redirect their conversation so he might covertly gain the knowledge he sought: how to kill the unkillable, though what he really wanted was just what he had said.

He wondered what Ulrich would taste like.

Zel couldn't risk using the actual latrines, since the room was communal. An outhouse in the alley was more commonly used by female patrons, but when Zel got outside, it was occupied. His urgent need brought him around back to a narrower alley, where he hoisted his skirts to relieve himself against the wall.

The heat in his eyes refused to go away, and he found himself sniffling and blinking rapidly to keep any actual tears from falling. He had to focus. He had to be smart. He *could* slip beneath their table to pleasure Ulrich like he had teased, like he had done for Rudy so many times, but if he did, he knew he would want more like he had never wanted anything before.

As Zel finished emptying himself of all he had drank, he could have sworn he felt eyes on him.

He whirled in the direction where he sensed someone, certain he hadn't hiked his skirts enough that anyone could have seen or realized the truth. But was someone there, hiding in the dark? Was some fool about to try robbing him? In case they were, Zel reached beneath his skirts to retrieve his dagger.

"Well now, look who's without her fancy dance partner."

Zel froze, for the voice had not come from in front of him where he watched the dark, but behind. He turned, not surprised to discover the oaf from earlier stumbling toward him. After likely spilling his guts somewhere nearby, the man hadn't run off with his tail between his legs. Unfortunate. For *him*. Because here Zel didn't need to worry about drawing attention.

"Whatcha gonna do with that blade, pretty petal?" the man asked, since Zel made no move to hide his dagger, and in fact raised it at the ready. Why did it always come back to that goddamned name? "Betcha I got something better to skewer you with." He reached down to grab his own crotch.

Charming. "I doubt it," Zel said, "but you are right that something needs to be skewered."

If Ulrich was the shadowed night, then Zel was what lurked within, striking before his prey could react, with a crouch and a spring upward, and then his dagger lodged right through the man's hand still holding his cock.

Zel twisted and yanked the blade free, but while the man would bleed out quickly, it was not as instantly fatal as other blows Zel might have struck. He watched the horror fill the man's face, let it sink in for what precious moments Zel could enjoy it that, no, the man was not going to survive this, but before the release of death, he'd have to endure the loss of his manhood. When it all finally became real to the man and he opened his mouth to scream, Zel sliced upward across his throat to silence him.

With a quick spin out of the way, Zel avoided the spray of blood that followed. The man toppled, too much in shock to clutch his neck, when he was already clutching his ruined genitals. The brutality of the kill would warn people it had been done by a Thieves Guild assassin. Not all kills required cleaners. Some were left as messages, and no one would know that Zel struck the blow.

He wiped off his dagger on the back of the man's shirt before re-sheathing it.

His ninth kill. The one that was supposed to be Ulrich.

If Zel didn't watch the light leave the man's eyes, did it count? Did he not want for it to count? Or did he want this to be the ninth, so Ulrich might not become a number at all?

"Anyone who would attempt to take another without permission deserves only death."

Zel spun again, first down the other end of the alley, where he had initially thought he sensed someone, but he still couldn't make out anyone hiding there. Then he spun the other way, where Ulrich was on approach, having dropped his guise and looking absolutely ravishing in the moonlight with how he sparkled like the magic he had made dance to the music.

Zel adjusted his skirts, unsure how high they had been while he put his dagger away, but Ulrich couldn't possibly have seen anything. Could he? Even if he hadn't, he had seen Zel coldly murder someone, leaving no second guesses about what the Thieves Guild truly was.

"M-my lord—"

"Might I ask, little cabbage," Ulrich began as he descended upon Zel without further glance at the body nor any care that it laid there, "for permission to complete the kiss you denied me inside?"

Heat flourished once more within Zel. Even beside a piss-stained wall and fresh corpse, the request for a kiss lost none of its magic. Perhaps it was the alcohol buzzing through Zel's brain, but he could imagine no other answer than a breathlessly uttered, "Yes."

And Ulrich kissed him.

ULRICH

Whatever extent of chastity's chains Zel had already shaken free of were made clearer by how explosively their tongues collided with that first precious kiss.

Zel was a malicious marvel, cold and calculating and precise. But the receiver of Zel's skills had earned it. Over the many centuries Ulrich's immortality had gifted him, he had learned that one truth remained in every age.

Some people deserved to die.

Zel was not one of them, nor was Ulrich's little cabbage deserving of a worse fate.

Ulrich clutched Zel to him, right hand no longer gloved, with black and sunken skin freely exposed and claws digging into the firm fabric and boning of Zel's corset. The heat from the slighter body against him, the rapid pulse of Zel's heart, loud and vibrating as their chests collided as passionately as their mouths had, was wonderful. This was no chaste peck, testing waters. Ulrich had been teased with a filthy promise of scuffed knees and an open mouth. Whether an honest declaration or drunken musings, it made him ravenous to have Zel, any part of his betrothed, as little or as much as might be offered.

Zel's panting in the wake of their kiss only increased that want.

"You do not think it vile what I did?" Zel asked.

"He was the vile one. You, little cabbage, have proved a harbinger of justice." Ulrich reached for Zel again but winced as the veins in his arm pulsed.

Zel saw the added glow, the pain it caused, and took hold of Ulrich's blackened hand. Still breathless from their kiss, Zel lifted the hand to press wetted lips to Ulrich's fingertips, and even drew one into his mouth, claw and all, keeping eye contact while tonguing it.

They knew Zel's hair plumped Ulrich's arm to life, as did Zel's blood. Now, it was proven Zel's saliva did the same, and Ulrich's arm wasn't the only part of him growing plump.

"Better, my lord?" Zel asked, for even when Ulrich's finger hit open air again, the lingering wetness kept the hand looking whole and alive.

"Remarkably so."

"You've never confirmed if there is a way to permanently save you from your pain."

"Besides you?" Ulrich grinned. "Only removing it."

"Your arm?"

"Yes. Then I would no longer feel its pain, for I would die."

Zel's eyes bulged at the admission. "But... how could it be removed if you are impervious to damage while you have it? Isn't its sacrifice what makes you immortal?"

"It is. But if a strong enough person of natural-born magic drained me of my power the way I drain souls..." Ulrich slowly used his black hand to pull Zel's braids out from within the cloak to stroke the bundle, thus keeping its plumpness even as the saliva dried. "I would be weak enough to make it possible." He tried to lean in for another kiss, but Zel withdrew.

"I... I'm sorry."

"Zel? What—"

A presence snapped Ulrich's attention down the other end of the alley. Someone was there. Watching? Listening? Maybe merely trying to stay out of sight and too scared to run, but as tempted as Ulrich was to slaughter whoever it was for intruding, he had no patience for further interruption.

"Come. We are not alone," he said, and after pulling Zel to him, he blinked them back to the tower.

Zel gasped at the sudden change in location and pushed from Ulrich's arms as if feeling guilty for having clung to him.

"Please, Zel, it is I who should be sorry, not you. I ask for too much when we are both intoxicated. I tried so hard to not want you."

"To... *not* want me?" Zel turned back to Ulrich.

What a pretty little liar Zel was. But much as Ulrich might want to give in to the temptations before him, he knew the truth, the real reason for Zel being here, and their little dance of push and pull was nothing but a ruse.

Wasn't it?

"It doesn't matter," Ulrich said, "because you do not want me. Not really."

"Ulrich..."

The utterance of his name, whispered back at him, when Zel more often said, "my lord," urged Ulrich to meet Zel's gaze.

"I do want you. I want you more than I expected I could ever want anyone."

There was no lie, no clever subterfuge in the rawness of those words. How... surprising. "I think you mean that. But then what causes you to recoil again?"

Zel looked at the floor.

"Is it that you truly wish to wait until we are wed to do more than kiss and tease one another? I do not believe that. Your desire is too strong. Even contrary to your mission." Ulrich held Zel's stare when their eyes locked again. "I do not fault you for your secret intentions here, little cabbage."

"You... you knew? Of course you knew." Zel squeezed watering eyes shut. "Yet somehow that does not feel like the worst secret I'm keeping. Because you would not want me if you knew all my lies. If you knew... the truth of your bride's birth."

Ulrich studied Zel, confused, until he realized how tightly Zel clutched the many layers of petticoats and skirts. "Oh, Zel. *That* you needn't ever have worried about." Ulrich approached and bent low enough to whisper intimately, "Since the day you arrived at my tower, I have been more than eager to discover my bride's cock."

Ten

ZEL

What had Ulrich just said?

"You knew that too?" Zel backpedaled, nearly toppling over onto the chaise when his legs hit it. They were in the main room, and being night with only the usual candles and sconces lit, the darker parts of Ulrich looked more contrasting than ever between shadow and light.

He didn't look angry though. He seemed confused. "Did you think I did not?"

"You wanted a bride."

"And a bride I received."

"I'm a *man*."

Ulrich scrunched his brow, seeming even more perplexed. "It is not always and certainly not only what lies between one's legs that makes one a man or woman, Zel."

"I don't understand. You don't care?"

"If you worry I have an aversion to cock, I can assure you I do not."

"But—"

"Did you not notice in the scenes I showed you that some of my courtiers from the past were male?"

Were they?

"I also told you that my favorite love story is between two men."

"*The Bard and the Fairy Prince* is about two men?" Zel had assumed the bard in the story was a woman. Fairy tale love stories were always between a man and a woman! "But you told my parents—"

"I told your parents that I would unite in marriage with their child should I find them worthy. I actually made no mention of wanting a bride. That was their assumption."

Zel felt like his knees might fail him at any moment. "You really do not care what I am?"

"Oh, little cabbage..." Ulrich's voice softened as he took Zel's hands. "I care that you are you. What else matters?"

This felt too easy, just like Ulrich taking to calling Zel by his preferred name after one and only one correction. "But... you still knew what was under my skirts. How?" He snatched his hands back, leaning as much away from Ulrich as he could with the chaise behind him. "You *were* watching me."

"I assure you I was not. I simply knew. I assumed this was how you see yourself, not a lie you sold me like pretending to not be an assassin. Just as names are powerful in this world, Zel, so too is self-perception, and one's own truth is the only perception of self that matters."

Zel's head was spinning. "I don't know what to say." Somehow, he was crying, tears streaming down his cheeks unbidden that until now he had managed to keep at bay.

Ulrich swept Zel into his arms and sat them on the chaise. Zel collapsed against him, sobbing without any sign that he would stop any time soon. He had never been able to discuss the truth of himself openly. Even with his parents it had been dangerous to do so for fear of being discovered. Zel was to pretend, and so he had.

But it hadn't always felt like pretending.

"Here, we are sobering, but we should be clearer headed for this." Ulrich pressed his left hand to Zel's forehead. "It can be a bit jarring, but you will feel better."

Whatever Ulrich did next, it felt sharp and made Zel flinch at first, but then the inebriation that had been lingering was gone. Ulrich pressed the hand to his own forehead and must have done the same for himself.

Being less fuzzy in thought, Zel was able to calm his tears.

"Forgive me for losing my composure." He took a breath and wiped his face. Ulrich kept him close, and it felt nice being nestled against him. "My parents assumed you would expect your bride to be a woman, so they raised me to be one. But I have also honestly felt like one at times, not because I've had to pretend. I'm... neither? Both? I don't know. I've never been able to truly think on it."

"Because of me," Ulrich said softly.

"*No.*" Zel turned in Ulrich's hold and looked up into his starlit eyes and all the ways he sparkled in the dark. "I don't think of it like that. They wronged you. You asked for recompense. We chose to deceive you instead of paying our dues honestly. Most marriages are contracts. As magically lucky as I may have been over the years, I never thought myself so fortunate as to find what my parents have."

Ulrich's head bent a little closer to Zel's at the admission. "I still have my secrets, Zel."

"Would that I could learn them all. In time I would like to. Starting with how you could ever want me knowing my true intentions all along."

"You were a very charming would-be assassin."

Zel laughed. "Please know that my heart's desires are greater than my duty. With all my secrets laid bare, I would start over and ask something of you, if you'll permit me."

"Ask, and we shall see."

For all the turmoil of this night, Zel did not hesitate to take hold of Ulrich's left hand and bring it up beneath his skirts to his bare knee. "If you truly want me despite knowing my deceptions all this time, I wish to withdraw my first request of you and ask you to take me to bed tonight." Zel kissed him with an upward surge and coil of his tongue.

Sober and seated now, it was no less thrilling than their first kiss. Ulrich returned the embrace, lips and tongue moving against Zel's, and his hand crept up to the start of Zel's thigh.

Then he paused.

"Zel, are you certain—"

"Please, Ulrich, let me have this. For me. Because *I* want it. If you do?" Zel blinked past the lingering moisture in his eyes and waited for Ulrich's answer.

He was stunning, and whatever terror he could evoke in others, when they were alone, Zel saw only Ulrich's beauty. "I do."

Zel huffed a laugh at the apt wording he'd prompted, and in the parting of his lips, Ulrich licked his way between them again. Now that they were home, sober, and bared open to one another, this kiss felt different, heated but tentative. Ulrich hadn't known another's kiss or touch in centuries. Zel hadn't known either from anyone other than Rudy. And because Zel's magic could ease Ulrich's pain, it made him feel special in a way he had never truly embraced before.

Ulrich's cursed hand plumped to life with a brush of Zel's braids, while his other hand stole higher up Zel's thigh. Self-perseveration honed from deflecting Rudy still made Zel feel like he needed to redirect the advance of that hand. But not this time. Not with Ulrich. Zel could allow the slow ascent and push of fabric, lifting the layers to reveal his calves, and knees, and thighs, which Zel parted to permit Ulrich's hand to move center.

Again, Ulrich paused.

"May I?" he whispered. "May I touch you where no one else has?"

"*Yes.*"

While it was the left hand with sharp nails, not claws, that found Zel's hardening length, Ulrich was still careful with their points as he curled his fingers tight and stroked with the base of his thumb up the shaft.

"*Oh...*" Zel moaned at the first tantalizing tingle. It was so different from touching himself, and without meaning to, he began thrusting into Ulrich's strokes.

Ulrich grabbed Zel's hips with his blackened arm and tugged, upending him onto the chaise. With Zel laid out, Ulrich lifted his skirts fully, up past the bob of his cock that he continued to stroke. The pad of Ulrich's thumb pressed the deepest and circled Zel's slit.

"*Ohhh...*" Zel moaned louder, head falling limp upon the pillow. There wasn't room to lie side by side, but Ulrich climbed atop Zel and straddled his knees.

He waved the fingers of his cursed hand, and several strands of Zel's hair floated out of his braids, causing some of the cornflowers woven there to fall like apple blossoms in the spring. Ulrich conducted the strands as he did during their daily routine, commanding the ends of the loose locks to wrap around his wrist. His claws were only as sharp as the other hand's nails when Zel's magic held the curse at bay.

Reaching between Zel's legs with his right hand then, Ulrich cupped and fondled Zel's sac while the other hand hastened its strokes. It was everything Zel had envisioned but never believed he could have with another, let alone with the sorcerer in the wood. He was soon set to panting, breaths coming shallower and far too constricted.

"U-Ulrich... I need this corset *off*."

It popped as it unlaced with another wave of Ulrich's fingers. *Much better.*

Zel's outer bodice was loosened as well, and though the layers remained, they gave way to the ascent of Ulrich's currently healthy hand dragging up beneath them along Zel's skin, higher and higher past his navel and ribs.

Nethers exposed under Ulrich's heated stare, Zel had never felt more seen. He heaved heavier breaths, nodding frantically when Ulrich paused.

"More?" Ulrich asked.

"*Please*."

"I would see your golden locks unbound around you first with fewer layers to hide your body from me."

"Undress me then!" Zel demanded. "You can loosen my braids as easily as you did my bodice."

"*You* can." Ulrich took Zel's hands, beginning a familiar motion, as if to remind Zel of the magic he could employ. "Unbind the braids yourself, while I savor your unveiling."

Zel's hair had already started to lift, but when Ulrich released him to begin the final unlacing and removal of his clothing, Zel hesitated. He had never controlled his magic entirely on his own.

"You can do it without me," Ulrich coaxed. His fingers, matching in appearance with some of Zel's hair still wrapped around his cursed wrist, were enthralling to watch. Pulling at the cords holding Zel's bodice together. Sliding the bodice from Zel's shoulders. Removing Zel of his petticoats.

"Y-you distract me," Zel said.

"You can do it," Ulrich repeated, continuing his slow disrobing of Zel's body. He paused to press a kiss to Zel's lips. "Go on, my darling little cabbage, my Zel... let down your hair for me."

The heat in Zel's belly spread outward in an instant, and as he raised his arms and flared his fingers, his hair began to dance. It lifted and unraveled itself, stretching above them like twisted fabric unfurling in the wind until its canopy was enough to block out some of the moonlight.

More cornflowers from Zel's tresses fell upon him, while his clothing was plucked away piece by piece. He must have looked like a nymph by the end, surrounded by blossoms, with the full length of his hair spilling from the chaise, no longer wearing anything other than his hiked-up chemise like a sheer shroud.

That and Zel's pendant were all that remained when Ulrich stopped. And the hairpin, lost in Zel's locks until Ulrich saved it. He set it aside and then fingered the pendant just as gently.

"Rudy had the honor of touching you, did he not?"

"He never knew the truth," Zel said. "Never touched me everywhere. No one has until you."

"*Where* did he touch you," Ulrich pressed, "that I might replace his lips and hands with my own?"

"Here." Zel touched his lips first, and Ulrich bent to claim another kiss. "Here." He tapped the side of his neck, and Ulrich sucked hotly at his pulse point. He wrapped a hand around Zel's throat as well, lightly where neck met shoulder, and licked his way up to Zel's ear.

"Where else?" Ulrich breathed upon where he had wetted.

"H-here." Zel touched his nipples, visible and pert where his chemise spilled open.

Ulrich latched onto one of them with a firm but not too pinching suckle.

"Oh!"

"Sensitive here, are you?" Ulrich circled the nipple with his nails.

"Y-yes." Zel worried his lower lip.

"I might keep you like this when I finally take you, for you are more ravishing in this garment than all the beautiful bodies of the world laid bare." He latched on to the other nipple, sucking ravenously. "Tangled up." He kissed back up to Zel's neck. "Debauched." He tongued Zel's ear again. "Eager." He lifted like he might descend for another kiss, but Zel gripped him by the back of his neck first.

"You have no idea how eager." Then Zel yanked him down to steal that kiss first.

Ulrich sank against Zel, and Zel felt the press of Ulrich's clothed cock. How hard he had become encouraged Zel to buck up, but Ulrich stilled him with additional weight. "Where else did Rudy touch you?" he asked.

"He wanted more... but never got lower than here." Zel touched his nipples again.

"Did you want him to?" Ulrich shifted beneath the hike of Zel's chemise to kiss and lick down his stomach. "Did you want him to touch you lower?" He kept going, past Zel's navel and the start of fine hairs.

"I-I wanted someone to... but not Rudy. It feels so much more incredible that it's *you*."

Ulrich swallowed Zel down, tongue lapping up Zel's underside and teeth grazing his veins. Zel yelped, the sound cutting off with a violent gasp. He had never felt so enveloped, so claimed, so *seen* again, as if he was his truest self in the moments of bliss between him and the one person who knew him as he was.

Ulrich teased Zel's head on each upward bob with more grazes of teeth and flicks of his tongue. Zel's hips thrust up instinctually to match that rhythm, body quaking as each swallow was accompanied by the teasing but persistent fondling of his nipples.

"*Ulrich...*"

"Do you need me to stop?" Ulrich asked between licks across Zel's slit. "Let you come? Or..." He licked lower to Zel's entrance.

"Don't stop! But I... don't want to finish yet. I want to last, so I can savor my... deflowering." Zel snickered, given he was haloed by cornflowers.

"Like this, Zel, you are a fairy from the deepest wood, luring in gullible travelers whom none could resist. Nor could I." Ulrich licked Zel's hole with an ardent twirl.

"*Please.*" Zel writhed against his laving. "Take me! Take all of me. Anything and everything you want from me."

"Then I will." Ulrich plunged in his tongue, and Zel was certain he would come right that moment, but before the heat expanding within him could fully combust, Ulrich withdrew and climbed back up Zel's body. He hovered in want of a kiss, but waited for permission, given where that tongue had been.

Zel dragged him down like before.

As they kissed, Ulrich lifted Zel from the chaise, leaving clothing and flower petals behind. Zel also felt a sudden weightlessness around his neck—his pendant miraculously having unclasped and fallen onto the chaise or floor with the rest. He couldn't begrudge Ulrich for having caused that to happen, especially when his possessive streak was all too attractive.

Zel heard the click of the key as they neared the magical door, though he imagined it must have been floating since Ulrich had both arms around him. When Zel pulled up from their kiss to look at their surroundings, they were crossing the threshold into a bedchamber like Zel's, but larger, with an even more opulent bed.

Ulrich's bedchamber at last, which once Zel had hoped to never see, and now longed to never leave.

Ulrich placed him on the bed. Just like in Zel's chambers, the ceiling was a mirage of shelter, for it protected them but showed through to the clear night sky. Had the stars ever looked so brilliant amid the beautiful unknowable heavens and a diversity of colors, all of which lived in Ulrich's eyes?

Zel glanced down the bed in search of that galactic gaze, finding Ulrich starting to disrobe. The heavens were not so unknowable for they existed right before him here in this bedchamber.

"Wait." Zel sat up. "May I unveil you now?"

"Of course."

When Ulrich had dismissed his disguise earlier, so too had he cast off his modern attire. He wore his sorcerer robes again, ageless in a way, and rich and regal. All he had removed so far were his boots and the sash around his waist. His silk-like robes in midnight blue hung parted, revealing the open line of his chest down to ankle-length pantaloons.

Zel moved to the end of the bed, causing his chemise to cover his bobbing length. He ached from how hard it was. The chemise was a tangled mess, open up top and hanging off one shoulder. As he knelt and began to undress Ulrich, the sorcerer lifted the fall of Zel's skirt up over the spring of his cock.

Zel flushed from Ulrich's desire to still see him, enjoying that anyone's eyes could be on him. That anyone could see him, truly see him, and not think he was something he wasn't.

Because he was...

He was...

Zel. And with Ulrich, he could finally *be* Zel.

Zel opened Ulrich's pantaloons first but didn't yet lower them. He reached up inside the robe and pushed it from Ulrich's shoulders. The reveal would have been perfect if Zel's hair that remained around Ulrich's wrist didn't catch in the sleeve.

Zel laughed and unwound the hair with a thought. But as it lost its contact with Ulrich's skin, the curse returned, and Zel finally saw how far up Ulrich's arm the shrunken blackness went. It reached past his shoulder, like fetid roots, clawing toward Ulrich's chest.

Immediately, Zel wound a section of hair back around Ulrich's wrist before the veins could pulse and cause him any pain. The cursed appearance did not disgust Zel, but he preferred when Ulrich's brow was smooth with relief.

How otherwise broad and toned and perfect Ulrich looked beat any other view Zel had beheld. Since Ulrich's face was smooth, Zel had expected little to no hair elsewhere, but a dark trail started beneath his navel.

Zel finished untying Ulrich's pantaloons, so they dropped to his ankles. The dark trail led to a thicker thatch around Ulrich's cock. Not dauntingly impressive but impeccable enough to inspire a moistening of Zel's lips.

"May I pleasure you now, my lord, as you did me?"

"Only if you continue to use my name."

"*Ulrich.*" Zel laughed again and scooted closer, batting his eyes prettily. "May I please suck your cock, Ulrich?"

"Yes." Ulrich's eyes darkened to near black.

Zel descended, reveling in the instant wafting of Ulrich's musk—moonflowers and sage again, like he always smelled. As unpracticed as Zel was at being bedded, this he could do with flair, and set to prove it with the hollowing of his cheeks, expert use of his tongue, and the sheer depth he could swallow that had always driven Rudy mad.

With Ulrich, it was so much better because Zel knew at the end of it all, he would be touched in turn and finally filled.

He hummed around Ulrich's thickening girth, batting his eyes up at Ulrich again as he did so and keeping his knees spread as he slowly began to stroke himself, just enough to keep his own thickness steady.

Ulrich watched it all with his darkened eyes, radiating possession and want more intensely than his sometimes-murderous aura. He wanted to devour, but it was not Zel's soul he craved.

He snatched Zel's wrist, removing Zel's hand from himself, which impelled Zel to also pull off Ulrich's prick. "I need to be in you. Now," Ulrich growled. "May I, Zel? *Please.*"

That Ulrich would plead while asking was everything. "Yes!"

Ulrich seized Zel by the hips, upending him like he had on the chaise, and tossed him up the bed with hardly any effort. He launched onto the bed after Zel and had his hips bent back in moments. The slick heat of his tip pressed to Zel's entrance, like he couldn't restrain himself. But restrain he did. He waited and lifted Zel's hand, fingers glistening with prerelease.

Ulrich waved his own fingers with their pointed nails.

"I could will the sharpness away, but I have a better idea. Wet your fingers for me."

Zel had done that before too, sucking his fingers or Rudy's to tease out a promise that would never come. This promise would.

He brought his fingers to his mouth and started to wet them with obscene precision. He knew to keep eye contact. To keep his mouth open just enough for Ulrich to see his tongue, and for the excess of spittle to pool at the corners of his mouth while a little dribbled free. When Zel judged them wet enough, he stopped, and Ulrich brought the hand down, down, *down* to between Zel's legs.

"Now... will you open yourself for me, little cabbage?"

Zel imagined Ulrich's tongue there again as he pushed his fingertips in first, then up past his knuckles, two fingers at once. His hands were small enough that he could easily take three. Four. His whole fist when he wanted to.

"You have done this before." Ulrich grinned.

Zel coyly bit his lip.

"Don't stop. But now… wet mine." Ulrich brought his own hand up toward Zel's mouth and offered his fingers to be sucked.

It was his right hand, which usually would have been black. Even without claws, Ulrich's nails were sharp, and Zel had to take them into his mouth more carefully. With special attention around the points, he otherwise sucked and wetted them as obscenely as he had his own, while slowly twisting his fingers inside himself, with hips rolled back to reach.

The fullness of fingers did not match what Zel wanted, but that satisfying pressure still made his mouth salivate. Ulrich's fingers were sopping when Zel finally deemed them ready.

"You should be open enough now to avoid unnecessary pricks." Ulrich brought his hand down and waited for Zel to remove his.

Zel's vision went fuzzy at the first slide of Ulrich's larger fingers inside him, and he arched his neck back with a moan. He was open enough to handle Ulrich's slow scissoring. No actual scissors-like points pricked him, and he could have laid like that, folded and fingered, until his vision failed him completely.

But Zel's need to be taken matched Ulrich's need to be in him.

"P-please… Ulrich…"

"Will you permit me, Zel?"

"Yes!"

Ulrich's fingers were replaced by the warm press of his cockhead, and as he pushed in, widening Zel to the point of bursting, he thrust up and surged down in one motion to distract Zel with a kiss. The pressure within was great, but Ulrich's claim on Zel was greater.

They rocked, and even while their lips were sealed, mewling whimpers left Zel's throat like a love song's refrain. He had never felt so heated. So full. So unable to control the noises emanating from him with each new thrust. The noises spilled from him as if Ulrich drew them out the way a bard drew music from the plucking of their lute strings.

Ulrich slid his arms beneath Zel to heft him closer, lifting him partway off the bed, which drove his thrusts deeper. His hair always seemed to float, swaying ethereally around him. But Zel's, unbound from his braids, started to float with it, like sunlight streaking across storm clouds. Zel's magic could manifest in the strands even when he didn't will it, as if each lock was an entity all its own.

He would swear their bodies started to float eventually too, like gods ascending. With the star-speckled sky above, they might as well have been, communing with the heavens in the safety of Ulrich's bedchamber.

"You are *marvelous*," Ulrich rumbled.

For the first time in Zel's orchestrated life, he believed that.

Heat flooded him, and again Zel was surrounded by moonflowers and sage, leaving him to wonder what he smelled like to Ulrich.

ULRICH

S*unshine*.

That was Zel's scent. Sunshine piercing through the dark, like lemon, vanilla, and a field of flowers that could only bloom when closest to the sun's rays.

Zel's walls—uninitiated until tonight—clenched around Ulrich as he finished, wringing out more of his seed to fill Zel, like he hadn't inside another in literal ages. To have filled such a radiant and worthy receptacle was to touch the heavens more than the feeling of any magic or soul devoured. More than looking up and seeing the sky above them through the enchanted ceiling.

More than Ulrich had ever known of real peace.

"I could almost believe in the gods while inside you," Ulrich whispered.

"With you... I no longer need any," Zel whispered back.

Ulrich tilted his head down to meet Zel's stare.

Adoring. Affectionate.

More.

"Your Rudy never did that?"

Zel laughed. "No. And I am glad, *so glad* that my first time was with you."

Ulrich laid Zel down from how he had lifted him by the hips. As Zel rested there, still with Ulrich sheathed inside him, he reached to stroke himself. He was still hard. Still unfinished. Ulrich couldn't have that, pleasant as it was to watch Zel's fingers slide along his shaft.

Ulrich pushed Zel's hand aside.

"Come for me, little cabbage," he said, but rather than stroke Zel, Ulrich slid out of him finally and shifted lower to swallow him like before. He sucked harder than earlier. Firmer. Fervent. He knew Zel was on the brink and wanted to swallow everything Zel had to give.

"U-Ulrich!" Zel cried when he spilled, and that cry may have been the sweetest sound from him yet.

Ulrich drank every drop and licked lower, beneath Zel's sac to clean up some of his own spillage.

"*Oh...* how I've fantasized about that," Zel murmured.

"These past few weeks, so have I."

"I think I could drift off to sleep like this."

"Then do so. I will take care of the mess."

"I may have to take you up on that."

Ulrich had never seen such peace on Zel's face before, like the peace he felt in himself. He was still bound to Zel by some of that golden hair wrapped around his wrist, but as Zel began to drift off, the hair unwound itself and became limp.

He would never let Zel see just how much the loss of the hair's touch pained him, somehow greater than it used to feel, having known reprieve. But he couldn't remain tethered to Zel every moment. Ulrich's curse was his to bear until it rightfully ended.

Soon.

He had decided. He was not going to offer Zel up to the terrible fate that would have awaited him if he hadn't passed Ulrich's tests. Yes, Zel was a killer. A thief. He had faults like anyone. But he was not vile, nor cruel, nor deserving of the condemnation Ulrich had been ready to dispense.

So no, he was not going to enact that part of his plan. What he'd expected of a child raised by thieves and murderers was not what he had received. But he was going to complete the main part of his plan and allow his assassin, his darling little cabbage...

To kill him.

Eleven

ZEL

Zel blinked awake slowly. He had slept more deeply in Ulrich's bed than he had in his own since coming here. Perhaps better than in his bed back home. The room materialized slowly as he opened his eyes, and although he assumed he was alone now, the memories of last night, of finally giving himself to someone fully and having all his desires fulfilled, would keep him company until—

"Finally awake, little cabbage?"

The bed dipped as a body rolled toward Zel, with long arms wrapping around him and tugging him flush against the powerful figure behind him. Zel almost didn't believe it when he glanced over his shoulder and found the violet eyes and starlight curls that framed Ulrich's handsome face. "You stayed," he said breathlessly.

"This is my room."

Zel snorted. "But you don't need to sleep. Do you?"

"I do not, but your warmth made it difficult to want to leave the bed." Ulrich lifted up enough above Zel to coil more possessively around him and claimed a kiss. It was a slow, indulgent, deep kiss that made Zel twitch between his legs with ripening hardness, just as he felt a similar reaction from Ulrich against his hip.

Zel deepened their kiss further, clinging to Ulrich just as greedily.

There were no secrets between them now. None from Zel anyway. He didn't have to pretend anything anymore. But that didn't mean he was free.

"Zel?" Ulrich questioned when Zel stopped reciprocating and tensed in his hold.

"It's nothing."

Ulrich frowned.

"Nothing I want to think about until I am more awake. I am still buzzing from last night and basking in the memory of your touch."

"Is that your way of saying you are too sore for another round this morn?"

"Ask me after breakfast."

Now it was Ulrich who laughed. "Breakfast in bed it is." He chastely kissed Zel's lips. "Unless of course you'd rather—"

"Breakfast in bed sounds wonderful. With coffee?"

"It is my pleasure to serve." Ulrich kissed him again before rising. He was naked as he crossed the room, striking in his powerful, otherworldly figure. His blackened arm with its painfully glowing veins while out of contact with Zel's hair didn't mar a single bit of him. Zel still wished it would stay healed, since it caused Ulrich so much pain, but he liked the feeling of claws across his skin.

As Ulrich conducted with his hands a few paces away, summoning a cart on wheels and all the trimmings of a hearty breakfast, including steaming coffee, he also manifested a robe to cover himself. Zel mourned the loss of the view, but Ulrich was still sensuous looking with the robe parted down to his navel. When he moved, rolling the cart toward Zel's side of the bed, his bare legs peeked through too.

"Does this please you, Zel?"

"Delicious looking." Zel eyed not the food yet, but Ulrich.

"You can taste more of me whenever you wish." Ulrich bent for another kiss.

No *rapunzel* was ever served with breakfast, but as Zel began to eat and enjoy his coffee, with Ulrich having pulled over a chair to sit opposite him at the cart and partake as well, he kept thinking about the lettuce. He ate it every evening and had done so all his life. Because Ulrich had wanted him healthy, robust, ripe with natural-born magic.

Natural-born magic...

Zel no longer feared Ulrich meant to consume his soul, but that phrase plagued him, and his appetite began to wane. Only someone with natural-born magic, like Zel, possessed what was necessary to drain Ulrich of his magic and leave him vulnerable enough to...

Zel set down the bite of bread he had been about to take.

"Is everything all right?" Ulrich asked.

"You said someone born of magic could drain yours the way you drain souls."

"I did say that." Ulrich set his next bite of food down too. "There are few ways such a thing could be done. Technically, someone not born of magic could accomplish the same, but it would take far longer for them to amass the amount of power necessary. The latter was how I became immortal to begin with."

"By amassing enough power to drain someone else?"

"In part. In my case there was more to the exchange." He waved at Zel with a curl of his blackened fingers and then spread them wide to show the bisected circle carved into his palm. "With continuous blood sacrifice, this symbol can grant long life, but long-lived is not the same as immortal."

Lothar. Now Zel remembered. Lothar bore the same symbol on one of his rings!

"For eternal life, a larger sacrifice must be made, and it must be willingly given."

"Willingly? Someone let you drain them?"

"No." Ulrich grinned. "Hence the curse. It would have consumed my entire body after forcibly draining someone. To keep the curse contained, I had to drain all of my closest and most powerful companions. My friends. It had to be them, for no one else was near enough to me in magical strength. It is unlikely anyone but someone as powerful as I was could have consumed enough souls or so quickly as to outrun the curse. Even I almost failed, but I was determined."

Zel recalled that the orphans who had remained with Ulrich the longest and who'd seemed the most corrupted over time had eventually vanished from the scenes of his past, and by the end, Ulrich had stood alone.

"For a long time, I felt no loss for betraying my friends, no regret," Ulrich continued. "The last I consumed, a man gifted in shadow magic, used to say, 'What's one more life if it's worth taking?' I said the same to him when I killed him, and he smiled before I took his soul. We had all grown cold and cruel by then. Only the physical pain of my curse prevented the numbness from overtaking me as the centuries passed. To drain my power now would require someone of equal strength, or someone born with magic, curated for many winters to expedite its growth."

"With lettuce from your own garden," Zel confirmed. "You weren't surprised nor upset to find my dagger or to discover me having dispatched that awful man last night, because as you admitted, you knew exactly why I came here."

"I should hope so." Ulrich held Zel's stare without blinking.

"You wanted me to discover all this, about how you might die, because you *want* me to drain you, to be powerful enough to succeed and... kill you."

"Such a horrified look on that sweet face. Is it not as fulfilling for you if your target wishes to die?"

Zel had never been quick to tears, but ever since the morn he'd broken down before his trek to the tower, his eyes could grow hot in moments.

"Forgive my awful jest." Ulrich rolled the cart out of the way and moved to the bed to sit at Zel's hip. "That was unthinking of me. But yes, I always knew why you came here, and that you are..." He brought his lips to Zel's ear and finished in a gravelly whisper, "such a fair lad."

Zel's eyes sprang wide at the triggered memory of the old woman he had quite literally run into on the night of his final assassination.

"A useful trick." Ulrich shrugged. "One I even taught to my apprentice. Disguises are always useful, but unassuming ones, weak, frail ones that appear less threatening, are better suited for manipulating others. I was just so curious to get an early look at you."

As surprised as Zel felt, the amazement quickly faded. Of course Ulrich had known everything all along. He had planned for this, for every step, every stage, to happen exactly as he had wanted it to. "But why? Why do you want to die? To give all this up. You have everything."

Ulrich sighed as if he had heard such reasoning before. "Immortality itself is more of a curse than most believe until they have it. I initially planned for you to drain enough from me to become immortal in my place—as punishment, not a gift. I assumed you would have been raised cruelly, deserving of such an end, being the babe of thieves and assassins, but you proved me wrong. You can be brutal when threatened, but everything in nature has defenses. The truly vile people of this world deserve to be dispatched, and I am one of those.

"When the time comes, you will still be able to drain enough from me that I can be killed, but you will not have to suffer with immortality unless you wish for it, and I plead with you, Zel, do not wish for that. It is the true curse even if it takes ages to realize it."

Zel's eyes were still hot, burning, but the scowl he formed kept any tears from falling. "You never wanted someone to marry."

"No. I wanted an end. But you almost could have made me reconsider."

"Then why don't you?"

"Zel—"

"Please, Ulrich." One tear slipped free, streaking down Zel's cheek, and as Ulrich reached to wipe it away, Zel grasped his hand and held it to his face, pleading, "Stay. *Live*. For me."

"Zel..." Ulrich tried again, but Zel spoke on, still holding Ulrich's hand to his face.

"At least let me say my piece before you answer."

Ulrich sighed again but nodded. "If you insist."

Zel brought Ulrich's hand to his lips and kissed the inside of his palm where the mark that had become his curse was carved. Then Zel tossed the covers from him and left the bed. Ulrich's gaze upon his backside as he strode across the room was potent enough to warm Zel's skin.

"If you want my attention on your words, Zel, you are making it rather difficult to focus."

Zel pursed his lips as he retrieved another of Ulrich's robes, leaving it, like Ulrich had, parted to just past his navel where he cinched it closed. "Try harder," he volleyed back. His still unbound hair dragged behind him like a train of spun gold. "Can you project into this room part of my past like you did your own?"

"You can project it yourself," Ulrich said. "You have more magic in you than you yet know how to wield. As with magically braiding or unbraiding your hair, simply will it."

Zel turned to take in the room, deciding how best to do this. He settled on facing away from the bed, with Ulrich seated behind him, and the room in front of them fell away. The bed remained as if on a precipice, and they were on a balcony like when Zel had learned the first truths of Ulrich's past.

Beyond, scenes began to play, and a city came into focus, Falchovari as it had been twenty winters ago. The view zoomed in through the streets to the Pied Pipers music shop. It was a clever name for the place, not only because their surname was Piper, but due to the multicolored or *pied* brickwork of the exterior, alternating between red, brown, and gold.

"Allow me to share with you my story this time," Zel said, and as he began his turn at the history lesson, emanating from within the shop came the sounds of a baby crying.

ULRICH

The first scene Zel displayed to Ulrich showed the panic that had followed his entrance into the world.

"My parents, Gregor and Sophie, told me that my cries pierced through their bedchamber walls, where my mother had allowed in only the physician, a male midwife who our guild master had secured for us."

Ulrich knew female midwives were more common. A male physician to assist with childbirth would have been reserved for the very wealthy.

"My father entered the room as soon as he heard me," Zel continued.

Ulrich stood to join Zel at the railing of the manifested balcony.

The physician was doing all he could to clean and bundle the infant Zel when he announced rather gravely, "I'm afraid it's a boy," clearly aware of the intended future for the innocent babe.

Gregor and Sophie exchanged frantic looks, before Gregor pulled a dagger. The physician still held Zel, but that did not deter Gregor from pressing the blade to the man's throat. "It is a girl," he said in warning, "a future bride to be presented to the sorcerer exactly as planned. Do you understand?"

"You cannot possibly hide—"

"*Do you understand?*" Gregor asked again.

The physician nodded, and once Gregor had retracted the dagger, he handed over the newborn Zel into his father's arms.

"Even my first moments alive involved a dagger," Zel said.

"How much time passed before your parents dispatched the physician?" Ulrich asked.

"Three weeks."

"Longer than I would have waited."

Zel snorted, and Ulrich cast him a wry smile.

Next, Ulrich watched Zel will the view of the past to zip forward in time.

"When I began to come into my own mind and understand things, I thought I *was* a girl at first," Zel explained as more scenes unfolded. "I didn't know to think otherwise. Eventually, my parents had to explain, pull me aside, make sure I knew not to play peek-a-boo under the skirts with any of my friends. They didn't explain all the details right away but slowly introduced me to the idea by saying I had a destiny to fulfill that required sacrifice. I was special. I had a great purpose. And that meant pretending to be something I wasn't."

The scenes shifted again to Zel in the undercrofts of the Thieves Guild with his parents and other various teachers.

"Then my training began to hone my body, my skills with movement and weapons. Once I neared womanhood—*man*hood—adulthood I suppose, I was taught how to make the boys want me."

"To better seduce me eventually?" Ulrich asked.

"Yes, but I did want to titillate the boys," Zel admitted. "That began long before I was taught to target them. I had always preferred being a girl over wanting to kiss one, so I never had to hide my attractions. But it was still all for you more than for me. My whole life has been about you."

The final scenes, most recent in Zel's life, came in rapid succession.

"Training my feminine wiles to seduce you. Training with blades to assassinate you. Even my education was all to better tempt you and win your favor for the sake of the mission. And though I found many of my own pleasures in it all, I hated that. I hated you before I knew you. Especially when I started to feel a deeper desire toward the boys, I resented you because I couldn't choose what I wanted. I hated having to be something I wasn't, and that every day of my life was dedicated to one future moment in time with one person I hadn't even met yet. It was only these past two or three winters that I came to accept my fate and resigned myself to not resent something I couldn't change.

"So, as I admitted during our first night together, I did eventually stop resenting you, stop hating you, and focused on what I had to do to get through this and to maybe have a life of my own on the other side of it." Zel turned from the scenes that had ended with his mother preparing him in her wedding gown for the trip to the tower.

He took Ulrich's hands.

"I never could have predicted how that one future moment in my life would end up being worth the difficult road to reach it, one small stretch of time enough to change everything and make me want so deeply that I cannot imagine drawing breath anymore without you there. My past had to be all about you, but I want my future to continue to be because it is what I choose."

"Zel—"

"My parents live under the thumb of the guild leader, Lothar." Zel squeezed Ulrich's hands tighter, refusing to let him pull or look away. "And he lives under the thumb of the evil Queen. We all do. Everyone's life is beholden to another in some way, whether they know it or not. But my parents have always found joy in life together despite that. I have never met another who made me feel like I could have what they do. Not until you."

Ulrich didn't try to pull or look away, but he looked at Zel seriously. "Do you truly know what you ask? Even when what you have said and shown me proves the point of why we should not be together? I molded you to be what I wanted—"

"No. You made sure I had the magic you needed to achieve the goal you thought you wanted. My parents and my experiences molded me. You lit the spark, but life fanned the flames. And where I could, I made my own choices. You want me not for who I could have been or pretended to be, but for who I am. Don't you?"

"Yes..." But that truth only made Ulrich's grief stronger, when he had never thought he could know grief again.

"Once I am immortal and you are weakened, instead of

succumbing to my blade, could you not replenish your magic over time?"

"I could. But listen to me—"

"If you had no desire for me at all, would you have bedded me?"

"Possibly." Ulrich's sorrow cracked with a grin, but Zel stared him down, clearly in no mood for levity. "No," Ulrich recanted.

"I had no intention of bedding you either. For different reasons initially, but because of who you truly are and what I have seen of your healing heart, I want you all on my own. Please, Ulrich." Zel took Ulrich's blackened hand with his left and reached with his right to cup the curve of Ulrich's cheek. "Make me immortal like you planned but stay immortal with me."

"Do not ask this of me, Zel. The last companions who trusted me regretted it. Even if my old apprentice does not, one can hardly consider it an improvement when you now call her the *evil* Queen."

"You... you mean your apprentice was the Queen?" Zel gaped.

Ulrich took Zel's hand from his face to hold both between them again. "How did you think she came into power? I gave it to her, but not before molding her into the perfect, terrible replacement. She had to be worthy, and back then I believed that meant she needed to be willing to step over anyone and everyone she cared for, even her own family, to maintain the power I taught her to wield. You say I did not mold you, but I did mold her, and you and others have suffered for it and continue to even now."

The admission made Zel hesitate, but stubborn youth that he was, his resolve returned. "Neither a guardian nor a mentor is responsible for their charge's choices."

"An easy excuse—"

"You eventually left that life and chose to be better."

"*Zel*. I am getting rather tired of you interrupting me."

Zel wisely snapped his mouth shut.

"Thank you." Holding Zel's soft, deceptively delicate hands did not make it easy to keep denying him. "You think I live a better life than when I was a tyrant? Devouring souls in the wood and luring unsuspecting beauties into my bed?"

Zel waited a moment before responding, as if to be certain he would not interrupt Ulrich again. "I was not unsuspecting. I asked to be taken to bed. And the souls you devour now know the risks of entering the wood and crossing onto your land. We are what molds us, but we can choose to break free of the cycle without choosing death for ourselves. Can't we?"

"That was not the plan."

"It wasn't mine either. But one does not plan when or with whom one falls in love."

Ulrich was too stunned to speak. His instincts, his experience, all he had come to know of Zel, told him those words were earnest. Ulrich had heard them before but from fanatics who worshipped him or those willing to say anything to earn his favor even if they actually loathed him. He couldn't say whether he had ever heard words of love spoken with heartfelt meaning, other than by his mother and the friends he had eventually killed.

It was Ulrich who reached for Zel's cheeks then, cradling his face. Against all sense that he should pull away now more than ever, he began to lean down.

Ulrich snapped back from the kiss he had been about to offer.

"What is it?" Zel asked.

"Trespassers. I can sense them on the grounds." Ulrich's connection to the tower and the land surrounding it made unexpected footfalls upon his property feel like someone walking over his grave, causing little pinpricks and tingles down his spine. "And judging by the strength of the feeling, there are several."

He waved a hand, and he and Zel were both dressed, with Zel's hair neatly braided, much as Ulrich hated giving up their routine of him brushing it first.

They had uninvited guests.

"You included my dagger, I hope." Zel reached under his skirt to confirm its presence—a single layered skirt, one of Zel's outfits he had made with the loom, complete with breeches and lacking a corset as he preferred.

"It is your choice if you wish to join me," Ulrich said, "but I assumed you would want to."

"Now and forever." Zel brandished the dagger. "I do not like being interrupted either, and we aren't done talking."

"I supposed we are not." Ulrich led the way out of the chamber into the main room where no trespassers had yet reached. "You are skilled, Zel, and much magic protects you, but you are not yet immortal."

"*Yet*," Zel repeated. "I will be careful." He lifted onto his toes to kiss the side of Ulrich's mouth. Then he charged for the stairwell, while Ulrich went to the window and leapt onto its sill.

When Zel realized he was not being followed, he looked back at Ulrich with a snort.

"You don't even need stairs, do you?"

"Not when I need to be swift." Ulrich dove from the window, descending to the garden like a bird of prey.

A gasp at his left when he landed alerted him to his first meal of the morn.

The attacker hesitated to strike a blow, leaving Ulrich an opening to lash out first. A fatal mistake. Ulrich had him by the throat, weapons dropped and mask down to suck out his soul in mere moments. As Ulrich finished the husk, he felt a tickle at his back.

He dropped the corpse and turned, summoning his magical fury to pulse around him with visible aura, which caused pure dread to anyone who perceived it. Two bandits stood before him, one closer, gazing in horror at her now bent sword that had failed to skewer him. The second held two handaxes and trembled as he threw one, then the other.

Ulrich caught them both.

The woman dropped her sword, attempting to flee, but Ulrich flung the handaxes into her back, dropping her at the other bandit's feet. Toppling over onto his backside, he stared wide-eyed at his own weapons buried in his companion.

She was dead, but Ulrich snatched the male up and sucked his soul out like the first.

Spotting a fourth bandit rigid with fear, Ulrich swept forward to descend upon her next, only for a dagger to lodge in the bandit's throat. From around the curve of the tower appeared Zel. He tore his blade free, and the bandit gurgled up blood behind her mask, staining the dark fabric a deeper black, before she crumpled forward.

"Three for me," Zel said, wiping his dagger on the bandit's back. Then he noticed the bodies left by Ulrich. "Guess we're even."

A yelp brought their gazes to the wall, where a new bandit had been about to leap into the garden. He didn't notice their stares at first, for his cry had been for the bodies strewn about. Then his eyes went from Zel to Ulrich, and he promptly jumped the other direction, back into the autumn weather of the wood.

"I believe I am about to pull ahead," Ulrich said, and leapt up after the bandit as easily as he had flung himself from the tower window.

When he landed outside the wall, he spotted the bandit zigzagging into the trees, smart enough to not give Ulrich a direct path to follow, but that would hardly save him.

Ulrich spared a glance at the wall, intending to open the way for Zel, but he saw atop the wall that Zel had scaled it after him. If there were more bandits about, Zel could handle them. Ulrich's job was to catch the one foolish enough to flee.

Once the bandits were dispatched with only cleanup remaining, Zel would inevitably speak his request again. How was Ulrich to respond? It had not been his plan to go on living and actually keep the bride he had lied about wanting, to stay immortal when he had thought it a curse for so long.

What surprised him was how tempted he was to turn that plan on its head. His immeasurable hours alone had made him long for the very end he'd toiled so hard to prevent, yet Zel's arrival had done the one thing Ulrich had thought impossible—brought life back into his monotonous existence, instilling a craving for that life to continue.

Ulrich caught the bandit and drained him like the others, positively bursting from the meal they had provided, but even multiple souls paled in comparison to how good it felt to touch Zel, to hold him, to even just be near him. It would be easy to say it was because of the *rapunzel*, the magic, the balm of Zel easing Ulrich's aches, but he enjoyed Zel's company too much to believe it was only that.

Letting the final husk drop to the ground, Ulrich was honestly considering agreeing the next time Zel asked for him to stay, when he heard Zel's scream echo through the wood.

Twelve

ZEL

Zel could convince Ulrich to stay, to be with him, to live with him forever, he could. There was no future he wanted more now that he'd had a taste of it.

With that thrill of resolve lighting a fire in his belly, Zel descended from the wall in search of more bandits, circling the tower in the opposite direction from where Ulrich had chased after the one that ran. Zel's knack for stealth, even without his cloak to hide his hair, had made it easy to sneak up on the bandits in the garden. He hugged the exterior wall to do the same as he moved toward the faint sounds of whispering.

The sun was beginning to rise, slowly brightening the clearing and surrounding wood. Zel couldn't yet see who owned those whispers, but he knew he was nearing them. It was no wonder Ulrich occasionally left a husk or two outside to rot if trespassers could be this foolishly brazen.

"This is our chance. The monster went the other way."

"*No.* Enough of this. She's not worth it!"

She?

"I'm going!"

"Louisa!"

A figure appeared, darting toward the wood, away from where Zel crept.

"Fine then!" the other huffed—and stepped around the wall right into Zel's path. His eyes sprang wide, face covered with a mask like all the others. "It's—"

Zel lunged forward, driving his dagger into the bandit's heart. It was a quick, clean, near instant kill, and he immediately tore his dagger free.

The bandit dropped to the ground.

"Bertie!"

Louisa and... Bertie? Zel knew—

A whoosh of air gave him seconds to react, and whether good instincts, magical luck, or both, he tilted his head just as a dagger flew past his face. The sting as the blade nicked his cheek filled him with equal shock and fury, and as he looked to the bandit who had been running away, before he could fling his own dagger back at her, something else flung from him instead.

Part of Zel's hair unwound from his braids and lashed out as if of its own accord, fueled purely by his anger and the reality of his cheek being cut.

No, he was not yet immortal.

But *yet* would not become *never*.

His hair wound around the bandit's waist like a whip and reeled her in with enough speed that no dagger flinging was necessary. Zel's dagger was ready when she lurched into its path.

"R-Rapunzel..." she uttered, and he realized why he had recognized those names.

Zel tore away the mask covering the woman's face. He knew

her—Louisa. They had never been friends, barely acquaintances, but Zel knew her and her beloved Bertold. These were not bandits foolishly targeting the tower.

They were from the Thieves Guild.

Zel's hair unwound from Louisa as miraculously as it had lashed out. She pulled herself from the dagger's blade, only to bleed out more quickly from its absence and almost immediately drop to her knees, falling right beside Bertie. The spill of their blood met the spill of Zel's hair on the ground, staining its gold with red.

When someone deserved death, whether simply an abhorrent figure or killed in self-defense, Zel felt justified in using his skills. He even enjoyed it at times. But he'd never killed someone he knew before.

"Zel—"

A hand clamped down on Zel's shoulder, and he screamed as he seized its wrist, flipping the offender end-over-end to land hard on his back in front of Zel. "*Rudy*?!" he snarled, stopping his dagger's downward arc just before it made contact with Rudy's skin. "Are you ma—"

"We came to rescue you!" Rudy scrambled to his feet, adjusting his disturbed spectacles. He was the only one who hadn't bothered to hide his face. "By God, Zel, what have you done?"

The others were all dead. Maybe a few had escaped before Zel or Ulrich took note of them, but the rest were dead. Zel had no true friends among the Thieves Guild outside of Rudy, but that was just it.

Rudy could have ended up slain or a husk too.

He still could if Ulrich found him.

"*Go*." Zel pushed Rudy toward the line of trees. "Get out of here! I don't need rescuing!"

"Of course you—"

"Get out—!"

"I saw you with him!" Rudy bellowed, jealousy marring his face as he snarled back at Zel, standing his ground. "Last night. At Hessen House. You killed someone and then kissed that monster right out in the open while standing over the body." The revulsion from Rudy caught Zel up short.

Two bodies were near their feet now, and many others lay beyond the tower wall.

Rudy glanced with a growing look of nausea at Louisa and Bertie. He had a pair of handaxes on his belt like many of the others, and knew how to wield them, but he had never had to use them against another. He had never killed before. "You didn't even bat an eye while slaughtering them."

"No. That's why I am the assassin, and you are the pickpocket." Because even if Zel had known they were from the Thieves Guild, he doubted he would have hesitated for long. Rudy's ignorance of the acts Zel was trained to commit was just another part of how dishonest their friendship felt sometimes compared to what Rudy believed. It made Zel ache again like he'd ached the last time they'd met outside the tower. "You were down the alley last night behind Hessen House? You saw..."

"I would never watch a lady!" Rudy looked at the ground with a faint flush.

Thank God. He must have looked away as soon as Zel hoisted his skirts, but he had still been there, spying. Before Ulrich, Zel had never liked the idea of anyone seeing him kill. His teachers, his parents, they were one thing, but Rudy had always seemed removed from the uglier activities of the guild.

Like that little girl all those weeks ago.

"You're not wearing my pendant." Rudy's eyes finally returned to Zel. "You were last night. Did he take it from you?"

"*No.*" But of course Ulrich hadn't included it when he clothed Zel. "In case you've forgotten, I was rudely awakened by an attack this morn and didn't have time to dress properly."

"And what have *you* forgotten? Do you remember why you're here? Because that didn't look like false seduction from where I was watching you last night. He is doing something to you, Zel. Changing you. Bewitching you!"

Zel readied another comeback but paused. "How did I not see you? I sensed someone there, but I only saw shadow."

The way Rudy tucked his arm behind his back proved he must be wearing some trinket of note. Zel snatched Rudy's elbow with his free hand, still gripping his dagger with the other, and yanked Rudy's arm into view. He wore a simple silver band on one finger. Modest as it appeared, Zel recognized it.

"Lothar's invisibility ring. He never goes anywhere without it. You *are* mad. Stealing from the guild master? Why? Why risk so much for me—"

"Because I love you!"

"*Zeeeeeeel!*" Ulrich's roar resounded through the trees, and Zel and Rudy both froze. If Zel hadn't worked his way around to the other side of the wall, they would already be caught. Ulrich would find them in moments.

"You must go!" Zel pushed Rudy again. "If he had caught you before I did, he would have sucked out your soul, do you understand?"

"Then he is the monster they say he is." Rudy stumbled back a step, but he wasn't fleeing. He wasn't leaving.

"We are monsters to the people we kill too!" Zel spat. "We don't even get to choose who we are sent after. The sorcerer only kills bandits who come asking for it, or thieves foolish enough to call in reinforcements he shouldn't have risked. *God*, you travelled all night, and for what?"

Rudy shook his head, still not turning to go. "He has bewitched you—"

"Rudy—"

"Rapunzel—"

"I love him!"

Rudy stood agape.

"I love him," Zel said again. "Because he knows the truth of who and what I am and wants me just the same. Could you?" He grabbed Rudy's hand once more and brought it between his legs to grip through his single layer skirt and breeches. "Because my name is *Zel*, not Rapunzel, and I am not what you think."

Moments passed that seemed to take ages, diminishing the precious few that they had, as Rudy blinked in confusion before, finally, his eyes snapped wide. Zel pushed him in the chest again rather than bear the sting of Rudy jerking his hand away.

"Go. The heart cannot be bewitched, Rudy, only won." Zel looked him square in the eyes, knowing that the only way to save his friend was to hurt him deeper than he yet had. "Even if you still want my heart after learning the truth of my body, you were never going to win it. He already has. Now go. Please."

Maybe because Zel had broken Rudy's heart so many times, Rudy's expression did not seem to change beyond numb shock.

"*Go*, before you say or do something that will bring down wrath upon you I will not be able to protect you from. And if you don't go, I might not even care that I can't."

ULRICH

The young man was retreating, however reluctantly.

However stunned to have learned Zel's well-kept secret.

So that was Rudy. Handsome even with spectacles. Maybe more so with them, for they suited his face. Yet Zel had chosen Ulrich, when this boy had risked nearly a dozen people just to ensure Zel's safety and sanity. For selfish reasons as well, given Rudy's clear love for Zel, but as tempted as Ulrich was to drain the boy for daring this rescue, he recognized how much Zel truly cared for him in return. Zel was doing everything he could to spare Rudy from Ulrich's wrath, so Ulrich would let Rudy leave.

What mostly convinced him to do so was wondering whether Zel would be better off with someone mortal. If not Rudy, someone else someday, for surely Zel would come to loathe an immortal life as Ulrich had, and eventually, he would loathe Ulrich too.

Of course he would. What a fool Ulrich was to have even briefly entertained otherwise. He knew what his answer had to be the next time Zel asked his question.

Ulrich gave Rudy just long enough to retreat before he swept toward Zel with his previous momentum. "Zel! Are you all right? I heard you cry out."

"I'm fine." Zel faced him with a false smile, not betraying his earlier panic. His partially unbound hair pooled on the ground beside the bodies and blood of his victims. "You caught the other one then? Were there more?"

Being close to Zel, with the rising sun's rays brightening his face, Ulrich noticed the cut on Zel's cheek. He reached for it immediately with his blackened hand. As with the prick on Zel's finger, contact with Zel's blood plumped Ulrich's hand to life, and even without removing his hand right away, Ulrich knew his touch healed the skin beneath—a symbiotic exchange, like two halves of a whole.

Zel nuzzled Ulrich's palm with a soft smile, but the warmth Ulrich wanted to succumb to was not his to bathe in. He had to accept the cold and drew his hand away, fighting the natural cringe when his skin returned to black and the pulse of his violet veins ached.

"I caught the one," Ulrich said, "and I do not believe there are others, but does your Thieves Guild grow so impatient?"

A flicker of Zel's panic returned. "You realized who they were as well? Lothar would not have sent them, so who knows why they would risk something so foolish. But regardless, we will not be giving the Thieves Guild what they want." Zel sheathed his dagger and took Ulrich's hands in his, as he had in the bedchamber. He was lying by omission to protect his friend, which only proved Zel's inherent virtue and Ulrich's lack of it. Zel did not even trust Ulrich enough to believe he could show mercy.

Why would he? Ulrich had never been... *good*.

"What happened to your hair?" Ulrich asked in regards to the red, unbound strands on the grass.

"My magic," Zel said. "It unleashed just when I needed it to catch one of my attackers. Quite the handy trick, if I can learn how to wield it purposely. I'm not sure I want to wind this bit back into my braids as it is." He lifted the section of hair with a grimace, given the blood already beginning to dry and becoming caked in his locks.

"Allow me. We can leave these bodies to the dirt." Ulrich waved a hand, and the blood sloughed off and seeped into the ground like ashes crumbling after a bonfire. Then he put his hand on Zel's shoulder and transported them into the washroom.

"Is the key still in your chambers?" Zel asked with a touch of concern.

Ulrich produced it with a thought, for he could always summon the key when needed. Its connection to the tower connected it to him.

Zel laughed, losing more of his heightened tension. "I shouldn't be surprised. You are always wondrous to me, every new thing I learn about you. Yes, even the parts that come with darkness," he answered as if Ulrich had asked the question.

Perhaps he had with his eyes while undressing Zel without the use of his magic. Why hurry a task that should be savored?

Zel's eyes were certainly easy to read before he said, "I am not yet immortal, but I could be, with but a taste of your magic willingly given when the time comes. Yes?"

"Zel..." Ulrich sighed. "Listen—"

"*No*. Do not deny me. It would be a curse to live forever alone, and I am sorry you have had to do so for ages and that those centuries tormented you, but it would be different together."

"I can teach you how to resist the last draughts of power that would make you immor—"

"I don't want to resist!" Zel stomped the washroom floor, fists clenching like the fiery youth he was. His hair, so much more a conduit for his magic now, echoed his agitation, like stalks of wheat swishing from the movement of animals walking between its stems.

Too much had transpired this morn, and Zel's strong façade was cracking once more.

"Please, if you have me kill you and leave me mortal, Lothar will take me for his bride in your stead, and he will not be as forgiving to discover what lies beneath my skirts." Zel said it just as the last of his clothing and armaments fell from his body and the truth of his radiance was laid bare. "We had hoped to overthrow him, but that would be impossible without your power."

The possessiveness Ulrich had felt for Zel many times stirred within him stronger than ever. He had assumed Zel would be rewarded, praised for finishing his mission, but this Lothar meant to take. Who wouldn't want to claim the loveliest of beauties for their bride?

Part of Ulrich wanted that for himself, but there was no right answer between them that wouldn't end with one or both of them hurt and regretful.

"Come," Ulrich said and took Zel's hand to assist him into the first basin. "I will let no such fate befall you, but for now, relax and let me wash your locks of the morn's troubles."

With a final frustrated quiver from Zel's hair, he complied.

Ulrich positioned the basins perpendicular to each other, so while Zel's body soaked in the first, his hair could be washed in the second. "We will use our remaining days to plan how to unseat this guild master," he explained, kneeling at one of the corners where the basins met. He spilled Zel's hair into the empty water like a cascade of liquid gold and washed it from roots to ends slowly for them both to enjoy the act. "I will consider the rest of your request before the month ends."

"Thank you." Zel relaxed as directed, sinking deeper into the basin, and tilted his head slightly to meet Ulrich's gaze, silently beseeching him for the kiss they had been denied when the guild members arrived.

The joy, the color and light that filled Zel's face when Ulrich gave him what he wanted almost convinced him to not let those words be the lie he intended.

But it was a lie, because if Ulrich did one selfless thing in his long life, it would be to save Zel from the folly of loving him.

Thirteen

ZEL

Much of the following days continued like those before. In the morn, Ulrich would brush out Zel's hair and help him to braid it with magic. They would share every meal together, with dinner always including a helping of *rapunzel*. They would go for walks, tend to the garden, share stories and music, but Zel's nights were spent in Ulrich's bed now instead of his own, and much time was spent planning how to enact upon Lothar the very assassination intended for Ulrich.

They would sneak into the guild, avoid larger concentrations of thieves and assassins, and attack Lothar while he was alone with only his sanctum guards to protect him.

Ulrich had not answered plainly yet about what would happen after Lothar was dead, but no longer would Zel accept a life carved out for him not by his own hand.

He had worried at first about Rudy, returning alone through the wood after bringing nearly a dozen with him from the Thieves Guild, but he must have been stealthy in his recruitment. Zel checked on Rudy the next day using Ulrich's orb, searching the halls of the guild until he found him and was content to see that it was business as usual for his friend, despite the missing members.

Rudy's next letter included:

Pity a crew of so many set out toward the Dark Forest without Lothar's permission and did not return. 'Tis a terrifying place, and I worry for you being so near it, my dear Zel.

Zel couldn't risk Rudy doing something else foolish, so he kept his reply vaguer than usual. He took minor comfort in that Rudy had made no mention, not even coded, of having discovered Zel's secret.

Only to Sophie and Gregor did Zel give hints that his mission had changed. He assured them that this was what he wanted and warned them in veiled terms to be ready for a siege upon the guild.

Zel refused to feel guilt for those he and Ulrich had killed in self-defense, but he did not want thoughtless slaughter of his peers. Nor did he wish to add to the weight on his shoulders that had always been more about fate than follicles.

Those follicles were not cooperating as hoped when Zel attempted to practice with them as weapons on purpose.

A faint swish was Zel's only reward as the section of hair he had sent outward like a lash missed its target and slapped against the wall. Winding it back into his braids was easy, and he did so each time, since it would have to be a surprise attack or prove useless. But no matter how second-nature it was to braid or unbraid his hair now, aiming it like a herder's whip was not so effortlessly learned. He had grabbed Louisa seemingly by instinct and could not repeat the results.

"I will succeed," Zel repeated his old mantra. "I am ready for this. I am fierce and beautiful and capable." His hair launched forward like a striking snake—

"That you are."

—and smacked the goblet he had intended to grab.

It happened slowly, like time paused as Zel held his breath, because the goblet was about to slosh its contents onto his letters, and would have if Ulrich didn't sweep forward like descending shadows and catch it before it spilled.

"Apologies!" Ulrich said. "I did not intend to startle you. Would you perhaps prefer the sparring chamber for these tests?"

"Why bother, when I can't even lasso a cup?" Zel wound the hair back into his braids with an angry whip that nearly slapped Ulrich like it had the goblet. "Sorry! My apologies now."

"You are frustrated." Ulrich steadied the goblet and turned to lean against the desk.

"Endlessly, it seems. A slow grab is doable, but slow will not serve us in the coming fight. If only I were as wondrous as you." Zel offered a wistful smile. "I would be if we could make me immortal before we raid the guild."

"As I have told you, much as I fear for your safety, we cannot. Some magic is little more than a parlor trick requiring no exchange. Some is fickle and demands precision to work as intended. Your magic must be at its utmost peak to drain mine, and that will only be at the appointed hour. The final night of our month together is a full moon, when the gods' eyes are most open."

"To look on us and grant me eternal life in the mingling of our power?" Zel felt calmer simply imagining it and moved toward Ulrich to find his place in the sorcerer's arms.

Ulrich opened them, parting his legs where he leaned against the desk, and gathered Zel to him. "Whether any gods truly look on us, I cannot say."

"It is no matter to me if they do or do not, if there is one human God or the many the elves worship, so long as we succeed."

"We will. For I am quite wondrous."

Zel snickered.

"You are wondrous too, Zel, just as you are." Ulrich kissed Zel's forehead, then his lips. Afterward, he looked at the desk. "Your letters are dry. Shall I..." But his words trailed off.

"What is it?"

"Only a curiosity. You sign your letters *Zel*."

"Why wouldn't I?"

"Rudy addresses you as such, usually, but your parents always address their letters to *Rapunzel*."

Even as only an explanation, the name made Zel sneer. He had begun to distance himself from it more and more while in Ulrich's company. "That is what they call me."

"They do not abide by your wishes to be called Zel?"

"I've never asked them to."

"Why is that?" Ulrich faced Zel again, as the letters folded themselves and flew out the window like usual.

"It's silly. They are the last people I need to ask, the last that matter, but I always shy from correcting them. Maybe when all this is over, I will say something."

"You needn't hesitate, Zel. You can be whoever you wish to be. Man, woman, neither, both. Whatever the answer, that is what I shall call you, how I shall see you, and others should too."

How the Immortal King of old could be so tender a partner, Zel would never understand, but however cursed Ulrich might see himself, his time alone had clearly softened him. Or maybe Zel had. "You still want me despite not knowing my own answer?"

"I would want you, Zel, even if you never know."

The tears, joyful ones always closer to the surface when Ulrich was this kind, flooded Zel's eyes with warmth. Never could he doubt that he loved this man, nor could he doubt why, even if Ulrich had yet to say it back.

Zel lifted onto his toes to kiss Ulrich more passionately than the tender peck he had been granted. In his fervor, some of his hair unfurled and wrapped around Ulrich's arms and legs, holding him bound.

"Sorry!" Zel gasped out of their kiss once he realized.

"Do not be." Ulrich's expression was startled, yes, but hardly fearful, as he looked at the wrappings that almost appeared like ribbon, tying his hands behind his back and his legs together. "It appears emotion is your trigger. Common enough with magic. You simply need to believe you can control it, and you will. Unless, of course, this is what you had planned for me."

Zel flushed. Tying up his sorcerer had not been his intention—he didn't think. Perhaps his hair knew better what his inner self craved. For now, he released Ulrich. "Practice would be safer first, but it is easier to believe in myself around you."

"Then why are you practicing alone?" Ulrich stretched his arms with an elegant flex once they were free. "I will be beside you for this mission, after all." He gestured pointedly toward the magical door.

Perhaps the two of them in the sparring room was the right idea.

A full turn of the key brought them there, and where Zel had continuously failed while practicing alone, he found it easier in Ulrich's presence to will his hair to obey his commands. Lashing out here to trip up Ulrich's ankles. Lashing out there to grab the sword from his hands. Lashing out everywhere, from multiple angles, and tying Ulrich up again with arms taut or bound behind him, and legs tied together too.

The way Ulrich grinned at Zel when he used the bindings to force the sorcerer to his knees gave Zel an idea for something very special for the night before they were to raid the Thieves Guild.

Something very special indeed.

ULRICH

Calling Zel wondrous did not do him justice. He was talented, generally collected, and as much as he had been honed into a vicious killer, a pure heart remained if a little tainted at its edges.

Zel did not wish for his freedom if it meant harm would come to his parents, or to Rudy, or to too many of his fellows, for Zel believed they were as trapped as he had been. Few joined the Thieves Guild for the fun of it, Zel had said, but because they had no choice. Especially in recent winters as famine took greater hold over the kingdom, people were desperate, and Zel cared what happened to them. He wanted a happy end for all.

It was sweet, and stung Ulrich knowing he could not give Zel all he longed for. But he could help unseat Lothar, free the guild for more charitable leaders, and pave the way for the better future Zel had earned.

That they could not do the ritual early was no lie on Ulrich's part. The spell was particular. And thankfully, Zel had not tried asking to postpone their raid until after the month was up, for he feared that if he did not return successful that very night, Lothar might take it for failure, lash out against Zel's parents, or besiege the tower at an inopportune moment.

The only answer was to go early the evening of Zel's final night and complete a different mission before returning to the tower to complete Ulrich's.

Since Ulrich had never been inside the Thieves Guild, they could not port directly there or to where Lothar might be, but as long as Ulrich got them into the city, Zel could lead them the rest of the way. Just like he had for their night on the town. Ulrich wished they could have had more nights like that.

But he would leave Zel a beautiful life, with all of Ulrich's treasures bestowed upon him.

Whenever they were apart during the final days, Ulrich worked to change his spells to accept Zel as their master. All would answer to him, including the shelf with Ulrich's dearest trinkets. It was the end Zel and his parents had hoped for. To win the tower, defy Lothar, and live happily ever—

"Zel?" Ulrich had entered the main room in search of him. It was nearing their evening meal, but instead of finding Zel bent over more letters or practicing his skills, there was no Zel, and upon the writing desk was a flickering candle.

The flame illuminated a piece of parchment. Next to the parchment rested the magical key, and written in Zel's neat scrawl were the simple words:

My bedchamber.

Ulrich wasted no time in giving the key a three-quarter turn in the lock.

Sunshine assaulted his senses even when the true sun was already setting.

Zel turned at Ulrich's entrance with an excited radiance in his expression like he had been waiting with bated breath. He looked stunning. He was ornamented like a king's courtesan, something Ulrich had once known well, and yet he couldn't imagine his heart had ever beaten faster when he looked upon one of them than the way it hammered in his chest now.

Hair even more immaculately woven than usual, Zel wore Ulrich's mother's hairpin but had also adorned himself with various bejeweled combs, rings, bangles, and necklaces—though not Rudy's, which he had not worn since slaying his fellow guild members and sending Rudy away.

If Zel wore anything beneath his loosely tied robe, it was well hidden. Magenta, violet, and gold made up the elegant silk garment, another item Zel must have created with the loom. It fell open, the sides nearly revealing the edges of pink nipples, and was cinched lower than his navel at his hips. A bejeweled belt glittered there as well, mostly hidden beneath the fabric.

Zel crossed the room to an end table beside the bed. He had a bottle of wine waiting, already poured into two goblets. "This is from the treasure room." He retrieved both goblets and offered one to Ulrich. "May I assume it is simply a good vintage and not poison or some strange elixir?"

Ulrich chuckled. He felt oddly under—over?—dressed in one of his usual sets of sorcerer robes. He accepted the goblet and clinked it against Zel's cup. "You may. Although such other options do exist in the treasure room, well labeled, I assure you."

Zel chuckled too, and they each took a sip.

It was one of Ulrich's most prized vintages.

"I could never find the right occasion to open it," he said, "especially since I had no one to share it with."

"You do now. Is this occasion worthy enough?"

Ulrich had been trying to not think on it much, but tonight was their final night, the last before their raid on the guild and the subsequent end of everything. The night before they said goodbye, although Zel did not yet know it. "I think it is."

They drank from their goblets again.

Ulrich had avoided Zel's bedchamber for privacy's sake, other than when he combed out Zel's hair. He enjoyed getting to see it in the evening like this, even if little had changed from how he had prepared it for Zel's stay.

Zel led him to the bed to sit upon it. "I thought tonight called for something special, but not only the wine."

"Oh?" Ulrich eyed him coyly over the top of his cup.

"I plan on testing more of my magic tonight. I have been practicing something new. I…"

"Yes?" Ulrich prompted.

"You knew when I lied to you, when I tried to beguile and seduce you. The latter bits were eventually not a lie at all, and yet, knowing I came here to betray you, you still gave me everything and encouraged me to embrace who I am. You gave me the freedom to succumb to you, safely, gladly, when I had never before been able to give myself to another. I wondered if tonight, you might give yourself to me. I still want you to fill me!" Zel swiftly clarified, harried enough that Ulrich chuckled again. "I very much want that, but I thought, this time, I might… lead."

"If to lead is what you wish, Zel, do so, and I will follow."

Zel finished another gulp of his wine, and Ulrich did as well. Then he took Ulrich's goblet and set both aside. He started by undressing Ulrich like he had on their first night together, peeling away his robes and underlayers article by article. Like each successive night since, Zel summoned a portion of his hair out of his braids to wind around Ulrich's blackened wrist, easing his pain and making him feel practically mortal again.

When Zel began to undo Ulrich's pantaloons, he kissed from Ulrich's lips down his chest and stomach, but once he had Ulrich bare, he did not yet continue the trail.

He batted his eyes up at Ulrich from low near his lap and said, "Would you please, Ulrich, lay upon the bed? I want you to know what it is like to surrender to another and trust them to do right by you, as you have given that gift to me."

To trust and to be trusted was not something Ulrich had known for a very long time. "I trust you, Zel." He gently took Zel's chin and coaxed him upright until their lips met. "I am yours to do with as you wish."

While Ulrich laid out as asked, Zel moved to the foot of the bed and untied his robe. The fabric fluttered from his body, proving he had adorned himself in even more jewels and precious metals, and that was indeed all he wore.

The hair unbound from his braids and lashed out like instantaneous whips, three added tendrils from the one already twisted around Ulrich's wrist now binding his other wrist and both ankles and stretching him like an X.

Ulrich heaved an eager breath as Zel climbed onto the bed between his spread legs, prowling with the same hunger and magnetism described of the fairy prince in Ulrich's favorite love story. It always *had* been his favorite, but this...

No. Ulrich could not entertain that. He could not have that. Tonight, let him focus on pleasure and not the pain to come with the month's end.

Once Zel sat on Ulrich's chest, the spring of Ulrich's cock bounced near enough to brush between Zel's cheeks. Zel's cock sprung likewise in response, as he rocked forward to drag his length between the swell of Ulrich's ribs.

Ulrich marveled at how the jewels enhanced Zel's natural beauty, glittering the way his hair seemed to glitter now, almost as ethereally as Ulrich's own. The clouds through the translucent ceiling, rolling in to cover the night sky's stars, did not spoil the view, for the best view was in the room with him.

Zel rubbed the carved, bisected circle on Ulrich's right palm, though the lines were barely there with his curse at bay from the contact of Zel's hair. Zel kissed him as he rubbed the faded lines like a reverent prayer. Then he began to descend like before, down Ulrich's chest, teasing purple-hued nipples, and lower down his stomach to the start of dark curls. Finally, when Zel was low enough, he licked from base to tip and twirled his tongue around Ulrich's cockhead.

He swallowed him once, twice, slow and deep, but mostly just to wet him, for he shifted up again until their cocks aligned. Zel took them in hand, a wide stretch of his fingers to encase them both, and rocked in time to his thumb digging into Ulrich's shaft.

The sight of Zel's flush cheeks and pink lips with the darkening clouds behind him made Ulrich sorely sorry he was not able to touch.

As if sensing that desire, Zel used his binding hair to bring Ulrich's cursed hand forward and pressed it to his cheek. He turned his head to kiss the palm and then sucked Ulrich's thumb into his mouth. Even already soothed from the bracelet of hair, the touch of Zel's saliva somehow eased it even further.

Releasing their cocks, Zel moved higher up Ulrich's chest again, still rocking so his shaft dragged up the skin. The movements of an assassin were often like those of a dancer, and Zel proved it with every undulating roll of his back and arch of his neck, graceful and precise. He shifted higher, while teasing his own nipple, and brought

Ulrich's hand to the other to circle the nub with the thumb he had wetted.

Zel shifted *higher*, bringing his leaking tip ever closer to Ulrich's lips. Ulrich wanted that and nodded the closer it neared him, until he was granted permission to taste. Zel bobbed between his lips, and Ulrich widened his mouth to take it. He wanted to run both hands under the dangling jewels and caress every inch of adorned skin.

This was Zel's night to lead, but Ulrich cupped the breast in his grasp more possessively than he had been guided to, hoping his wishes might be known.

Zel seemed to sense that too and slowed the roll of his hips feeding Ulrich his cock. The hair brought Ulrich's other hand to Zel's body, and with magic and momentum, conducted the whole of Ulrich's palms and fingers to stroke up Zel's skin from hip bones to neckline and down again.

Zel whined, pulling his tip from Ulrich's lips with a shiver. He slid down, *down*, and licked up the wet trail left in his cock's wake, all the way back to Ulrich's lips. He tasted himself with a plunge of his tongue. Then his hair pulled Ulrich's arms taut back into the X.

Ulrich mourned the loss of Zel beneath his hands, but as Zel slid down, down, *down* again, Ulrich's head teased once more between his cheeks. Zel rocked himself there slowly, sliding Ulrich's tip up along his pucker and past it, but not yet in. He kissed Ulrich as slowly as his subtle thrusting.

When he finally lifted, he seemed to take in the whole of Ulrich's curls spread out around him like a mane. "You are so... beautiful," Zel said, as he pushed down on Ulrich's tip at last, and the head slid in smoothly, swallowed by Zel's rocking.

"As are you... and quite open, I feel."

"I prepared myself for you... thinking of your hands... your tongue." Zel flicked his own out to lick Ulrich's lips before sliding it deeply between them again. He thrust down on Ulrich little by little. "I am going to fuck myself on your staff... long into the night... and all you need do, is enjoy."

"Long is optimistic."

Zel laughed, continuing to slowly swallow Ulrich with his stretched but contracting passage. Bound by Zel's hair while Zel had his way with him, Ulrich not only felt the pressure of Zel's hands or the squeeze of his thighs the further back he sat, but the caresses of more of Zel's hair unleashing on him to join the fray.

Ulrich moaned at the swipe of its silken texture along his sac and delicately around the curves of his buttocks. He rarely moaned, and honestly could not recall the last time he had but it must have been centuries ago.

The minutes stretched on like that, impressively long despite Ulrich's teasing, until it was clear that neither could last much longer.

"Come in me, Ulrich," Zel said, after he had taken all of Ulrich in an endless series of thrusts and continued to rock feverishly. "Come in me!"

"You come first."

Zel's eyes flashed wider like emeralds shimmering.

"Show me what I would not let you do our first night. I want to see you bring yourself to rapture."

The clouds had grown darker above Zel, making him shine all the brighter like the first rays of dawn. He sat taller as he wrapped his fingers around his cock. He had to slow his thrusts upon Ulrich to stroke himself, or perhaps he did so to make sure Ulrich lasted longer.

Ulrich grew closer by the moment with how Zel tightened around him with each leisurely pump and play of his thumb through the prerelease at his tip. It made Ulrich want to suck that pink head into his mouth again and kiss Zel's pretty pink lips right after. Saliva built in his mouth at the thought, and he grew closer and closer—

"U-Ulrich!" Zel came first just like Ulrich wanted, and with it the heavens opened with a crack of thunder and sudden torrent of rain—that came right through the ceiling!

Zel cried out in alarm, instantly drenched.

Oh, how his magic had grown, for that had not been Ulrich's doing.

"What is happening?" Zel laughed, immobile atop Ulrich.

"Someone has become quite powerful to break my enchantments. Finish me, Zel!" Ulrich urged with a buck of his hips. Some of Zel's release had reached Ulrich's chin, and he swiped out his tongue to taste it before the rain washed it away.

If Zel smelled like the sun, then he tasted of it too.

Zel's rocking picked up again as he wrung out the last of his release within the downpour, and the hair Ulrich had felt caressing him found every bit of tender tissue it could fondle until Ulrich burst too.

Only after he had come within Zel did all those tendrils, almost as if they had grown sentience, wrap tighter around him to lift him from how he had been spread. They launched him upright, inviting him to embrace Zel, and as he finished giving Zel everything he had, he licked the dripping rainwater from Zel's throat.

They were soaked, with the bed and floor quickly becoming the same. Even with their black and gold hair plastered all around them like tethers to each other, Ulrich thought Zel had never looked more radiant.

He repaired the enchantment to save them from the storm, but before he could dry them, Zel said, "When you clean us, don't dismiss all of it. I want to keep some of you inside me tonight."

"As you wish, little cabbage."

They stayed like that for a while, still drenched but kissing and licking the water from each other. Content as Ulrich was to keep his length inside Zel all night, they did eventually need to untangle, but he did as asked, leaving some of his release within Zel when he cleansed them of their mess and lingering dampness.

Slowly, Zel summoned his hair back into his braids, squirming in seeming contentment, as Ulrich gathered him close for them to lay side by side.

"Did you enjoy that as much as I did?" Zel asked.

"You need to ask?"

"Sometimes, it's difficult to imagine I could be anything special to you. You must have been with so many others."

"I was. And while pleasure could be achieved, there was always something missing." Ulrich stroked Zel's back between the dangle of jewels, and Zel tilted his head up to meet their gazes. "I had no love for myself, no love for anything, and so all the world seemed numb and tasteless, like my senses had been muted. Until you brought color and life back into it."

Zel's smile was an added burst of radiance, but it quickly faded. "*Back* into it means there was color once. With your friends?"

"Yes, but long before the events I showed you, I knew a different kind of happiness."

"With your mother?"

Such a clever cabbage to have guessed right. "I would rather not think on that tonight. Color and true undiluted happiness in this gray world can be found right here, and I wish to think on nothing else."

"Then here is where we shall stay." Zel tilted his head higher for a kiss and whispered, "I love you, Ulrich."

He had implied it before, and Ulrich had heard him admit as

much to Rudy, but to hear it said directly to him stung worse than Ulrich expected.

Or perhaps that was the sting of tears in his eyes.

"Beautiful Zel, you are a singular entity in this world." Ulrich petted Zel's hair, lulling him with magic to fall asleep faster than he would have naturally. Only after Zel drifted into slumber did Ulrich whisper back, "I love you, little cabbage."

He could not possibly live without Zel after this. Which was why he did not plan to. He would not live at all after tomorrow night, and Zel could have a happy life with someone else someday who would be far more deserving.

Ulrich could only hope that Zel forgave him once this was finally over.

Fourteen

ZEL

Our dearest Rapunzel,

Your father and I await the return of our beloved child with open doors whenever you next darken them. We know the sorcerer will have found you worthy as your final day with him wanes, and we hope to celebrate your marriage soon.

Though little has changed in the day-to-day lives of our friends and neighbors, trust that they miss you dearly, as do we.

-Your Enduring Mother

The day had come. Everything was set. The coded message from Zel's parents implied they were ready as well, and that Lothar's schedule should be as usual, given the wording of "little has changed in the day-to-day." The hope was to reach Lothar stealthily with minimal encounters, but should fighting commence, Ulrich was a powerhouse, and Zel was confident in his skills with a dagger, as well now in his skills with his hair.

How much easier it would have been to simply blend in and walk freely as guild members with Ulrich disguised as one too, if Zel had not been the most recognizable of members, and everyone knew he should be at the tower—or only returned with the sorcerer's head. They had considered feigning that as well but couldn't be certain if Lothar would keep the audience private or invite the whole of the guild to celebrate.

With evening on approach, Zel doubted his parents would read a reply letter before events transpired, but he sent one anyway.

Mother & Father,

I will see you soon. I love you both. But please, from now on, call me Zel as others do, for Zel is who I am.

-Your Devoted Child

Ulrich ported them into the city at sunset. Before they left, Zel used the orb that could see anywhere its wielder had been to check every corridor and room he could within the Thieves Guild. But although he should have been able to see inside Lothar's sanctum, since he had been there before, he could not. One of Lothar's many trinkets must have been blocking outside magic. That did not bode well, but they had to trust Zel's parents were correct that Lothar would be there as usual.

They blinked into existence in a back alley rarely frequented by foot traffic, like the one they had used when heading to Hessen House. This one was closer to Pied Pipers—Zel's home, with living quarters above and an entrance into the Thieves Guild through the storeroom. The shop would be closed for the evening, but all doors would be unlocked, just as Zel's mother had hinted at when she'd written "open doors."

Perhaps Zel was being sentimental, but it seemed fitting to wear his pendant from Rudy beneath his remade assassin garb, which he had crafted using the magical loom. He hadn't brought his original outfit to the tower, but he had mimicked it with the finer fabrics from Ulrich's treasure room, made it better, even allowing his hood to be a more vibrant violet because it still blended well with the shadows and Ulrich had said the hue looked lovely on him.

Ulrich donned no base disguise to dull his brilliance but wore a similar outfit to Zel's to hide the sparkle of his hair and the aura about him that no one could miss when looking upon his visage. Their outfits were enough that if anyone spotted them darting through the dark, they would assume *Thieves Guild assassins* and leave them be.

There was still some brightness to the sky as the sun dipped below the horizon, but once Zel had his bearings of which street they had appeared on, he knew the most shadowed paths to reach his home. They arrived without anyone seeing them, finding the back door unlocked as promised. Inside, everything was still.

"Do you know where your parents might be?" Ulrich whispered.

"They would not want to rouse suspicion, so they could be on missions if they were given any or simply below, waiting on the evening meal with other members. If able to, they will have helped clear the way for us." Zel was certain of that much, even if they had not been able to speak plainly in their letters.

He led Ulrich quietly through the back of the shop. The storeroom was on the other side, so they passed the stairs leading to the living quarters along the way.

Ulrich paused to look up the steps. He had covered his face, just as Zel had, but his violet eyes still glimmered.

"Up there is where you lived?" he asked.

"All my life."

"I would have been interested to see your room someday."

"I would be interested to have you in it."

"So I can see it?"

"So I can *have you* in it," Zel repeated, and pulled Ulrich down to his slighter height, lowering both their masks so he could press a kiss to Ulrich's lips. "Later," he promised.

"Yes..." But Ulrich seemed hesitant, distracted.

"Do you doubt we can do this?"

"No guild master could best me, but I am allowed to worry about you, little cabbage."

That meant the world to Zel. It truly did. But he knew his worth, and he wasn't about to falter right on the cusp of having everything he had ever wanted—and much he hadn't even dared to dream about. He brandished his dagger with a grin. "Do not doubt my skills any more than you doubt yours. We will win. Then we can be together as we have earned."

Zel hurried ahead. The storeroom was as quiet as the rest of the shop, but as soon as he lifted the hatch into the undercroft, noise filtered up from the members below. Zel's instincts were to pull his braids out from under his cloak and stroke them to calm his nerves, but he should not need such a crutch any longer.

He would succeed.

He was ready for this.

He was fierce and beautiful and capable.

And so was Ulrich.

Zel held a finger to his lips, and Ulrich nodded. They each pulled their masks back up, and Zel descended first. Ulrich had the power to cast great magic, but anything too flashy might draw attention, and even he might be overwhelmed if the whole of the guild turned on them. So they snuck, down the ladder and into the belly of the guild.

The undercrofts in general had wards against the use of magical trinkets inside its walls, other than those sanctioned by Lothar. How much easier this might have been with some of those at their disposal, such as the orb to peer around corners even if not into Lothar's sanctum, but at least it would take something far more powerful than a mere ward to prevent Ulrich from using his powers.

Zel flattened Ulrich against the wall with an outstretched arm as a pair of guild members moved past the doorway where they stood. It was a small alcove they were tucked into, a well-known one, but no one should have been headed there to go up unless it was Zel's own parents. He and Ulrich waited, and when no voices sounded near, Zel peeked out into the hall and glanced in both directions.

Clear.

Lothar's audience chamber, his sanctum, was only a few twisting turns of the undercroft halls away, but they needed to pass the entrance into the primary common room to reach it. Between Zel's skills and Ulrich's ability to practically be shadow, their footfalls made no noise, but a single mistake could raise the alarm.

Zel motioned to Ulrich when they neared the common room. He was to sweep Zel past it fast enough that hopefully no one would see them.

"Let's get him then! He'd hate to miss poultry night!" a voice boomed from inside, as two large shadows neared the inauspicious doorway.

Ulrich's hand came down upon Zel's shoulder, and when he glanced back, it was Ulrich who held a finger to his lips. Silently, he outstretched his arm past Zel, the black and cursed one, and as if from his clawed fingertips, mist formed like violet smoke. It took on the shape of a slinking cat that approached the door and scurried inside.

"By the depths—!" the same voice exclaimed, for the cat must have darted right past him.

"Catch the beast!" another announced, and the pair could be heard heading deeper inside.

Ulrich kept hold of Zel's shoulder and coaxed him forward. When they were but a step from the entrance, a force like a great wind pushing him launched Zel past the opening so swiftly that he nearly gasped. They paused on the other side of the door, but no sounds came from inside to indicate anyone had spotted them. Those within were too busy chasing the cat.

It was comforting to have Ulrich's hand remain as they continued. A phantom cat would not keep the guild members occupied forever, and Zel did not know how long it would stay formed, but they only needed to make it a few more turns.

He kept his ears craned for any signs of someone approaching, but though he would have sworn no one was around the next corner, he was proven wrong when he nearly collided with an ample chest. The buxom woman must also have been an assassin to have moved so silently, but when her faint yelp of surprise turned from confused eyes on Zel, whom she must have recognized even with his face covered, to suspicious ones on Ulrich, Zel punched the hilt-end of his dagger into her windpipe.

As the woman choked and stumbled backward, Ulrich swept in

front of Zel and touched his left hand to her forehead. Zel cringed when she went limp, but he could see her breaths and the pulse in her neck, proving she was only unconscious. Ulrich tucked her body into a nearby alcove, prompting them to move more swiftly onward before anyone could discover her.

At last, the next turn would take them to the chamber outside Lothar's sanctum. Ulrich halted Zel again, gesturing past the doorway to a mirror on the opposite wall. With a wave of his fingers, the mirror tilted at an angle that reflected the room.

Two guards, which Zel had expected.

Since there was no one else around, Ulrich cast another spell. They had discussed this one beforehand, but Zel was always in awe of Ulrich's magic, so much greater than any he had seen before his time at the tower.

Similar to the mist that had formed the phantom cat, wisps unleashed from Ulrich's fingers, but rather than become violet or mold into any shape, it vanished as it moved toward the door. After a few moments, two distinct thuds were heard.

They hurried on, thankful that neither of the now sleeping guards had fallen across the entrance's threshold. Most Thieves Guild entrances were open archways, but this one had a door. Zel could not hear anything within, as the walls and door were thick. Inside should be two more guards, Lothar, and possibly others if he was in audience with anyone, such as for a mission debrief or torturing information out of a target.

Zel and Ulrich shared a nod, then Zel threw the door open for Ulrich to rush in first.

The room was dark when Zel dashed in after him and soon became pitch-black when the door closed in his wake.

"There is no one here," Ulrich said.

"How can you tell? I can't see anything."

"See as I do." Ulrich covered Zel's eyes with his cursed hand, and when it moved away, Zel's vision could pierce the dark.

The only thing in the room was Lothar's empty throne.

Zel lowered his mask. "But why post guards when he isn't even here? It doesn't make sense."

"Are there other entrances?" Ulrich lowered his mask as well and drew back his hood, moving toward Lothar's chair.

"None. Where could he be?" Zel spun in place, admittedly panicking. They had contingencies for facing more enemies than planned, but everything had hinged on Lothar following his routine and being here.

"There is a piece of parchment on that chair," Ulrich said as he neared it.

Zel squinted after him. While he could see, the room was still dim to his senses. There did appear to be something on Lothar's chair, like a waiting note. "What does it say?"

Ulrich picked it up and read aloud, "Not so powerful now, are you?"

"Ul—!"

But Zel's warning cry came too late. Whatever trap had been set sprang into action with Ulrich lifting the note, causing half of a metal cage to spring up from the floor, just as its second half fell from the ceiling. The two halves met so swiftly, Ulrich merely clanged against the bars when he reacted and tried to move.

"Can't you—" Zel vaulted toward him, but Ulrich had clearly been thinking the same thing, for though he seemed to attempt to become shadow and slip through the bars, all that happened was a brief aura of shadow erupting from him that immediately snuffed out.

Ulrich grabbed the bars but lurched his hands back a moment later when they started to sizzle. "Iron. Enchanted specifically to nullify magic."

Zel reached toward the bars too but hesitated to touch them.

"Don't," Ulrich confirmed. "They will hurt you too."

"But how do I get you out?"

"You don't."

The voice sent a biting chill through Zel's chest. He turned to see the door opening behind them, permitting Lothar to enter—flanked by Zel's parents carrying torches. Sophie and Gregor stared blankly, their actions stilted and strange as if not moving their own bodies.

They were wearing control collars!

"How did you—"

"How did I know to not trust them?" Lothar said, as Sophie and Gregor lit the sconces on the walls to brighten the room. "Because I knew to not trust you."

His smirk was insufferable as he approached after closing the door, effectively trapping Zel with the enemy. If he had ever truly had magical luck on his side, that luck had run out.

"The Queen has many trinkets she has bestowed upon me for my services with the guild. This is one, and quite a useful one for spying." Lothar pulled a gilded hand mirror from his belt, similar to Ulrich's but gold instead of silver. When he aimed the glass at Zel, it did not reflect him nor the sanctum but an entirely different view, as if through the eyes of another.

It was the Thieves Guild common room. Zel could even see background commotion of members wondering where the phantom cat had gone, which Zel imagined had vanished as soon as Ulrich was caged.

But whose eyes was the mirror seeing through?

"Rudy..." Zel answered his own wondering, for he knew few others with glass over their eyes, and starting the night of Zel's final mission, Rudy had worn brand-new spectacles.

"Mirrors with various uses are one of the Queen's favorite tools." Lothar tucked the mirror away again, since it had done its job and trapped Zel in his hubris. "I saw everything young Rudy did. Like you killing your own people at the tower. I heard everything as well. To think, you went and fell in love with that monster."

"You are the monster," Zel spat. He had to think. He had to subdue Lothar somehow.

"I would have made good on my promises, you know," Lothar said. "You couldn't even do that, after all I've done for you and your parents these past twenty winters. But, if you submit yourself to me now, perhaps I can be lenient."

Ulrich shook the bars of his cage behind Zel, and when Zel glanced at him, the fury in Ulrich was palpable. He might not be able to wield magic from there, but he had not lost his luster nor the ominousness of his aura. He kept his blackened hand around one of the bars, even as it sizzled again.

"At least you did part of your job," Lothar sneered, "since it seems the sorcerer has also fallen for you. But then, who am I to be surprised, when you are so desirable." He seized Zel's chin with a sudden lurch, causing Zel's hood to fall back. Though he instinctively brought up his dagger, Lothar caught him by the wrist. He squeezed so hard that Zel yelped and dropped the dagger to clatter on the stone floor. "I was a little jealous watching my pretty petal's lips wrap around young Rudy's prick so lustfully."

The anger at hearing that pet name again was almost as strong as Zel's revulsion at Lothar's touch. Since Rudy had worn his new spectacles that night, Lothar had been able to watch them.

"Do not blame him. He thought the spectacles a gift. He didn't know about the mirror or how I manipulated him to keep an eye on you with some well-placed doubts about your safety. Honestly,

I don't even care that things have ended like this. I'll still have the tower and its secrets. And you will still be mine. Whether by free will or with a collar of your own."

Ulrich raged against the bars again. "You will not touch Zel!"

Lothar threw Zel aside, nearly causing him to trip. His dagger was still at Lothar's feet. He could use his hair, but how? When? Any move he made had to be the right one, or he would lose the advantage his hair granted him.

Gregor and Sophie flanked the door, having secured their torches into empty sconces. Should Zel free them for reinforcements or focus on Lothar? He had to decide. He had to act! But it had to be at the perfect moment, or everything could be lost.

"I will touch what I want to touch," Lothar mocked, grinning at Ulrich through the bars. "But first, to deal with you."

ULRICH

Zel had lost his dagger and seemed to doubt making use of his hair, likely because his parents were involved now, enslaved by Lothar's collars.

Ulrich had to rein in his anger toward this wretched man—and toward himself for having fallen prey to such an obvious trap. For all their sakes, he had to help Zel regain his resolve.

"Iron, even enchanted this powerfully, cannot kill me," he informed the overconfident guild master.

"Oh, I know, but this cage can prevent you from using your magic while you're in it, which is all I need for now. I will keep you here until I learn how to kill you, since it seems my assassin failed."

"How did you know I would be caught in this cage instead of Zel?"

"It was a gamble. But if things had been reversed, I still had my bargaining chips." Lothar kicked Zel's dagger back toward the door. "Sophie, take that. Then, dear Pipers, restrain your daughter."

Zel faced his parents with a start. Their subjugation complicated what might otherwise have been an easy win. Zel was well trained, but his heart was his weakness and the reason Ulrich knew he deserved better than a cursed life in that tower, however blissful it might seem for a time.

Sophie, who Ulrich remembered well even with the addition of twenty winters and the scar on her cheek Lothar had given her, claimed the dagger and sheathed it among several others on her person. But neither of the collared Pipers made a move toward Zel.

The truth of their stillness almost made Ulrich snort. They had no daughter, not as far as they knew—nor as much as Zel had decided yet.

"I *said*," Lothar barked impatiently, "restrain Rapunzel now!"

The pair immediately marched toward Zel. Pity he got closer to the truth that time.

Behind the blankness of their eyes, Ulrich saw the real Gregor and Sophie watching in panic. He could see the honest warring in Zel's eyes too, whether to choose Ulrich over the two other most important people in his life.

"Don't," Ulrich said, shaking the bars again, much as the iron stung him. "Do not let him taint you, Zel, with the vileness you managed to rise above."

"Rise above?" Lothar scoffed. "Do you think the hands of that girl so clean?"

Zel's head snapped back toward Lothar, even as his parents advanced. There was the true Zel, stronger than the fear that hobbled him. "No one's hands are clean in this world, Lothar," he snarled, "but the blood we stain them with is not created equal."

Golden tendrils lashed out from Zel's braids, unravelling to act as whips that wrapped around Lothar's arms and legs and brought him to his knees.

"And I am hardly a *girl*."

There was Ulrich's little cabbage, unbreakable and dazzling.

Gregor and Sophie descended in their attempt to restrain Zel, but he used his hair to keep them back too. Most of it was focused on subduing Lothar, some of which he was tightening more and more around Lothar's throat.

"P-Pipers," Lothar croaked, "use Rapunzel's hands to cut the hair!"

"What?" Zel faltered at the order. While before his parents were merely trying to detain him, now they drew their weapons. "I-it can't be cut!"

"It can by you," Lothar rasped.

He knew. He must have gotten the information out of Sophie and Gregor.

Ulrich hesitated to call out again and distract Zel while his attention was already split, but he knew how much more there was to Zel than his hair. Even the massive amount of it wasn't enough to keep Lothar down and fight his parents off at the same time, not when he was clearly hesitant to harm them.

They both went for Zel's right arm, forcing one of their daggers into it, and wrenched it around to aim for the hair at the base of his neck.

"Wait!" Zel struggled, as an initial tendril was quickly sliced. "It houses my magic! If I don't have all my power, you will never be able to kill him!"

"Pipers, hold!" Lothar ordered. In Zel's distress, the hair had loosened some of its grasp on the guild master's throat.

Zel was caught in a grapple with his parents, who although halted, had a good grip on his arm and could cut the remainder of his hair with only a few hacks—or slice open his jugular if he moved wrong. "My hair is part of a ritual necessary to drain the sorcerer enough to weaken him. If you cut it, he will find a way out of that cage long before you find another way to end him."

Oh yes, Ulrich would, he thought as he continued to grip the bars, sizzling skin be damned, and watched for openings to offer words of encouragement.

"Then will you submit to me?" Lothar glared from where he remained on his knees. "Or do I need to have your parents kill each other in front of you for this treachery? With but a word, I can have them turn their weapons on each other's throats."

"Zel..." Ulrich called to him softly, and held his stare when their eyes met.

"It is them or him, Rapunzel. And do not doubt young Rudy will quickly follow. Work with me to end the sorcerer, and I will let the rest of you live. Defy me, and your parents' blood will be the first spilled."

Zel closed his eyes, but then, with an exhaled release of tension, he said, "No, to be enslaved would be no life at all." His eyes snapped open with their own severe glare at Lothar. "I will never submit!"

"Cut the hair, Pipers. Then fight each other to the death."

"No!" Zel struggled valiantly against them, but his hair fell in swiftly sliced clumps until all that remained was a bob at his shoulders.

Ulrich shook the bars again, for he saw the defeat on Zel's face despite the fury he had displayed in his defiance. That Ulrich could do no more than watch was worse agony than all his centuries of solitude.

Zel's parents released him, immediately prying away the hair that had been wrapped around them. Lothar began to as well, now that the hair holding him had gone limp. Zel had moments to act before his parents turned on each other, and before Lothar disentangled enough to be a threat.

"Once they are dead," the guild master said, "I will put one of their collars on you. But you will not be allowed to die. No. You will make a lovely pet for all to see that there are worse fates after crossing me."

Ulrich felt the fire in him grow hotter like an echo of his blistering palms, for though he could not help directly, he could speak the truth that Zel had failed to realize. "Zel! Your hair may have manifested your magic, but *you* are the source. You. And no force but your own disbelief in that can ever stop you."

Their eyes locked once more, and with resolution fighting away the tears in Zel's eyes, he gave a short, decisive nod.

Energy erupted from him with something almost like his hair tendrils, but these golden whips were made of pure sunlight.

The spectral hair tripped Gregor and Sophie before either could take any determined swipes at each other and returned to Lothar as fresh bindings, keeping him on his knees. Zel grabbed his distant dagger with the incandescent hair as well and lurched it back into his hand—his left, since his right still held the dagger pressed into his palm by his parents.

He was marvelous to witness as he stalked toward a shocked Lothar, a true force of nature, even more powerful than Ulrich could have anticipated. He had never felt so proud.

"You menace—"

"That's right," Zel said, staring at one of Lothar's hands that his tendrils of light forced to the floor and yanked outward. Lothar wore several rings, but one in particular Ulrich recognized, for the symbol carved into it matched the bisected circle on his own palm. "I remembered why that symbol looked familiar when I saw Ulrich's. Long life, is it?"

"Pipers—" Lothar attempted to call out, but Zel leapt forward, brandishing both daggers that he crisscrossed to slice together through Lothar's wrist, removing his hand. "Noooo!"

The rapid aging was instant, as with any such trinket that was a pale comparison to how Ulrich had become what he was. Zel's parents remained paused, awaiting their next order, but no order would come.

"You *bitch*!" Lothar seethed, having become an old man in his seventies with his silver hair falling out in clumps, a worthy retribution of Zel's having been cut.

"Actually..." Zel knelt in front of Lothar, who was bound by tendrils to the point of being forced into a subservient bow, "I was born a boy. Raised a girl. And apparently, have grown to surpass both."

"Pi—"

Zel sliced across Lothar's throat.

Lothar gurgled blood, but when he was about to go limp, Zel grabbed him by his remaining hair to hold his head upright and watched the light leave his villainous eyes.

"Hush," Zel said as those eyes dimmed. "We do not mourn our marks. They are already dead."

Perhaps this was the moment when Ulrich had never felt prouder nor more enamored by his betrothed.

As soon as Lothar was dead, gasps sounded from Zel's parents. Their collars unlatched on their own, and the pair tore them from their necks before descending upon Zel.

"Sweet child!"

"You were marvelous, Zel! Marvelous!"

They embraced him, one on each side, uncaring of Lothar's blood nearing them as they knelt. Zel's sunlight tendrils dissipated, and he had already dropped Lothar's head, but his daggers clattered to the floor now too, as he surrendered to their embraces and wept.

It was some time before Zel spoke, but even still caged, Ulrich wouldn't have considered interrupting them. He gave them their moment, finally prying his fingers from the bars so his wounded skin could heal.

"Did you call me Zel?"

Gregor and Sophie laughed.

Then Gregor, who had spoken the name, said, "We read your letter."

"Right before that bastard collared us," Sophie added.

"We had heard you correct others, of course, but we assumed you preferred for us to use your full name, or you would have corrected us too."

"We would have listened," Sophie affirmed. "Even if we had chosen the name ourselves, your preference always would have trumped ours."

With more tears threatening to pool in Zel's eyes, whatever he might have been about to say was cut short by the door bursting open and a dozen or more Thieves Guild members entering. Someone must have noticed the unconscious bodies.

"How do I free Ulrich?" Zel demanded, leaping to his feet.

"Fifth stone up, centered behind the throne," Sophie said. She and Gregor both stood, freshly drawing their weapons to defend against anyone foolish enough to go after their child.

Zel wasted no time rushing behind the throne to find the stone and pushed it into the wall. *Fitting*, Ulrich thought, as the two halves of the cage parted to free him. 'Twas the similar depression of a stone in a wall that had started all this.

Ulrich let his aura pulse from him like a rolling purple mist through the room, and any of the guild members who had seemed twitchy backed up as if fighting the urge to flee.

"Your leader is gone!" Ulrich announced, as Zel stalwartly came to stand beside him, "but you needn't make an enemy of me. Swear allegiance to your new leaders, the Pipers, and I will spare you. Refuse, and you will answer to me instead of their blades."

An eruption of surprise filtered through the ranks upon recognizing Lothar lay dead on the floor and the sorcerer stood in their midst, but barely a member hesitated before taking a knee and holding their weapons blades-down toward the Pipers in fealty.

"Spread word among your ranks of what happened," Ulrich ordered, even as more members continued to arrive. They too all dropped to one knee, even not knowing the full story. Ulrich looked to Zel. "We must finish preparations at the tower before the hour grows late."

"Of course."

"What are you going to do?" Gregor asked them.

"What all this was leading to," Ulrich said, "and it requires Zel's magic, which remains strong. You needn't worry for his safety. Not with me."

Almost as if the gods had planned it so, young Rudy appeared in the doorway with the next collection of guild members.

He did not take a knee.

"I will see you again," Zel promised his parents.

Someone in the crowd muttered, "Did the sorcerer say *his* safety?"

But Ulrich swept them back to the tower, barely allowing Zel to hear Rudy's final cry.

"Zel!"

Fifteen

ZEL

Lothar was dead. Zel's parents were safe—and they had called him Zel. Why he had ever doubted they would heed his wishes seemed so silly now. The Thieves Guild might not be able to act independent of the Queen, but that was another day's fight.

The night was theirs.

And Ulrich would soon be Zel's.

"Do we need to await an appointed hour?" Zel asked once they'd returned to the tower.

"The appointed hour is now, for we must finish before midnight."

"We have plenty of time."

"Yes..." Ulrich seemed to hesitate, frozen where he stood.

"You are certain the loss of my hair won't affect the ritual? Ulrich? Are you well? What else—"

Ulrich lifted him by the waist and kissed him.

All Zel's anxiety over this night flooded out of him. So much had remained bundled up inside him, even with the battle won, but to feel Ulrich's claiming lips and hungry tongue, the rest fell away like Zel's hair had fallen at his feet.

"I am not sure if we have enough time for *that*," Zel hummed, "but I could be persuaded."

"I am afraid not." Ulrich chuckled.

"Afterward then." Zel kissed him again. Outside of that awful cage, Ulrich was a godlike presence, equally sparkling and shadowed like an entity of the night sky, but something else seemed to be dimmed in him for his lips turned downward once this new kiss broke. "Why do you look sad? Did... did my brutality with Lothar change your view of me?"

"Never. Nothing could." Ulrich held Zel's cheek, and though the fullness of Zel's braids was gone, his bob of hair still brushed Ulrich's blackened fingers and brought them to life. "Ferocity in response to being wronged is justified. And as your parents said, you were marvelous, Zel."

"Then is it my hair? Do you miss it? I do. It must look awful right now."

Ulrich held Zel's other cheek and kissed him gently. "You are as radiant as ever."

"Then tell me what we need to do so I might shine even brighter."

"You have partaken of my *rapunzel* for twenty winters, and thirty days longer while in my presence. You have proven worthier than I ever could have imagined and made it to this preordained night. The rest now is simple."

Ulrich drew them back from the center of the room and raised a hand, drawing in the air what then manifested on the floor as glowing violet symbols.

A bisected circle large enough for them to stand in, only this time, in the center of the line was a smaller circle interrupting the division. Ulrich led Zel into the glowing ring, positioning Zel in the top half and Ulrich in the bottom.

Energy surged within Zel as soon as they were situated, as if the symbol of prolonged life—an exchange of it, given the center circle?—heightened the magic about to be shared.

Zel thought perhaps he heard something outside, but Ulrich clasped his hands, keeping Zel's attention on his beloved. He had the sudden wish that he was in his mother's wedding dress instead of his assassin garb, but there would come a time to don it again.

"We entered this circle together, and so all you need to do now, Zel, is to absorb my magic with a willing kiss."

"How though? What do I do differently than a normal kiss?"

"For me, it became second nature after ages of feeding on souls. For you, once our lips are sealed, imagine you are drawing out my power, feeding on my aura, my essence, my soul, and it will begin to enter you."

"That's it? I just have to imagine it?"

"Same as when you use your magic to braid your hair. Will it, and it will be."

Whatever haunted Ulrich's eyes as Zel clutched his hands, lifted onto his toes, and invited Ulrich to once again lean down and press their mouths together, Zel knew that his devotion, his *love* could banish it. This kiss was softer than the others, and at first, Zel wasn't sure how to begin other than enjoying the connection. He tried to imagine drawing out of Ulrich all the beauty and galactic splendor the sorcerer exuded, to drink it down like wine.

The first surges of power stole Zel's breath away, and he pressed their lips together more firmly. The next was less a torrent and more a steady flow. He fought to maintain that capacity, taking it in like being flooded with... light? Joy? No wonder devouring the essence from another soothed Ulrich's pain. It felt incredible.

"That's it," Ulrich said when Zel paused for breath, "just like that, little cabbage."

Zel tugged Ulrich closer, sealing their lips again, though neither crossed the line of their respective halves of the circle. He returned to draining Ulrich's magic at the same steady pace, but there seemed to be no end to it. The longer the exchange continued, the more Zel could feel how much there was to take. The more he took, the better it felt to taste the next gulp.

And the rougher Ulrich's blackened hand felt.

Zel paused once more, this time to look at their clasped hands. Ulrich's cursed one was not merely sunken, it was more skeletal than ever, like the skin had rotted to black bone.

"It is all right. You are doing splendidly," Ulrich said, but the strain in his voice caused Zel to look up again.

Despite seeming in pain, Ulrich glanced at either side of Zel's head and smiled. Zel hadn't realized it, but his hair was growing.

"Keep going," Ulrich urged.

As boundless as Ulrich's magic seemed, when Zel returned to kissing him, he started to sense an end to it, like an echo following the sustained stream to indicate when the well would finally be dry. As Zel drank it in, slower and slower, he felt the growth of his hair cascade past his shoulders and down his back. It was returning to its previous grandeur with the consumption of Ulrich's potent power.

Zel willed some of its strands to coil around Ulrich's wrist, and Ulrich sighed in contentment, relieved of his pain. But when Zel peeked down at the hand, it only looked slightly revived, not whole the way it usually reacted.

The well was nearly dry already. There was something very tempting about the last few swallows, promising more than the pleasure and fullness and power Zel felt, but he feared succumbing to that hunger and not being able to stop.

Then Ulrich stopped them both.

"That is enough."

Ulrich's knees gave way, and Zel clutched after him. Though he felt an insurmountable strength within him now, he let them slowly sink to the floor. It wasn't only Ulrich's shriveled arm that looked worse for wear. The whole of him looked awful, pallid and limp with the loss of his glittering vivacity. "Was it too much?"

"N-no. It was exactly enough," Ulrich answered weakly.

"I am immortal now?"

"No. And you will not be."

"What...?"

Ulrich's head lulled like he might pass out, and Zel swiftly lifted him, using his newfound strength that amazed him once he had Ulrich in his arms. He carried him with ease to the chaise and laid him down like Ulrich had laid down Zel when first exploring the truth beneath his skirts.

Violet eyes fluttered back to alertness, more a mauve-like brown now.

"I... will not die from this."

"Thank God. Then what—"

"I will not die... until you remove my arm and let the curse consume me." Ulrich tapped the dagger in the sheath on Zel's belt.

"No."

"You no longer have to fear the wrath of your guild master. You can live whatever life you want now, Zel, powerful, practically untouchable, but still mortal. And I am vulnerable enough to finally die."

"I will not kill you." Zel shook his head. "Please don't ask that of me."

"I wish I did not have to, but I am too weak to do it myself. It is why I needed an assassin to begin with. This is the only opportunity I will have to be set free. Take my arm, and the rest of me will rot."

"Please... *please*." Zel climbed onto the chaise with him, hating how the cursed arm was still mostly black and shriveled even with his hair wrapped around it. The arm dangled from the chaise as if useless. "Would immortality truly be a curse if it was with me? If we were together? Please, Ulrich. I love you."

"And I love you, my little cabbage." Ulrich lifted his head enough to press their foreheads together. "But you ask for forever after only a month in my company. What if you came to regret that choice?"

"Whether a life of twenty years or thousands, love can strike just as suddenly and is no less worthwhile. Or can you tell me you have ever felt for another as you feel for me?"

"I cannot."

"Did you even truly miss another's touch until you had mine?"

"I did not." Ulrich smiled softly.

"Then what I ask makes more sense than what you ask of me. *Please*, Ulrich. Stay."

Ulrich's eyes gazed at Zel with perhaps more wonder than ever before. "So clever for one so young. Perhaps with you, Zel, forever would not be a curse. But are you sure of what you ask of me—and of yourself?"

"*Yes*." Zel nodded.

"If you are certain, if you have no doubts in you at all, then—"

The sing of a rotating blade cutting through the air came faster than Zel could react. As he sprung upright, shielding Ulrich from whatever was coming, it did not occur to him to protect the part of Ulrich hanging off the chaise.

A handaxe lodged into Ulrich's cursed arm beneath his shoulder, severing everything beneath it.

"Noooooo!"

As the remaining blackness and violet veins began to spread throughout the rest of Ulrich's body, the power in Zel unleashed with such a fury that he levitated off the chaise. His regrown hair spiraled around him like mythic snakes and lashed out at the attacker in the window, who Zel only realized was *Rudy* in the same instant that his hair threw him from the tower.

Zel swept forward to give chase like a streak of sunlight the same way Ulrich could move like shadows. Rudy had climbed the tower using a coil of Zel's own severed hair left at the Thieves Guild and tied it to a grappling hook. That must have been what Zel had heard earlier—the hooks lodging into the stone.

As Rudy plummeted, slowing his descent by still haphazardly holding onto the rope of hair, Zel extracted the grappling hook just as Rudy landed, so his final descent was harsh enough to stun him. Zel leapt from the window, descending like a blazing star, hair wildly whipping around to grab hold of the perimeter wall and launch him over it to land where Rudy had fallen.

"Whyyyyy?" he demanded, imagining he must look as awesomely fearsome as Ulrich once appeared to all those who crossed him.

"He bewitched you!" Rudy coughed, holding his ribs like a few might be broken. *Good.* "He must have! He must have bewitched you! He's a monster!"

"I love that monster!" Zel snarled. Outside at this hour, the area should have been cast in darkness, but Zel's figure lit up the clearing as though it were midday. "Now I am one too. How could you have gotten here fast enough—?" he started to ask, but with how Rudy had fallen, he noticed in the stretch of Rudy's shirt the chain of a necklace beneath it—gold like Zel's.

Zel fell upon Rudy and ripped the necklace out from under the fabric. It was an identical emerald pendant to the one Rudy had given to him.

"This lets you port to somewhere nearby wherever its twin is, doesn't it?" he guessed.

Rudy's glance aside said all Zel needed to know, but still Rudy added, "And return to where I started when I wish it."

"And here I believed it such a thoughtful gift." Zel grabbed his own pendant, broke its chain as he tore it free, and threw it at Rudy to join the other.

"I only wanted to be close if you needed me!"

"I do not need you! Why do you persist when you know I can never be your bride? I am no woman, Rudy!"

Rudy looked up at Zel with the worst of emotions, because it was soft and kind and full of devotion. "Who or what you are could only ever be beautiful to me and worthy of my love. Learning your secret could never change that. But do you truly love *him*?"

Why now, when Ulrich might be dead already, did Zel spare tears for his friend? He could feel them making his eyes grow hotter than his anger.

"Please, Zel, I only ever wanted to see you happy and safe," Rudy continued. "Even if not by magic, how can you be certain the sorcerer hasn't been manipulating you by having you locked away with him all this time?"

That at least made Zel smile. "Because I wasn't locked away. I have had more freedom this past month with Ulrich than in my entire life. Even if I had been free to love you, Rudy, I never could have as more than a friend. But I do love him. I was never bewitched, and the only one manipulated between us was you, letting Lothar control you with whispered lies. Can you understand that? Can you respect my choice? Or were you only ever my friend in the hopes of one day convincing me to be more?"

It clearly pained Rudy to be asked that, even seemed to horrify him. "I would always still be your friend, Zel."

"Lothar said you didn't know your spectacles could spy on me."

Rudy's look of horror intensified, proving he had not. "I assumed they did something, or he wouldn't have given them to me. But I didn't—"

"I don't have time to hear more." Zel looked up at the tower, then back at Rudy. "I want to believe you. I want to always be friends. To love each other as friends. But you better hope he is not lost to me, or I know not what I will do to you in the moments that follow."

ULRICH

Ulrich had lost all sense of time. Whether Zel had been gone moments or hours, he did not know. The curse was spreading rapidly, with pain worse than any he had ever known coursing through him, originating from where his arm had once been, but making him throb everywhere each time he gasped for breath.

This was what he had wanted. This was what he had planned. But now, in his final moments, knowing he might never see Zel again, he realized he would give up every good year of his distant past along with the monotonous torture it became if he could simply touch Zel's cheek once more and see his smile.

Yellow light shimmered before Ulrich's vision, and he turned to it, struggling to focus. Golden hair, a sweet, feminine smile...

But that was not Zel.

Was it?

"Ulrich!"

That was Zel, calling from the window. He had returned, but who was this golden apparition? And now there was a hint of orange to its left, now green to its right...

How was all this color spilling into the tower in the dead of night?

"Ulrich?" Zel was touching him, holding him, but Ulrich could barely feel it. "How do I fix this? Can I return some of the magic to you?"

Ulrich was struggling to stay conscious, let alone think clearly. "I-I... do not know."

"Please. Let me try." Zel leaned over him and pressed his lips to Ulrich's.

He barely felt that either, and at first, nothing seemed to be happening. Soon enough, however, Ulrich felt the presence of the magic Zel was attempting to force into him. The way it soothed him only for the throbbing pain to immediately return was such cruel mockery. Zel was giving him too much, yet none of it was making a difference.

With Ulrich's arm gone, such efforts were too late.

Zel kissed him harder, tried to push his magic into Ulrich faster, but it only meant he was left gasping breathlessly too.

"Z-Zel..." Ulrich sputtered with a turn of his head. "Stop. It isn't working. You will only die with me."

"Then I will die—"

"*No*," Ulrich commanded, wincing as the effort sent a fresh spike of pain lancing through him. He tried as much as his dwindling lifeforce would allow to focus on Zel's face, but more colors had joined the first, red and blue now, and they were taking on clearer shapes behind Zel. Figures. *Faces* that Ulrich remembered so well...

Not the cruel grimaces and unfeeling sneers from what had become of his friends—what had become of him—but the grown men and women they might have been if those young orphans had accrued more than power and the corruption that accompanies it.

Ulrich had seen this version of them in their final moments as he'd sucked the last of their magic and souls into himself, like phantoms of what had been lost.

"No more," Ulrich said, perhaps as much to them as to Zel, if they were even truly there or just visions borne of his rotting mind. "I will not have my life extended in exchange for yours."

The pause in Zel's attempt to replenish Ulrich's magic was already allowing the curse to spread faster again. It was better this way than for Zel to ever end up as they had.

"Perhaps eternity would have been worth it with you at my side, little cabbage... but to live without you for even one day would be my worst torment yet. My life... could never be worth the loss of yours."

"Then how about mine?" a new voice called.

"Rudy! What—"

"I couldn't stay down there and leave you to weather this alone. You are my friend, Zel, and I wronged you. I wronged your beloved." As he came into view, his eyes moved from Zel to Ulrich. "Please let me fix this."

No. Ulrich tried to speak it, but his voice had left him with the renewed spread of the curse. Consuming Rudy would be no better, even if it was a friend's *willing* sacrifice.

Unlike Ulrich's.

Was this truly them? Like blurry colored lights with faces fading in and out, as barely discernible as Zel's familiar features, though still clearer than Rudy's unfamiliar frame. Was it them... waiting for him to finally join them as the boy whose greatest exploit was once his superior skill at infusing trinkets with magic?

"No, Rudy... it won't make any difference," Zel's voice quaked. "If my magic is not enough... if *I* am not enough, then... then n-nothing..."

"I am so sorry, Zel—"

The room exploded in color and sudden focus.

Then it faded again.

What...?

"There has to be something we can—"

Another explosion of prismatic brilliance, and Zel's radiant face appeared in perfect clarity, which Ulrich could see was twisted in anguish as he wept.

"Zel, look!" Rudy exclaimed. Ulrich could see him clearer now too, something about those bursts of color having cleared his mind, however minutely. "It's your tears! The curse recedes whenever one falls on his skin. If we had more or something else—"

"My blood!" Zel unsheathed his dagger and carved it across his palm.

Wait! Ulrich wanted to protest, too addled to understand why Zel would do such a thing, but before he could object, Zel pressed the smear of blood on his palm to the spot where Ulrich's arm had been cleaved by Rudy's axe.

The brilliant prism of Ulrich's vigilant friends exploded in a blinding light, but with their departure, he thought perhaps he heard a voice.

"What's one more life... if it's worth living?"

When the light finally returned to normal for Ulrich, he knew the curse had abated to what he imagined was merely scar tissue above where he no longer had an arm.

He had not felt such peace in... more centuries than he could hope to count.

He also had a terrible throbbing in his head and a general ache about his body that he had not known in just as long. It was a far cry from the pain of almost dying and a different sort of ache than his arm used to cause, one honestly easier to tolerate because it was corporeal, grounded. Ulrich felt oddly freed and unburdened by having to experience it, not as powerful as he once had been, but not devoid of magic either.

And although it took a moment longer to register than his aches and throbbing head, Ulrich also realized that Zel was kissing him.

When Zel pulled up, Ulrich could only stare at his golden betrothed in rapturous wonder. "I... I think I'm mortal."

Zel laughed. "I think I'm normal again. Well, what I was before the ritual."

"You are still radiant. But you wasted so much magic on me."

"It wasn't a waste. Your eyes and hair sparkle again."

"The hair might be from perspiration," Ulrich joked. "But if my eyes sparkle, Zel, it is because they are looking at you." He touched Zel's face, touched the unbound fall of his hair, wild and regrown. It didn't ease his pain, for that particular ache was forever gone, but it soothed him all the same. The new aches, he could tolerate. He would never have his arm back, but it was no longer his curse to bear.

A worthy sacrifice for what he had gained, so much more than the sacrifice he'd made so long ago.

"If Rudy hadn't noticed my tears revitalizing you, I might not have realized the answer soon enough." Zel looked over his shoulder to where Rudy stood, farther away than his voice had sounded, like he'd backed up a pace or two once Ulrich reawakened.

Ulrich allowed himself a moment to enjoy that the young man might be frightened of him. Or Zel. Or both. Perhaps he was mostly regretful and loath to face them, given his eyes were on the floor.

He also held his side, as if his ribs were bruised or broken. A fall from and subsequent climbing of a several stories tower for the second time were sure to do that.

"Please don't thank me," Rudy said to his feet. "All would have been well if I'd just listened to you, Zel. I am so sorry. I didn't..." He trailed off, and only then did he glance up, first to look at Zel and eventually at Ulrich. "I don't think I ever truly knew what love was until I witnessed the two of you. I was such a fool to think I knew better, yet you were willing to die for each other. You love each other, no bewitching necessary. I am truly, truly sorry." He again glanced at his feet before turning as if to go.

"Rudy!"

Rudy hesitated but didn't look at Zel.

"I am still so angry at you, but I meant it when I said I hope we can always love each other as friends. It might take me a while to fully forgive you, but I want to try. *Eventually.*"

Rudy snorted and finally did look at his friend after the teasing way Zel said that. "If you someday think me worthy of your forgiveness, I'll be here. Well, I'll be home." He took out of his pocket what Ulrich saw was a pair of pendants like the one he'd given Zel. A matching set, it seemed, and Zel was no longer wearing his.

"Here." Ulrich held out his remaining hand from where he lounged on the chaise. He wasn't ready to get up yet, but he could do this much, since he knew the type of trinket this was now. It only betrayed its magical aura when near its twin. "Those won't work while you're in the tower, but I can fix that."

Hesitantly, Rudy came forward and placed the pendants in Ulrich's palm. Ulrich only needed one.

To the naked eye, he did nothing to it other than smooth his thumb over its emerald surface. Then he handed both pendants back to Rudy.

"Thank you." Rudy glanced once more at Zel and vanished, returning to wherever he'd been when he followed Zel here.

As Zel better situated himself on the chaise at Ulrich's hip, he helped Ulrich to lay back more comfortably. Ulrich must have looked weak and worn, if Zel was treating him so tenderly. He certainly felt it.

"What now?" Zel asked. "Do you think you could live one mortal life with me, even if we can no longer have forever?"

"I believe there are some very specific words for times like this. About happiness. And an ever after."

Zel grinned. "Like in *The Bard and the Fairy Prince*? The tower could still be our home."

"But a place to retire to when the day is done, not to lock ourselves away in like hermits. There is still the Thieves Guild left in turmoil, and an evil Queen who believes she controls it. Even with a change in internal leadership, her reign remains, and I am in no condition to rise up against my old apprentice."

"Is that what you would have wanted?"

"I do not yet know the extent of my magic that remains, but I know I must live now or be left to rot. I feel strangely invigorated to do more than wallow another several centuries—or decades as the case may be."

"I am with you for all of it, for any of it, Ulrich, if you are with me."

"As my... bride? Or shall it be bridegroom?"

Zel scrunched his nose in adorable thought. "If there was a term that combined the two, I think that would be most fitting. I might have to invent one."

"Well then, little cabbage, for now, I shall call you my beloved."

"I love you, Ulrich." Zel bent down and kissed Ulrich gently.

"I love you, Zel."

Ulrich was indeed drained, but with rest, he knew he would recover. He wished he had enough energy left to kiss more passionately and drag Zel down onto the chaise with him, but that would have to wait for another night. Any night, every night, hereafter.

"At least Rudy can inform my parents that we are well. Tonight, I want only you." Zel tucked himself beside Ulrich. They didn't quite fit, but that was another sacrifice Ulrich was willing to make.

Ulrich lifted his remaining arm to wind around Zel's shoulders. "Whatever comes next, we can take what joys we please and maybe even do some good from the shadows."

"Do some good?" Zel tilted his head at Ulrich. "Hm, I wonder what that would be like."

"As do I." On the chaise, in quiet repose, at least for now, Ulrich captured Zel's lips once more.

Epilogue

ZEL

"Zel!" Ulrich called, while seizing one of the thieves they had been contracted to stop.

Already sensing the third thief's approach after finishing incapacitating the second, Zel needed no warning. With a quick pivot and lurch of the dagger from the second thief's shoulder, Zel lashed out toward the third with a graceful spin.

The dagger plunged between the third thief's ribs. Not a clean kill, but Zel had been avoiding vital areas on purpose. These were the worst kind of thieves, for they had been stealing food meant to be rationed and distributed fairly, a necessity as the Great Famine continued to worsen. They deserved for their final moments to be slow agony.

Zel looked down the alley as Ulrich drank the last few wisps of life force from the first thief. After feeding in such a way, there was always a flush of his old, more powerful aura, added sparkles in his hair and bright glowing galaxies in his violet eyes.

Souls no longer fed his immortality, nor were they required to ease any pain. Devouring them was simply efficient and a good deterrent by leaving behind husks. It also kept Ulrich's magic stores from depleting, and while that might not extend his life indefinitely, it helped ensure a healthier and longer mortal lifespan, and Zel wanted Ulrich around for a good long while.

"That one can live." Zel nodded at the second thief unconscious against the wall.

The third, still skewered on Zel's blade, struggled to pull free of it or to at least turn and see what approached him from behind. Too late. Ulrich was already there, and when the thief tilted his head back, Ulrich loomed over him to claim his soul too.

Ulrich looked rather fetching in his own assassin garb to match Zel's. Zel had kept the outfit made with the magical loom, complete now with a skirt-like tunic to add a feminine edge to otherwise masculine clothing. All of Zel's outfits were thus now. A mix of both. For everyone finally knew the truth of Zel's birth.

That *they*—Zel—was a mix of both too.

As the husk of the third thief dropped, Zel pulled their dagger free from the desiccated ribs. Ulrich bent down to meet Zel's slighter height and shared the final swallows of the thief's life force with a kiss.

Zel drank it down as eagerly as they enjoyed Ulrich's tongue and lips and embrace. Zel's right hand might still hold a dagger, but the left clutched Ulrich, wrapping around the metal bicep of Ulrich's false arm.

His right, that had once been cursed, was gone now, replaced with one made from metal, like a steel skeletal arm from just past the curve of his shoulder to equally skeletal fingers, covered in a long sleeve and a glove. Zel could feel its distinctness beneath their grip. Ulrich had crafted it using a forge from the treasure room similar to the magical loom.

He had also used the forge to craft the bands he and Zel wore on the fourth fingers of their left hands, twisted gold like the plaiting of Zel's braids.

Ulrich had begun to use more of his magical items as another way to conserve what power remained in him. Because of the loss of his immortality, his garden was not as potent as it once was. If a woman with child ate the *rapunzel* now, her babe would not be magic born, but the garden still produced the most robust of produce and continued to grow even in the depths of autumn, as if springtime remained forever around the tower.

Zel licked their lips as the kiss ended. Sharing the stolen life forces did not make them feel as powerful or as untouchable as drinking Ulrich's magic during the ritual, but like they might live two or three times the length of a mortal, which was fine by Zel so long as that life was lived with Ulrich.

"Are we done here?" Ulrich asked.

The second thief was starting to rouse. Then he was very much awake when he registered the nearby husks of his companions.

"Do not be in too much of a rush to join them," Ulrich warned the man. "Run along now. So says the Queen."

The unsanctioned thief skittered away as told.

The thieves and assassins from the Thieves Guild still answered the evil Queen's summons and carried out missions, but they were much more than her lackeys now.

Zel cleaned their dagger and sheathed it while Ulrich retrieved the sack they had been hauling for their next destination.

"You don't mind still carrying out the Queen's dirty work?" Ulrich asked.

"Not if the targets deserve it, and stealing from the hungry counts as deserving in my book."

"Agreed."

Occasionally targets who did not deserve death or brutal warnings disappeared in other ways, so the Queen never knew they had not been dispatched. Also occasionally, assassinations she hadn't authorized were carried out and blamed on those she did want killed. It was a gamble, but a life well lived required risks.

The only way to unseat a tyrant wasn't to wait for them to grow a conscience or grow bored enough to change, but to undermine them with the power of the people little by little with every small act they could. In the turmoil of a famine, it wasn't easy, but Zel and Ulrich both knew well how to be patient. And it was going to take many more than just them to see the end of the evil Queen's reign.

Noise from the mouth of the alley drew Zel and Ulrich's attention. A young couple stood stunned, having come upon them clearly by accident. Old Thieves Guild rules said to leave no witnesses, but they didn't serve the old rules anymore.

Zel grinned and held a finger to their lips.

The couple nodded and hurried away. People in these streets knew the winds of change were upon them. Zel and their parents would not be like Lothar. If any friends or family members of those slain ever embarked upon revenge quests against the Pipers, Ulrich, or the guild, they would not win. Because they had far too much to lose to let anything be taken from them again.

"Shall we?" Zel turned to Ulrich.

"We shall."

ULRICH

"Magic Man!" one of the children announced when Ulrich and Zel entered the orphanage. The title was close enough to "sorcerer," Ulrich supposed, and certainly better than most of his other monikers.

The sack Ulrich carried was filled to the brim with food from his garden. They brought it weekly as added sustenance for the children, but it wasn't solely altruistic, since the matron of the orphanage was a Thieves Guild whisperer and gave them information on activity in the city. An adequate step on the road to being...

Good.

"Am I reduced to a charlatan and clown to you?" Ulrich asked grandly, but as he pretended to protest, he summoned the vegetables from the sack to float through the air, sending them toward the kitchen past the amused looking matron, but saving one small tomato to float in front of the child's face like a large red nose.

The child giggled and pawed at the tomato, which Ulrich released from his enchantment to allow it to be caught.

"You better share that," Ulrich warned, and the child ran off with a fervent nod.

They did not know most of the children well, but there was one particular girl Zel had an affinity for. She often pulled Zel aside, chatting excitedly. Zel explained once that they were responsible for her father's death, but Zel had spared her, some of which Ulrich had witnessed himself before appearing to Zel that night in the guise of an old woman.

The girl wanted to join the Thieves Guild someday, as a pickpocket if not an assassin. Zel was hesitant to give her any promises, but Ulrich could tell the girl would not be dissuaded. 'Twas the way with tenacious people once they set their hearts on a certain path.

Ulrich had been such an orphan himself once.

The children had no fear of him. Most would stare in simple awe, even after a filling night such as this one when Ulrich's power glittered about him similar to the old days. The matron was another story, but her unease in Ulrich's presence did not prevent her from passing to him tidbits of interest for the guild, while Zel chatted with the girl.

They could not stay long, but Ulrich enjoyed the unburdened expression he saw on Zel's face while they were here. When once Zel had been looked on with jealousy by those who saw *rapunzel* delivered to the Pipers' doorstep, now Zel and Ulrich provided for those who had little.

"You realize I could simply magic the food here each week," Ulrich said when Zel joined him again near the front.

"And use up your stores unnecessarily? Nonsense! Besides, I enjoy the visit."

"As do I."

"Does it remind you of when you were younger?"

"A little. Hopefully, there are no future budding immortal monarchs in our midst."

"Don't tempt fate!" Zel chuckled.

"*You* did." Ulrich looked upon his beloved. "As did your parents. And how grateful I am for all of it."

Zel flushed, still made bashful at times by Ulrich's adoration. They might believe they were born with magical luck, but if one were to ask Ulrich, he'd swear the real luck was his.

"I am especially thankful that you had your parents, whereas these children and I did not."

"You never did tell me what happened to your mother," Zel noted. In the golden bundle of Zel's braids, although their hood currently hid it, remained the emerald encrusted hairpin once worn by Ulrich's mother.

"I never knew who my father was," Ulrich admitted. "My mother might not have known either, given the many she sold herself to."

Zel's eyes widened, as Ulrich had anticipated they might when finally told this tale.

"When I was still very young, one of her customers promised her a better life if she ran away with him, but he had no interest in children. She chose a better life."

"But... you still kept the hairpin and considered it precious to you."

"The time I had with my mother was precious. I grew to understand why someone might give up everything for a better life for themselves, and I still do not hate her for it. But it is your parents who are the ones worth emulating, Zel. In Lothar's sanctum, when the other members of the guild rushed in, they did not hesitate for a moment before guarding you and helping you free me. They saved themselves with our pact, but even then, before you'd first screamed your way into the world, they made that decision to save you. I am glad you had them, and because of them as much as your own precious nature, you grew into a paramour worth keeping."

Zel smiled like the sun they always reminded Ulrich of and wafted up that familiar scent of sunshine too as they lifted onto their toes to kiss Ulrich. "I am glad as well."

"Master? Mistress! Uh..." A different little girl had come over and tugged on Zel's tunic.

"How about *Zel*?" Zel corrected.

"Are you hurt, Zel?" She indicated a bit of blood on the surface of Zel's bracer.

"Oh! No, I'm fine. It isn't mine," Zel added in a whisper.

The girl nodded with wide eyes before running off.

Ulrich snorted as the two of them made for the door. "You are still a little wicked, you know."

Zel didn't for a moment deny it.

They hit the streets again to return to the Thieves Guild. Ulrich could still port them anywhere he had been before, but he saved that for returning to the tower, where they slept, took most of their meals, and enjoyed private time together.

They did often, however, enjoy their evening meals at the Thieves Guild with Zel's parents. Such was the plan tonight.

"Mission accomplished, I assume?" Sophie kissed Zel's cheek upon their arrival.

"Orphans fed and thieves made an example of," Zel confirmed.

"Still taking good care of our treasure?" Gregor asked Ulrich, gripping his forearm in decisive greeting. He made a point of doing so each time they met, like a challenge to himself to never show hesitancy.

"Always, but they too take care of me." Ulrich did not throw in Gregor or Sophie's faces that they had once owed him a debt. He had come out the better in the end, after all.

Gregor had taken to calling Zel their "treasure," which Ulrich considered a fitting endearment since neither "son" nor "daughter" was appropriate any longer.

Because of Zel and Ulrich's frequent presence in the halls, a small indoor garden had been started in the kitchen capable of growing some of Ulrich's same hearty vegetables—including the very *rapunzel* that had once been stolen from him. Although he had explained that much of its magic was depleted, and it was safe for anyone to ingest, few members other than Zel's parents had dared to try any yet.

Twenty winters was not enough to forget someone melting apparently.

Sophie and Gregor had taken to leading the guild with fervor. They were well liked by other members, much as many had been wary and oftentimes envious of Zel. Some still were, for different reasons now given Zel's magic and being wed to the fabled sorcerer in the wood instead of having slain him. But because Zel's parents took far better care of everyone than Lothar had, envy was mostly overshadowed by loyalty and respect.

The Queen knew the Pipers as her liaisons now. When next her messenger had requested a mission, they had presented themselves as having taken down Lothar for her sake because he'd been planning to become her immortal equal and overthrow her. Whether she believed them or not, her following message had given them her blessing for the change in leadership—so long as they continued to be her puppets.

As far as she knew, they still were.

The Thieves Guild was bustling as usual, but as Zel had stated numerous times, more joyful than it had ever been under Lothar's rule. The primary common room was packed with members, but none were yet dining, having waited for their leaders to join them. A head table was reserved for the Pipers and their generals who oversaw each unit—the pickpockets, the elite thieves, the assassins, the guards, the whisperers, and the cleaners.

Zel and Ulrich, the lone pair instead of a solo general, led the assassins.

There was also a member allowed at the table who oversaw the youngest recruits.

Rudy appeared just as the rest of them had taken their seats. He gave his nightly report before joining them, explaining that recruitment to the new Thieves Guild was going well. They had to be more covert than ever or risk the truth of their end goals getting back to the Queen, but though it might take a long while, Falchovari would see a day without an evil Queen or other immortal monarch. The time had come for something kinder, even if the road there would not be without its share of blood and wickedness.

Ulrich bore Rudy no ill will. He knew the motivation for Rudy's actions had been love, and he could not fault someone for loving Zel. It was Zel who had made the decision to forgive Rudy, and Ulrich would always abide by Zel's choices.

Rudy had also made private amends to Ulrich, and in a way that had been quite surprising. He'd caught Ulrich alone at the Thieves Guild a few days after the night of the full moon, when Ulrich had recovered enough to return to the city with Zel, who had refused to do so without him.

"You are giving me the pendants?"

"For you to keep one and to give one to Zel, should it not be too distasteful a gesture."

When Rudy offered the pendants, he had bowed low, something no one had done in Ulrich's presence since he was king.

He still awaited further elaboration before accepting the gift.

"Because, um..." Rudy had glanced up timidly upon being left waiting, "this way, the two of you can always be but a thought away from each other, should you ever be separated. It's something that should be shared between beloveds, not used in secret by a supposed friend." He lowered his hands holding the pendants but did not rise from his bow. "I have apologized so many times, and Zel professes to have already forgiven me and tells me to stop, but it never feels like enough. That's when I realized I hadn't ever truly apologized to you, not alone, not between just you and me. So, please know how much I mean this when I say I am so sorry, Lord Sorcerer, for all I did that endangered your happiness with Zel."

"Thank you, Rudy. You are allowed to call me Ulrich, you know, as I often remind guild members. You are also allowed to stand up straight and look me in the eyes."

Rudy had done so with the usual hesitancy he displayed around Ulrich, but once his posture was upright again, Ulrich outstretched his hand for Rudy to give him the pendants, which he did. "Um, may I ask...?"

"Yes?" Ulrich prompted patiently.

"How did you change the pendants' properties, or whatever you did to them, to allow them to work while inside your tower with only a touch? I suppose elves, and especially one as powerful as you, are just that attuned to such things?"

"In part. There are also interesting tricks to magical enchantment."

"Oh?" Rudy's earnest eagerness had intrigued Ulrich.

"Would you perhaps... like to learn?" he'd offered. "It has been a very long time since I had an apprentice to pass such knowledge to."

"I would love that!" Rudy's hesitancy seemed to have been forgotten in the face of his excitement. "I've always had an interest in magical trinkets. Though Lothar did sour me on them a little."

Ulrich had gestured for Rudy to follow him out of the alcove where they'd been having their exchange. "It'll be good for me to teach someone again." And this time, he would be a far different mentor.

He had been thus far, and Rudy was an attentive student and a devoted friend to now both Zel and Ulrich.

So, since Sophie and Gregor sat at the center of the head table, with trusted generals to their left, Zel on their right, and Ulrich next to Zel, the only open seat was on Ulrich's other side.

Which Rudy gladly took.

GREGOR

Though weeks had passed since the events of that fateful month without Gregor and Sophie's beloved Rapu—*Zel*—Gregor still found it odd at times to be seated at the head of the Thieves Guild between his wife and treasured child, while on Zel's other side was the very sorcerer they had all once feared.

Now, Zel's husband.

Ulrich was no less frightening than he had been those twenty some winters ago, even with his magic diluted. But then, Gregor, Sophie, and Zel were frightening in their own rights. Sometimes the world demanded fearsome figures. The only question was how and upon whom to use such menacing auras.

Rudy received no pulse of it from Ulrich, even as Zel joined the pair in conversation as amiably as if nothing had changed since they were childhood friends. Gregor was glad to see the pair remain close despite all that had transpired. He was also glad to see Ulrich's friendship with Rudy continue to blossom.

Sophie's hand came down on the table to rest over Gregor's, and he turned to look at her, radiant as ever, beautiful as their child, with a fair face and deep warmth in her eyes, and just the right edge of a vicious twinkle to be set loose when necessary. The scar on her cheek, faded as it was after so many winters, in no way marred her. She was Gregor's treasure too, and together, they had brought something special into this world, something strong enough to perhaps be one of the catalysts to change the kingdom forever.

Whatever the three had been discussing, Ulrich suddenly erupted with a boisterous laugh, bringing Gregor's attention back to them.

Perhaps strangest of all while sharing such meals was the peace Gregor felt. The kingdom was still in the grips of the Great Famine. Much was uncertain with the evil Queen's reign still bearing down on them. But a flicker of hope was present, like the rare chance for a wish upon a star.

One of the more recent pickpockets to have achieved full membership passed by the table with a coquettish bat of her eyes at Rudy, which he responded to with a faint blush and hesitant wave.

"What say you, Rudy," Zel said, louder than he'd spoken during their previous conversation but not so loud as to alert anyone beyond the head table, "have you imparted the most important lesson to our newest member?"

"Which one is that?" Rudy asked.

"*Only empty pockets need filling.*"

Rudy's blush turned bright vermillion, which told Gregor he was better off not knowing the hidden meaning.

Perhaps even Rudy was finally free to find a love of his own. Such a fate was not for everyone, but for those destined for it, for those who could not imagine a life lived without romantic love, there were few greater joys than finding it. Gregor knew so intimately, glancing again at his wife and leaning toward her to steal a kiss, just like this whole adventure had begun with a different attempt at theft.

More than anything, Gregor was so glad that their Zel, their surprising and miraculous babe, had found that same happiness.

Watching Zel finally remove their cloak and drape it over the back of their chair, Gregor noticed the pendant he recalled from when Zel first left for the tower. He also noticed that Ulrich wore an identical one now, which had not caught Gregor's attention before tonight.

"Did you gift your husband a matching pendant?" Gregor asked Zel. "Or did he create one to match his bride?"

"It's a bit more complicated than that," Ulrich answered, and he and Zel shared a companionable look with Rudy. "And I will remind you, Gregor, that Zel is my beloved, not my bride. I never did ask for a bride."

"So we will be reminded of until we are old and gray," Sophie interjected. "I would be angrier at ourselves if not for the outcome. But perhaps the greatest magical luck of all, beyond the power of any *rapunzel* was how our Zel still found their way to their true self."

Gregor looked again to Sophie with the adoration he felt for her that would never fade, for she had summed it all up perfectly—and saved him from his error.

"Are we to hear a song from our Pipers tonight?" one of the guild members shouted from the crowd, drawing all of their eyes forward.

"That could be arranged," Sophie answered.

"After we eat!" Gregor added with a chuckle.

"Aw, come on!" Another stood, raising her hands to urge others to join in the cajoling.

"One before!" the first called.

"While the food is served!" the second agreed, since attendants had begun to bring out the night's fare now that their leaders were seated.

Gregor met eyes with his wife, their treasure, and the sorcerer in turn. "I suppose we might manage if our patron can assist?"

With a nod from Ulrich, a flute and two violins were summoned. Gregor claimed the former, while Sophie and Zel took up the latter, and the three stood.

"Care to lend your voice as well?" Zel asked Ulrich more quietly.

"With you in private, my love, certainly. Not here."

Gregor had a feeling Zel would wear Ulrich's reluctance down eventually.

"Your composition, Zel?" Sophie asked, and Zel started right in as agreement.

> *"In the stillest night,*
> *at dawn's break,*
> *a voice began to lament;*
> *sweetly and gently,*
> *the night wind*
> *carried to me its sound."*

Gregor watched Zel's eyes fall upon Ulrich as the family continued to perform.

> *"From that lonely pain,*
> *my heart wept*
> *and tears flowed down like rain,*
> *cleansing the flowers,*
> *lovely and small,*
> *to no longer grieve alone."*

> *...and for a long time, they lived happily and satisfied.*

Grab the 8-book series at mybook.to/GriMM

Little Red Riding Hood by TJ Rose

Zel by Amanda Meuwissen

Hansel and Gerhardt by W.H. Lockwood

The Elves and the Shoemaker by Emory Winters

Cinder by D.N. Bryn

The Frog Prince by A.M. Rose

Rumpelstilzchen by Sam Northman

Snow White & the Seven Little Miners by Kit Barrie

About the Author

Amanda Meuwissen is a queer author with a primary focus on M/M or gay fiction and romance, including LGBTQ+ Fantasy #1 Best Seller, *Coming Up for Air*, LGBTQ+ Horror #1 Best Seller and #1 New Release, *A Delicious Descent*, Gay and Fantasy Erotica #1 New Release, *Last Courtesan of Olympus*, and many others. She lives in Minnesota with her husband, John, and their two cats. All other books and social media for Amanda can be found at linktr.ee/amandameuwissen.

Claim a free eBook teaser by joining Amanda's newsletter here: amandameuwissen.com/newsletter

Also by Amanda Meuwissen

Tales from the Gemstone Kingdoms
Fairy Tale / High Fantasy Series

A Delicious Descent
MM Horror Retelling of Dracula

Coming Up for Air
Merfolk Dark Urban Fantasy

...and more at various retailers and amandameuwissen.com